RESUSCITATION

Book 2 of *Racing the Reaper*

JERRID EDGINGTON

Master Koda Select Publishing

Resuscitation
Book Two of the *Racing the Reaper* Series
An MKSP Book/February 2015

Published by Master Koda Select Publishing, LLC
ISBN-13:978-0-9905878-7-3
Originally published in eBook form by Master Koda Select Publishing, LLC in 2014

Master Koda Select Publishing functions only as the book publisher and as such, the ultimate design, content, editorial accuracy, and views expressed or implied in this work are those of the author.

Cover Design: Cover design © Rebbekah White
Images
   Angel Wings: Stock footage provided by Kimmet/Pond5.com
   Ambulance: Stock footage provided by 4@leaf/Pond5.com
   Paramedic: Stock footage provided by bluevis/Pond5.com
   Young Beautiful Woman: Stock footage provided by Wisky/Pond5.com

Printed in the United States of America

www.masterkodaselectpublishing.com

THANK YOU!

First of all, I want to thank you for taking the time to read my books. You are the reason that I write and I can't thank you enough. I also want to thank Kim Emerson, owner of Master Koda Select Publishing for believing in me and teaching me so much about writing.

If you enjoyed the book, please post a review on Amazon. You can also reach me at authorjerridedgington@gmail.com for any questions or comments that you would like to make or follow my blog at www.authorjerridedgington.com.

DEDICATION

I dedicate this book to all the men and women that put their lives in danger so that others may live.

ONE

JAMES COMPRESSED THE pregnant woman's chest who was splayed on the warm asphalt of the two-lane highway while Jacob called for a helicopter.

The volunteer fire fighters that freed her from the car stood around watching. Jacob was thankful for them, but he was agitated they weren't more aggressive in offering assistance. It was a matter of minutes before the baby the woman was carrying would also die.

They were on a highway in the middle of the woods. The road wasn't well-traveled. The sun peeked through the plush green trees that lined the curvy road, casting various shaped shadows on the asphalt.

Jacob glanced at the other vehicle. A man's body slumped over the steering wheel with the windshield caved in and the glass pierced into his skull. The steering wheel buckled from the impact of his body being flung into it—he hadn't been wearing a seat belt.

Jacob grabbed his cell phone. He couldn't control his trembling fingers as he tried to push the numbers on the keypad. Taking a deep breath, he tried to control his anxiety. Slowly he exhaled through pursed lips and dialed the emergency room at Magic County Hospital. After several rings, a woman answered the phone.

"ER," she said abruptly.

"This is Jacob, on Medic-57. I need to speak to the doctor, now!"

The clock was ticking and they didn't have long before they would

1

lose the unborn child, too. Once a patient went into cardiac arrest from trauma, they had less than a one percent chance of survival unless they were on the operating table. If the mother wasn't breathing, neither was the baby. Jacob's primary concern was what could he do to save the baby? Would CPR be sufficient until they were able to get her to the hospital? They were forty-five minutes away from the closest facility and the helicopter wouldn't fly a patient in cardiac arrest because there wasn't enough room for them to be able to continue resuscitative measures. Their options were limited to only one and he needed the doctor on the phone. Jacob paced back and forth next to his partner, James. With each compression, the woman's head bobbed up and down.

The operator sighed. "Hold on."

A moment later, a man picked up the phone. "This is Doctor Young."

Jacob's throat constricted. "This is Jacob on Medic-57. We're on scene of a head on collision with one confirmed fatality. We have a pregnant female who is approximately eight months pregnant. We lost pulses a moment ago, and we're forty-five minutes from the nearest hospital. What do you want me to do?" Life or death calls brought out the best in him, but the added element of having a child's life in his hands terrified him. There was silence on the other end of the phone. "Hello? Are you there?" Jacob felt as though a vacuum had sucked the air from his lungs.

James pumped frantically on the woman's chest. Beads of sweat from his forehead slowly traced down his face and fell onto the lifeless woman's body.

"Yes. I'm here. How long has she been in cardiac arrest?"

"Less than a minute. My partner is doing CPR on her now."

Doctor Young cleared his throat. "You have two choices. I can talk you through a field C-section, or you can do nothing and the baby will die. There's nothing you can do for the mother. She's already dead."

The thought of cutting into the woman's abdomen horrified Jacob. "I'm not trained for that! I don't know the first thing about performing a C-section."

"Look, I know you're scared, but that baby will die if you do nothing. That is a guarantee. At least if you try, the baby has a chance at life."

Jacob sucked in a deep breath. He didn't have time to think. He had to get control of himself. *I should've called in sick today.*

"Do you have access to a scalpel?" Doctor Young asked.

Jacob grabbed the OB kit with shaking hands and ripped it open. The scalpel dropped to the ground. He reached down and picked it up. "Yes, right here," he said holding it. He wiped the sweat off his forehead with his arm. Seconds ticked away, lessening the chance for the baby's survival.

"Do you have any betadine on your ambulance?"

"Does it matter if we disinfect her stomach?"

Doctor Young sighed. "Good point. Now, take your scalpel and cut a vertical incision from her Xiphoid process down to her pubic region. Don't cut too deep. You don't want to perforate her bowel."

Jacob put the phone on speaker and laid it down on the ground next to him. He pushed the scalpel into her skin, being careful not to go too deep. Adrenaline surged through his body. Afraid of doing serious damage, he was careful how far he slid the scalpel into her stomach. The urge to slice her stomach open and pull the baby out was overwhelming. As the blade pierced the skin, a small trace of blood trickled from the entrance wound and down the side of her swollen abdomen.

"How is it going? Have you made it through the first layer of tissue yet?" Doctor Young asked.

"I'm trying," Jacob answered nervously. His hands trembled as he slid the scalpel down the woman's abdomen. A thin line of blood traced his incision. He concentrated on not allowing the CPR that James was performing to distract him. As long as her heart was being compressed, oxygen rich blood was making its way to the baby.

"You're doing fine. There is going to be quite a bit to cut through. But Jacob, you need to work fast."

As if there wasn't enough pressure, now I have to go faster?

The tone in Doctor Young's voice renewed the urgency that he needed to work faster. The only chance the baby had to survive rested solely on his shoulders. After making the initial pass, Jacob cut a little bit deeper. Blood pooled, making it difficult to see where he was cutting. A wave of nausea rolled through his stomach. He choked down the urge to vomit and refocused on the task.

"There's a lot of blood."

"Get some gauze and wipe it away," Doctor Young instructed.

Jacob sat the scalpel down on the woman's abdomen, reached into the jump bag, and retrieved several small white packages of gauze. He ripped them open and blotted the blood, clearing a visual path. The scalpel bounced on her stomach with each compression. Picking up the scalpel, Jacob continued cutting. After several passes, bowel and intestines came into view. Jacob grasped the organs, lifted them up, and pushed them to the side. Just underneath, a semi-pink mass appeared. A sigh of relief slipped through his lips.

"I think I've made it to the uterus."

"Good. You'll need to cut through that carefully. Remember, there's a baby inside of there."

Jacob's hands shook uncontrollably, making it difficult to hold onto the scalpel.

Calm down. You can do this.

Pushing the scalpel ever so lightly into the mass, he started to cut through. A moment later, a large gush of fluid flowed out of her abdomen.

Oh no! What have I done?

"A lot of fluid came out of her."

"What color is it, Jacob?"

"Clear."

"Okay, that's good. That's the amniotic fluid. Carefully continue your incision, but hurry. You're running out of time."

Cautiously he continued to cut through the uterus. A few moments later, dark hair from the top of the baby's head appeared. A momentary sigh of relief pushed his fear away; he was close.

"How are we doing, Jacob? Is the incision big enough for the baby to fit through?"

Jacob grabbed more gauze to soak up the remnants of the fluid. How is Doctor Young able to stay so calm through this?

"Yeah. I think so."

"Now you need to reach in, grab as much of the baby as you can, and pull it out."

"Am I going to hurt it if I pull too hard?" Jacob wouldn't be able to live with himself if he caused permanent damage to the small child. This life was innocent. He'd made it this far and didn't want to turn back now.

"Not any worse than if you do nothing and the baby dies."

Jacob sensed the urgency in the doctor's voice. He focused on what to do next. He reached in, grabbed the baby, and tugged on the small body. The baby wasn't budging—he panicked. "The baby won't come out!"

"Listen to me, Jacob. You have to pull that baby out and do it *now!*"

The baby was sliding off into certain death. With one last heave, he pulled as hard as he could. The limp and blue baby slid out of its mother's stomach. James stopped doing CPR, grabbed the umbilical cord clamps, placed them on the cord, and cut through it once it stopped pulsating.

"The baby is out!"

"Good. I don't hear it crying. Have you stimulated it?"

His greatest fear was lying lifeless in front of him—a baby that wasn't breathing. Jacob retrieved the bulb syringe and suctioned out the baby's mouth and nose—still no breathing. James grabbed the baby and with his large fingers, compressed its small chest. His hands were twice the size of the baby. It was so little and frail. Jacob had done the impossible and successfully performed a C-section. He couldn't bear the thought of losing the baby now.

Dust flew from their leather boots as the two men ran toward their ambulance. Jacob got inside first, reached down and helped James into the back. He placed the baby on the cot and continued to compress the chest. The silence in the ambulance was deafening. His chest constricted against his thumping heart. Vertigo hit him full force and he grabbed the cot in an effort to steady himself. He forced himself to suck in a deep breath.

Jacob grabbed a bag valve mask, hooked it up to oxygen, and ventilated the baby; it was a boy. With each squeeze of the bag, his chest expanded, filling with oxygen. While performing CPR with one hand, James placed the cardiac monitor leads onto the baby's bare chest; a green flat line scrolled across the screen; his heart wasn't beating. Grabbing the pediatric kit, Jacob pulled out the laryngoscope and an endotracheal tube. As he slid the straight blade of the scope into the tiny mouth, he couldn't see anything past the baby's large tongue. He repositioned the laryngoscope, lifted the tongue out of way and the white vocal chords appeared. With ease, he slid the tube past them and then secured it to the baby's ashen colored face with a tube holder.

After what seemed an eternity of performing CPR, a blip appeared on the cardiac monitor, then another one. Jacob's heart skipped a beat. He stared at the monitor and his breath quickened.

"Come on, little man. You can do it. Fight!" Jacob pleaded.

In rapid succession, the baby's heart rate scrolled across the screen. Jacob reached down, squeezed his brachial artery, and felt a strong heartbeat. The corners of his mouth tugged upward and a small smile traced across his face.

James stopped compressing the baby's chest.

The color of the baby's trunk changed from ashen to pink. His small arms moved intermittently, but he still wasn't breathing on his own. After a few minutes the baby's arms and legs also changed from ashen to pink.

The emotional workout almost brought Jacob to his knees. In the near distance he heard the familiar sound of the helicopter approaching. This was music to their ears; if only they could've arrived sooner. James slid a needle into the baby's small arm. He was able to establish an IV on his first attempt, a rare accomplishment on a newborn child. After he secured the IV, he leaned back against the wall of the ambulance, his breathing slowing to a normal rate.

The flight crew, once on the ground, approached Jacob and James with their flight cot and equipment. After giving them a brief report, they whisked the baby away, and ran across the asphalt toward their air ambulance. Moments later, they were airborne.

James and Jacob sat down on the bumper of the ambulance. The emotional stress took a toll on their bodies. For several minutes, neither of them spoke. Several of the volunteer firefighters walked over and congratulated them. Jacob couldn't feel proud for what they'd done. They were able to save one life, but they also lost two others. The odds of the baby surviving were grim. He wasn't sure if the CPR was effective enough to keep blood blowing to the baby's small body.

James placed a hand on Jacob's shoulder. "Great job, man. I couldn't have done it."

Jacob rested his elbows on his knees. He tried to be a macho man and not let his feelings get the best of him, but he couldn't hold back. The floodgates of emotions opened and unleashed their unforgiving fury upon him; he wept.

After a few minutes, Jacob peeled off the blood soaked gloves, and dropped them on the ground. He dried his eyes, walked over, picked up the cell phone, and pressed it against his ear.

"Hello? Can you hear me, Jacob?" asked Doctor Young.

Jacob dried off his eyes and cleared his throat. "Yes. I'm here. Sorry. We handed the baby off to the flight crew."

"Is he okay?"

"Yes. We got him back."

"They saved the baby!" Doctor Young yelled. He could hear shouts of joy and people clapping in the background. In the midst of the chaos, for a brief moment, Jacob was happy. Realizing they faced a grim situation, kept their composure, and were able to give the baby a chance, he smiled.

"You did a great job. I'm proud of you."

"I wish I could feel good about it, doc. Thank you for your help." Jacob hung up the cell phone and slid it back into his pants pocket.

James followed Jacob over to the mother's body. James pulled a sheet over her up to her head. Jacob knelt down next to her body, studying her face. Her face pale and lifeless, yet so peaceful and angelic. Not more than an hour ago, she was driving down the road probably thinking about what color to paint her baby's room. Now, she was dead. It saddened him to think the child would never know his mother. He reached down and pulled a few strands of dark brown curls out of her eyes.

"You have a son. A beautiful little boy. I'm sure you'd be proud of him. I'm so sorry we couldn't do more to save you." A tear trickled out of the corner of Jacob's eye.

James took the sheet and pulled it over her head.

Jacob stood while looking down at the woman. "I'm in a lot of trouble now. I just did something paramedics aren't allowed to do and I may lose my license."

TWO

JACOB OFTEN WONDERED why Becca killed herself, instead of him. The images of the bullet passing through her head haunted his dreams. He spent nights waking up in a cold sweat and screaming as he awoke from the horrific nightmares. He believed that was her way of making him feel guilty for the rest of his life. How selfish of her! He'd never dealt with someone who had a deranged mind and didn't know how to sort through the emotions it caused him. Understanding what was going through her head was a question without any hope of answers. He would never forget her or that fateful day.

After selling his house, Jacob moved to Boise Idaho. He'd been living there for two weeks, but still hadn't seen Bridge - his whole reason for moving there. He knew she worked at Magic County Hospital as an emergency room nurse, but getting her phone number proved unsuccessful. Hospital policy this, hospital policy that. He ran into a never-ending wall of denial when it came to her. There was so much he wanted to share with her.

Once he had settled in, Jacob gained employment at Magic County EMS. They ran double paramedics on the ambulances, which was a welcome change. It cut the call volume in half, for charting purposes anyway. The biggest difference between Boise, Idaho and Phoenix, Arizona, besides the treacherous heat, was that the fire department didn't have paramedics, only EMT's. The system placed him in charge of all medical and trauma calls. The fire department was very helpful. They took care of the basic tasks on scene, freeing Jacob and his partner to concentrate on advanced assessment and skills.

As time wore on, the never-ending sleepless nights slowly subsided. Often though, a smell or a sight would remind him of his long lost friend, Stitch. What he wouldn't give to have five minutes to say he was sorry for fighting with him before he died. He would carry that burden with him for the rest of his life.

Jacob prepared for work. He still thought about the pregnant woman they lost, but thankful they were able to save the child's life. The local media grabbed the story. Jacob and James were painted as heroes; he didn't feel like one. Under strict instructions by the director, Nate, they weren't allowed to speak to the media. Their department had a Public Information Officer who handled all media requests. Jacob wasn't interested in speaking to them anyway. He wasn't a glory hound. If his participation on a call was forgotten, he felt he did his job. After gathering all of his personal belongings for his next twenty-four hour shift, his cell phone rang.

Jacob fished it out of his duty pants pocket and flipped it open. "Hello?"

"Good morning. It's Nate. I need you to come into the office and see me before you go to your shift."

"Okay. Is there something wrong?"

"We'll talk about it when you get here. Your shift will be covered until we're done."

"I'll be there in ten minutes."

"Sounds good. See you then."

Jacob hung up the phone. Nate was the director of Magic County EMS. Usually it wasn't a good thing when he called someone to his office. He was the type of director that wasn't heard from unless a problem occurred. Jacob wasn't surprised. He'd been expecting Nate's phone call. He knew it was time to face the music and explain his actions. Paramedics aren't allowed to perform field C-sections, but he didn't regret his decision; he saved a child's life.

Jacob gazed at the terrain filled with lush green trees. It was a welcome change from the desert landscape he was accustomed to. The scenic background heightened his mood. Rush hour traffic, even at its peak, was substantially lighter than in Arizona. The commuters were friendlier and often waved. In the desert, the only waving people did was with their middle fingers. Perhaps it was the heat.

Jacob arrived at the main station. His stomach tensed with the anticipation of what Nate was going to say to him. He would stand by his decision, regardless of the repercussions. His only alternative was to do nothing and watch the baby die. He couldn't do that in good conscience, because he was in the business of saving lives and that's exactly what he did.

The Central Station was a large tin building, white in color with minimal landscaping that failed in comparison to Alliance Ambulance in Arizona. The door to Nate's office stood alone from the main entrance of the building. He approached the door. Trying to shake off the nervousness, he took in a deep breath, and walked inside.

Nate sat at his large oak desk sifting through a stack of papers. He looked up and his eyes ordered Jacob to sit in a chair at the front of his desk. Nate was in his early thirties. He stood six-foot-five, slender, with short brown hair. He had only been a paramedic for five years, but was quite successful at the political game, which helped him obtain his position as director. Jacob knew that many of the EMT's mocked Nate for climbing the ladder so quickly. He wasn't known to flaunt his new position in front of the seasoned paramedics, but they still resented him.

Jacob sat down. "What the problem?"

Nate leaned back in his chair and draped his hands across his stomach. "You certainly have made a splash in your short time here. My phone hasn't stopped ringing since your field C-section."

Jacob looked at him, confused. "I wish that call never happened. I didn't want to cut into her stomach, but if I hadn't, the baby would've died."

Nate rocked back and forth in his chair, staring at Jacob. "I have some bad news. With all of the media attention you've created, State EMS has opened an official investigation into your call. I'm being pressured to fire you."

Jacob sat up stiffly in his chair. "What do you mean, fire me? I did what Doctor Young instructed me to do. I didn't do anything wrong." He knew there was going to be some backlash for performing the procedure, but fired? He didn't feel he deserved that severe of a punishment.

Nate leaned forward in his chair resting his elbows on the desk. "You've forced me into a difficult situation. I understand why you did what you did. State EMS sees it differently."

"Please tell me, what did I do wrong?"

I'll tell you what I did wrong. Nothing!

"They're alleging that you went outside of the State's approved protocols for paramedics."

A shiver shot up his spine. "I disagree. There may not be a protocol for an emergency field C-section, but I operated under a doctor's order. He instructed me how to do it step by step."

"Nothing has become official. For the time being, I suggest you keep your nose to the grindstone. I've been ordered to have all of your charts reviewed until this situation is resolved."

Jacob tried to speak, but his tongue was stuck to the roof of his mouth. He was in the middle of an internal battle. His heart was telling him to stand up for his decisions, but his mind said differently. *Pick and choose your battles.* "What happens now?"

"Business as usual. Go to work and I'll let you know what State EMS has decided."

Jacob sat for a moment, trying to control his anger. He felt it was unfair. How could they discipline him for following a doctor's order? After all, he *did* save a baby's life. He wasn't going to go down without a fight. If he had to, he'd go to the papers and every news station in town. They were already tagging him as a hero. Surely, they'd be interested in knowing he was being persecuted for saving a life. He wanted to throw that into Nate's face, but held his tongue.

It may not come to all of that. I need to calm down.

Nate looked at him. "You want something?"

"No."

"We're done here. Get to work." He looked down at the stack of papers on his desk.

Jacob leaned forward in his seat, hesitated for a moment, got up, and stomped toward the door. He grabbed the handle and looked back at Nate. "You know this is unfair. I did exactly what any other paramedic in my shoes would've done."

"Life isn't fair."

Jacob shook his head, stepped through the door, and slammed it shut. The sound of the metal door slapping against the frame echoed through the air. His pleasant mood was long gone. Looking back at the call, if he were to have it to do over again, he would've done the same thing. It was a bittersweet moment.

Pulling into the parking lot of the station, he noticed James talking to a man he didn't recognize. James patted the man on the shoulder, looked up, and pointed toward Jacob. The man walked quickly toward Jacob's truck. He strolled across the lot with a purpose: arms swaying at his sides, eyes red and puffy. He walked in front of Jacob's truck and stood looking at him. Jacob hit the brakes abruptly to avoid running the man over. His truck jostled back and forth before settling to a complete stop. A rush of anger washed over him as he slammed the truck into park and watched the man stomp toward the driver's door.

"I've been waiting for you," the man said.

"I'm sorry. Do I know you?"

The man's eyes welled up with tears. "No. But my son does," he said choking down tears that threatened to spill down his cheeks. His upper lip trembled. He inhaled deeply, glancing around the parking lot.

Jacob had no idea who the man was. He got out of his truck and stood in front of him. Behind the man, James stood with tears in his eyes.

What's going on?

He approached Jacob, grabbed him, and flung his arms around him. The man's grip caused Jacob to have trouble breathing. The man wept uncontrollably. He released his grip on Jacob and stepped back. "I just want to thank you. Because of you, my son survived."

Jacob looked at him quizzically. Once he realized whom the man was, his chest constricted and a knot formed in his throat. Guilt pushed through his body. He wanted to apologize for letting him down, and not being able to save his wife. He tried to open his mouth, but couldn't form any words. A man he'd never met before held him, crying. He yearned to take the man's pain away.

"I'm Matt Blankenship. You took care of my wife the other day." He hung his head and cupped his face with his hands.

Jacob placed his arm around Matt. His heart sank for him. He whispered, "I'm so sorry, sir. I wish we could've saved your wife, too. I can't imagine the pain you're suffering."

Matt stepped back and dried his eyes on his arm. "You must think I'm some kind of wimp."

"No. Not at all. If I were in your shoes, I'd be the same way. How is your son?"

Matt cleared his throat. "He's doing well. I don't know how I'm going to do this alone—I can't do this. I need my wife." His shoulders bobbed and tears trickled down his cheeks. He reached up and covered his eyes with his hands once more.

Jacob looked over at James. They stared grimly at one another. He wasn't sure how he could console him. He was broken and lost. Jacob didn't have any kids and couldn't fathom his pain.

"I don't understand why God let this happen. How could he take away the one person I would rather die than live without?"

Jacob often asked himself that question. Why did God take people away so quickly? Being that he struggled with that as well, he didn't know how to answer. "Look," he said, "all I know is you have a son now. He needs you more than anything. It's horrible that you lost your wife, I know, but you will have a part of her with you every day. Each time you look at him, you'll see her. Your wife will live on through your son."

"There is something I wanted to tell you. I'm naming my son after you. Without you, he would be dead, too."

Jacob swallowed hard. Just when the urge to cry had left him, it came rushing back like a raging river. He didn't feel worthy of the honor. "I don't know what to say."

"There's nothing for you to say. If it wasn't for you, I would've lost two loves in my life, instead of just one."

Jacob choked down the tidal wave of emotions that crashed over him. The one constant he had learned in his career was that every day was an emotional roller coaster. There were peaks one minute and desolate valley's the next. Learning how to sort out and accept those feelings was a difficult task. He often worried that the field would get the best of him and turn his heart cold. He had to stay subjective, and keep his goals in focus, saving lives. At times, he didn't know how to do that. The last thing he wanted to happen was to lose his love for the job. He'd seen many paramedics burn out and stop caring. He didn't want to become another statistic. Jacob's one redeeming quality was he didn't turn to alcohol to numb the pain he endured on a daily basis. Without any other outlet, he feared it would be a matter of time before he succumbed to the emotional beatings, and he would fall victim to a crutch like many others in his profession.

Matt dried his eyes once more. "I have to get going. I need to go see my son, but I wanted to personally thank you. I am forever indebted to you." He walked up to Jacob, hugged him once more, and then left.

Jacob looked over at James. "What a way to start a shift, huh?"

James smiled. "Yeah. I feel bad for that man. Why did you have to go see Nate?"

"The state is investigating the call. My career may be over."

THREE

JACOB MILLED AROUND the station trying to keep busy and his mind off the pending investigation. The field C-section was reeling through his brain. Nate was steadfast that it was the wrong decision, but Jacob didn't agree. Before he cut into the woman's abdomen, he knew it was a life altering decision. He strolled across the newly installed hardwood floors. The sound of his boots thumping on the floor echoed off the walls. The television caught his attention. Images of the gruesome wreck scrolled across the screen. Jacob stopped, confused. He didn't recall anyone with a camera on scene, but he focused on following Doctor Young's orders.

Jacob's stomach grumbled; he hadn't eaten yet. His appetite decreased and he had difficulty sleeping since the call. Images of the woman with her abdomen laid open were burned into his mind. Each time he smelled burnt rubber, his mind raced back to the call. Most people would seek out professional help and attend a Critical Incident Stress Debriefing, but not Jacob. He didn't believe in them. After his first CISD meeting, he swore he would never attend another one. He hadn't gotten anything from the meeting other than his feelings were ignored. It angered him how the nursing staff were allowed to talk about their grief, but he wasn't allowed to.

Jacob looked over his shoulder. "You hungry?"

James stared at the television, not answering.

Jacob turned back around and finished watching the report. They

17

didn't say anything about EMS or what they'd done. They just talked about the double fatality. He was grateful for the strict privacy laws. Most likely, the media tried to obtain information from the hospital, but he knew they wouldn't divulge anything. Jacob didn't want his picture splashed all over the media, painting him a hero. He didn't feel like one.

Once the report was over, James shifted his attention back to Jacob. "Yeah, I'm hungry. Let's get something to eat."

Jacob followed him through the station and out to the ambulance bay. James preferred to drive, and Jacob didn't mind. The silence in the cab was deafening. Neither man was in a social mood. Trapped in the quiet solitude was the best place to be sometimes. Each man had to find a way to deal with the emotions and accept they'd done the best they could.

After finishing their lunch, they headed back to the station. It was another beautiful day in Boise, Idaho. Jacob felt good about his decision to move there. The scenery was more vibrant than that of the desert terrain. The people were much friendlier here—which was a welcome change. Jacob hadn't blamed people for being so grumpy; living inside an oven brought out the worst in people.

Their unit tones blared over the speakers. "Medic-57, what is your location?"

Jacob leaned down and picked up the radio microphone. "We're about to pull back into our station."

"We have a call for you at 310 Lake Drive. You have a thirty-six year old female unconscious, unresponsive, but breathing."

"Medic-57, copies. Show us en-route."

James switched on the lights and sirens. He flipped a U-turn in the middle of the road and raced toward the address. The cars in front of them pulled over to the right. There was another thing Jacob liked about Idaho; people yielded the right-of-way to emergency vehicles. That was a welcome change. Jacob sat in the passenger seat and ran scenarios through his mind. He liked mentally preparing for a call. It was a skill he learned from his former partner, Trent. His philosophy was if you were prepared for the worst, you wouldn't be caught with your pants down around your ankles.

After navigating a few turns, they arrived at the address. The fire department was on scene and James pulled in behind the large red truck.

One of the firefighters raced out of the front door of the home, nearly falling down the few short steps that descended from the front door.

"She's not doing well. She's unresponsive and her breathing is erratic. I don't know what's going on, but there is a softball size mass pulsating in her abdomen," he said. Perspiration beaded on his brow and traced down the side of his freshly shaven face.

The men jumped out and ran to the back of their ambulance. Jacob didn't like to speculate, but from what the firefighter said, it sounded grim. His chest tightened and his heart thumped. A surge of adrenalin coursed through his body.

James flung open the back doors and stopped. "We forgot to tell dispatch we're on scene."

Jacob looked over his shoulder at the firefighter. "Can you tell dispatch for us? We need to get inside."

"Sure. No problem."

James tossed the cardiac monitor and their jump bag onto the cot. Jacob pulled it out of the back of the ambulance and together they briskly walked toward the front door of the residence. Another firefighter met them at the door, jogged down the steps, and grabbed their equipment. Jacob slid a pair of gloves over his sweaty palms.

A frantic man met them when they entered the house. His eyes were wide and filled with fear. "You have to help her! Please help her!"

"Where is she?" James asked.

"She's in the bedroom," he answered as he turned and led them through the house.

Jacob and James followed the man down a long hall to a large bedroom. An attractive woman was lying on a large bed and her auburn hair draped over her shoulders. Jacob noticed her pale color and ashen lips. Two firefighters were next to her obtaining vital signs.

"What's going on?" Jacob asked.

"Husband found her lying in bed. She wouldn't respond to him, so he called 911."

Jacob approached her and placed cardiac monitor leads onto her pale and pasty chest. Her eyes were closed and breathing was erratic and irregular. He lifted the bottom of her shirt and looked down at a softball-sized mass pulsating in her abdomen. This was a first for his career.

"What's her history?" James asked.

"Nothing pertinent...." Before the firefighter could finish his sentence, the woman's husband stormed into the room.

"Why are you still here? You need to get her to the hospital. Quit screwing around and get going," he said through gritted teeth. His jaw was tense and his eyes narrowed.

"Sir, we need to figure out what's going on before we attempt to move her," Jacob said.

The man walked over and grabbed Jacob's arm. "You listen to me and you listen good. My wife needs to get to the hospital. If you don't quit screwing around and get going...so help me God, if anything happens to her, I'll hold you responsible!"

Jacob ripped his arm free of the man's firm grip and looked him squarely in the eyes. "Sir, we have tests to do and you coming in here demanding things isn't making it any easier. Back off and let us do our job!"

The room went eerily silent. The two men stared at one another. It resembled a scene from a show down at the OK Corral. After a moment, the man took a few steps back without losing eye contact with Jacob.

"Please gather any medications she takes and place them in a bag," Jacob asked.

The floor shook as the man stomped out of the room. Jacob shook his head and then continued placing the cardiac monitor onto the woman. He empathized with the patient's husband and understood why he was uncooperative; he was scared, but his actions were impeding their ability to take care of her. He would apologize to the man later, after they safely delivered her to the emergency room.

"Can you guys get the cot in here and ready to load her?" James asked.

Two of the firefighters left to retrieve the cot. Once the monitor was on the woman, Jacob turned toward James. "Her heart rate is pretty low. What's her blood pressure?"

James leaned over and pumped up the blood pressure cuff. After a few moments, he looked up at Jacob. "It's 86/60. She's in bad shape."

Jacob leaned in and felt for a pulse—it was weak and thready. "Low heart rate, low blood pressure, and a pulsating mass. You thinking what I'm thinking?"

The color left James' face. He sighed and shook his head.

"Abdominal aortic aneurysm."

They realized she didn't have much time. If the aneurysm burst, and she wasn't on an operating table, she would die in a matter of minutes. They readied their equipment as the two firefighters returned with the cot and positioned it next to the bed.

"We need to be careful while moving her, guys. We don't want to do it roughly. She's in critical condition," Jacob said.

The men grabbed the sheet she was lying on and carefully moved her over to the cot. Jacob looked down. The mass was still pulsating in her abdomen.

The woman's husband stormed back into the room holding a plastic bag full of medications. "What is taking so long? Get her to the hospital, now!" he shouted.

Jacob glanced over his shoulder. "Sir, we're getting her ready for transport. We have to be careful right now. If we rush, she could die."

The man dropped the bag of meds onto the floor, shook his head, and left the room.

"Let's get moving," Jacob ordered.

They lifted the cot and pushed her toward the living room. The woman was breathing, but still unresponsive. Jacob looked at the cardiac monitor and her heart rate remained low.

If we don't hurry she isn't going to make it.

His stomach tightened. Having a critical call didn't happen very often. They were behind the eight ball; her chances of survival were slim to nil.

Once outside, Jacob looked over his shoulder—the woman's husband paced back and forth next to his car shouting into his cell phone. One of the firefighters lifted the cot and placed her into the back of the ambulance. Jacob jumped up next to her and prepared the supplies he needed to start an IV. James walked around to the side door, got in, placed her on oxygen, and took her blood pressure again.

A grim look came over him. "It's 78/56 and her pulse rate is slowing."

Jacob knew it would only be a matter of moments before the aneurysm burst, filling her abdomen with blood, and plummeting her into death.

The patient's husband ran up to the back of the ambulance

screaming, "Why are you still here?"

Jacob looked over at two of the firefighters. "Close the doors!" His patience had grown thin. Now the man was getting on his nerves. It wasn't bad enough they had to try to save the woman's life, but the added stress from her husband was too much.

One of the firefighters slammed the doors and the ambulance shook side to side. Jacob could hear the man screaming several profanities at them.

He pushed by the firefighters and flung open the doors. "You listen to me. If anything happens to my wife, I'm going to hold you responsible."

Jacob made eye contact with him. He forced a breath through his pursed lips, calming himself. "Sir, we're doing everything we can to help her. If you don't mind, we are wasting valuable time.""

The man glared at Jacob and then slammed the door shut.

"Can you believe the nerve of that guy?" Jacob pushed his frustration down and refocused on the unconscious woman in front of him. Time was of the essence, they needed to be at the hospital, now.

James looked up. "I don't blame him, but enough is enough. You about ready to go?"

Jacob slid the needle into the woman's arm and she didn't move. Once he taped it down, he hooked a bag of saline to it. The drips ran in rapid succession into the tubing. Her blood pressure was low, but he needed to make sure she didn't receive too much fluid. It would put more pressure on the already weak aortic artery. Once her blood pressure was above ninety systolic, he would slowdown the fluid.

Jacob wiped the sweat off his brow. "I'm ready. Let's get going to the hospital. Have a firefighter ride back here with me just in case I need the extra hands."

James nodded and stepped out of the back of the ambulance. He approached the woman's husband. "We're going to be going with lights and sirens sir, so don't follow us. You go normal speed and we'll get her there as quickly as possible."

"Whatever," the man said, as he turned and ran to his car.

"We need one of you guys to ride in with Jacob."

One of the firefighters climbed into the back of the ambulance. Once the door was shut, James ran up to the front and got into the driver's seat. He reached down and grabbed the radio microphone.

"Medic-57, to dispatch."

"Go ahead, Medic-57."

"We'll be en-route to Magic County Hospital, code three. Can you call the ER and inform them we're bringing in an unstable female patient with a possible abdominal aortic aneurysm? Our ETA is ten minutes."

"Dispatch copies."

James flipped on the lights and drove toward the main road. Once he was at the intersection, he turned on the sirens and waited for traffic to yield to him. After the cars complied, he pulled out and raced toward the hospital. He looked in his side mirror and noticed the patient's husband was following closely behind him with his flashers on. Jacob looked out the back window and couldn't see his headlights he was following so closely.

"You see this, James?"

"Yeah."

While James navigated the traffic, the patient's husband came dangerously close to the back of their ambulance. James looked in the rear view mirror and could see the grim look on Jacob's face. He could tell she wasn't improving. A car pulled out in front of James and he had to hit the brakes to avoid a collision. Looking at his side mirror, the patient's husband nearly rear-ended them.

James had enough. He grabbed the microphone. "Medic-57, to dispatch."

"Go ahead, Medic-57."

"We have a family member that is following us too closely and nearly hit us. Can you dispatch an officer to get him away from us, please?"

There was a long pause on the radio. "I see your location on the computer. There's an officer a few blocks away from you. We'll take care of that."

"Medic-57, copies." James replaced the microphone in the rocker.

A few moments later, a police car flipped on his lights and swung in behind the patient's husband. He pulled over to the side of the road, jumped out of his car, and shouted at the officer. James turned his attention to the traffic in front of him and continued to race toward the hospital. The corners of his lips tugged upward forming a smile.

The firefighter sat in the CPR seat nervously watching the patient. He was young and it was obvious he didn't have any experience. Jacob glanced at the monitor. The heart rate that scrolled across the screen slowed. Forty…thirty…twenty…ten…and then a green flat line streamed across the screen.

"Crap," Jacob yelled.

"What's going on?"

"She just coded. How far out from the hospital are we?"

"Six minutes." James looked in the rear view mirror and saw the firefighter compressing on the woman's chest. Jacob pulled out the intubation kit. James knew it was only a matter of minutes and she would be dead. He pressed down on the accelerator and sped toward the hospital.

A few minutes later, they arrived at the hospital. James picked up the microphone. "Medic-57 to dispatch, we're out at the hospital."

"Dispatch copies."

James ran to the back of the ambulance and flung the doors open. Jacob had the woman intubated and the firefighter was doing compressions. Fluid dripped rapidly into the tubing. The mass that once pulsated in her abdomen was gone.

"I think we're too late," Jacob said grimly.

"You're probably right," James answered.

He grabbed the end of the cot, with the firefighter continuing to do CPR, and pulled her out of the ambulance. The men pushed the cot toward the ambulance entrance. A nurse directed them to a trauma room that had several medical personnel in it.

"How long has it been since she coded?" a doctor asked.

"Eight minutes," Jacob answered.

Each person grabbed a part of the sheet. "On my count. One-two-three," the doctor ordered.

They lifted her limp body over to the empty bed. One of the nurses took over compressions while another nurse hooked up the various wires to the patient's chest. The doctor glanced at the cardiac monitor mounted on the cart.

"She's in asystole. How long has she been down now?"

"Almost ten minutes," Jacob answered.

The doctor grimly looked at everyone in the room. "I'm afraid there's nothing we can do. Does anyone object to calling it?"

The room became eerily quiet. Everyone looked at one another, but no one spoke.

"Time of death is 12:45." He pulled off his gloves and walked over to James and Jacob. "You guys did a great job, but there's nothing we could've done. Her aneurysm must've ruptured. Even if it had happened here, I doubt she would have had a different outcome." He patted Jacob on the shoulder and left the room.

The staff began to disconnect the wires.

Jacob and James looked at one another. They tried to save this woman's life, but failed. Jacob hung his head, turned around, and walked toward the nurse's station.

James looked over at the firefighter. "Thank you for your help. We appreciate you."

"No problem. Guess I'll see you on the next one." He turned and walked out of the emergency room.

A few minutes later, the patient's husband stormed through the door of the emergency room. A bead of sweat rolled down his forehead. "What's going on? Where is my wife?"

The doctor walked from behind the nurse's station. His forehead crinkled. "Can I help you, sir?"

The veins in his forehead pulsated. "My wife. Where is my wife?" the man shouted.

"We have several patients. Can you give me more information?"

He looked over at Jacob and James. "Those jerks are the ones that brought her in. Thanks for getting me pulled over by the police. I'll be calling your supervisor."

"Sir, I need to speak to you privately. Follow me," the doctor said.

A silence rolled through the emergency room. Everyone stopped what they were doing and stared.

"I will not go anywhere. Where is my wife?"

The doctor approached the man and placed a hand on his shoulder. "Sir, you need to come with me, please."

The man pushed his hand away. "No. Take me to my wife."

The doctor stepped back. "Sir, I'm sorry but your wife passed away. There was nothing we could've done to save her. Her condition was grave. Is there someone we can call for you?"

The man's face turned pale. "What are you saying?"

"I'm sorry. There wasn't anything we could've done differently to change the outcome."

He turned toward Jacob and James. His eyes narrowed. He stomped toward them and grabbed Jacob by his shirt.

"Get security in here now," the doctor yelled.

The man got inches from Jacob's face. "I told you that if anything happened to my wife I was going to hold you responsible. She's dead and her blood is on your hands. You're going to pay for this!"

He let go of Jacob, turned around, and stomped out of the emergency room.

FOUR

JACOB ROLLED OVER. He had another sleepless night. It was tragic what happened to the woman, but he knew in his heart there wasn't anything they could've done. Her fate was decided before they arrived on scene. Still, he felt horrible for her husband's loss. He told Jacob he was going to pay for his wife's death. His blood ran cold as he thought back to the last time someone had said that to him.

"You're going to be sorry for this, Jacob. You're making a huge mistake!" Becca yelled as the officer disappeared into the crowd with her in tow.

He rolled out of bed to the sound of his cell phone ringing. He picked it up and saw the phone number for the main station. It was his day off. Why should he answer it? Against his better judgment, he flipped open his phone.

"Hello?"

"Hey, Jacob. It's Nate. You have a second?"

Jacob sighed. *You're the last person I want to speak to right now.* "Sure. What's up?"

"I just got off the phone with state EMS. They've decided to have an official hearing to determine if any legal action will be brought against you."

He saved a baby's life. What more did they want? "What happens now?"

"They've set the preliminary hearing for tomorrow. You'll need to come down to the main station at one o'clock today to speak with the attorney the county has assigned to you."

An attorney? Is that necessary?

Ever since he chose the medical field, he had faced many obstacles, which made him question if he'd made the right decision in his career choice.

"I'll be there." The weight of his career pressed down on his shoulders as he flipped the phone closed. He only had a few hours until he had to be at the main station. He dressed, grabbed a bite to eat, and headed out the door.

Outside a horde of reporters and news cameras waited. They were firing question after question at him in rapid succession. The camera flashes were blinding. Through the mob, Jacob caught a glimpse of his truck. As he pushed his way through the reporters, across the street, he saw Becca. Frozen in his tracks, his heart beat as if it were going to jump out of his chest and his mind was racing.

How is this possible? Becca is dead.

He took a moment to adjust his eyes to the flashing lights of the cameras. When he looked again, she was gone. Jacob rushed past the reporters and jumped into his truck. He had difficulty finding the ignition—his hands were shaking. Reporters swarmed around the truck, banging on the windows. When he gained control of his hands, he put his keys in the ignition and started the engine. Throwing it in reverse, he sped out of his driveway. Reporters jumped out of the way, narrowly avoiding being run over.

As he drove toward the main station, he couldn't shake the image of Becca. Of course, she was dead—he saw the bullet pass through her skull, but that reporter looked just like her. He never sought out professional counseling to cope with the trauma of Becca's death. He was a strong man and didn't need help. He worked to gain composure and clear his head. He had bigger problems to deal with—his career depended on it. His cell phone rang. He fumbled in his pocket trying to retrieve it.

"Hello?"

"Hey, man. It's James. I just heard what's going on. Why haven't they called me in?"

That was a good question. "I don't know. I guess because I'm the one that did the cutting."

"This is ridiculous. They should be pulling us both in. I'm sorry, man. This isn't right."

Jacob couldn't agree more. "If I had to do it all over again, I would've done the same thing without hesitation."

"If circumstances were reversed, I don't know if I could've done what you did. You're much braver than I am."

Jacob laughed. "I don't know about braver. Maybe just not as smart."

"Ha ha."

"Anyway, I'll call you when we're done."

"Sounds good, man. Good luck." James disconnected the call.

Jacob and James were forging a strong friendship. The years in the field took its toll on James' marriage and he was now divorced, but he was a proud father, and spent every day he had off with his boys. Jacob was envious.

Over the past year, Jacob had been through enough adversity for a lifetime, but he still felt unprepared for this meeting. As he pulled into the parking lot of the main building, sweat popped out on his brow. He parked his truck and sat there, staring. Delaying the inevitable wasn't going to change the fact he had to go inside and face the music.

He got out of his truck and approached Nate's office door. With each step, a crescendo of nerves crashed around him. No matter what happened, he was going to stand his ground, and defend his choice. He twisted the doorknob and entered. Inside, an older man sat across from Nate chatting. The two men took notice of Jacob and turned their attention to him.

"Thanks for coming in, Jacob. Take a seat, please," Nate said pointing to a chair next to the older gentleman.

Jacob followed Nate's request. The man next to him was in his early sixties, had grey hair that was short and well kept, with a goatee colored dark brown. His face etched with lines of his age and set apart his piercing blue eyes.

Nate leaned back in his seat, resting his arms across his stomach. "This is Mr. Burgess. He'll be the attorney representing you in the proceedings."

Mr. Burgess leaned over, offering his hand. The attorney avoided eye contact, looking instead at his polished shoes. That didn't settle well with Jacob. His father always told him if a man wouldn't look you in the eyes, he had something to hide.

Jacob took his hand. "Nice to meet you, sir."

Mr. Burgess retrieved papers from his briefcase, put on a pair of glasses, and drew a long look down the end of his nose at the documents. "So Jacob, do you understand what's going on here?"

"Yes. State EMS is being unfair about what I've done."

Mr. Burgess's eyebrows rose. "That's an interesting statement. Is that what you think they're doing?"

Nate leaned forward in his chair, resting his elbows on his desk.

"What else would you call it? I saved a baby's life. Doctor Young talked me through it."

Mr. Burgess grabbed an ink pen and scribbled on a piece of paper. "Doctor Young, did you say?"

"Yes."

"How did you get the order to...." He flipped through several pieces of paper. "Perform a field C-section?"

Jacob shifted nervously in his chair. "I used my personal cell phone to call him."

Mr. Burgess looked over the top of his glasses at Jacob. "Did you call in on a recorded line?"

Jacob sat back in his seat and thought for a moment. "I'm not sure."

Mr. Burgess took his glasses off, sat them down on the stack of papers in his lap, and shook his head. "We have a problem. If it wasn't on a recorded line, it will be his word against yours."

Jacob hadn't thought about that. "He wouldn't say otherwise, would he?"

Mr. Burgess and Nate glanced at one another. "Jacob, you have to understand it's not what you know, it's what you can prove. If for any reason this Doctor Young decides to say he didn't give you such an order, you'll be solely responsible. I've been looking through the state approved protocols. Paramedics aren't trained, nor approved for such a procedure."

Jacob choked down the nausea that threatened to climb up from his stomach. The realization of what was happening weighed heavily on him. This could be the end of his career.

Mr. Burgess took off his glasses and leaned toward Jacob. "Look, my job is to protect you the best I can. I have to look at the worst-case scenario. I haven't spoken with Doctor Young yet, but he will be subpoenaed to testify at the initial hearing. Honestly, even with his testimony stating he gave you the verbal order to perform the C-section, the state could still pursue legal action."

Jacob's brow furrowed. "I'm being persecuted for doing the right thing?"

Mr. Burgess looked back at his shoes. "Possibly."

Never in his life did he think he would be faulted for saving a life. The anger inside of him ignited. Jacob refused to admit fault. If it cost him his career, so be it, but he would be able to sleep at night knowing he'd done his job to the best of his ability. Even if the state didn't agree.

"I will get back to you with what Doctor Young says. He's my next visit," Mr. Burgess said. He stood, gathered his paperwork, and shook hands with Nate. "I'll be in contact."

Nate looked grimly at Jacob. An uncomfortable silence settled over the room. "That didn't go so well. At this point, there's nothing we can do about it," Nate said.

"Are we done here?" Jacob asked.

"For now. After Mr. Burgess calls me, I'll be in contact with you." He leaned forward in his seat. "I know I've been hard on you over this. I'm in a difficult position, but I commend you for having the guts to save that baby."

Jacob got up from the chair. "That will make me sleep better at night." He walked through the door and out of Nate's office.

Jacob didn't sleep well that night. Images of the accident raced through his mind. He couldn't shake having seen Becca standing in the front yard. It wasn't possible that she was there—she was dead. He rolled out of his bed. In the short time he'd been in the field, he suffered many sleepless nights. The endless tragedies would drive most men crazy. He often wondered how strong of a man he was, if he could handle the rigors of the medical field.

On autopilot, he drove to work. This was exactly what he needed, something to take his mind off his problems. Working on the ambulance was his escape, his own world. No one could hurt him there. Taking care of other people's problems helped him forget his own. It was better than climbing inside of a bottle, or worse yet, turning to drugs. He didn't want or need the fake resolution those routes of escape offered. He was stronger than that.

The sun was shining, birds chirped, and people were blissfully going about their day. Surrounded by all the beauty Mother Nature had to offer lightened his mood. Getting in contact with Bridge was proving to be difficult, but he was still glad he made the decision to move to Idaho. He just hoped that when he was finally able to connect with her that she would be happy to see him.

James was sitting outside the station talking on his cell phone when Jacob arrived. He had a disgruntled look on his face. Jacob wanted to pry, but decided against it. He didn't know the man that well yet. As Jacob neared the station, he noticed James pacing back and forth, running his hands through his short hair. His jaw was tense and eyes narrowed.

"I don't agree with that at all. I was there, too. I see. Well, I guess there's nothing else to discuss. Goodbye," James said as he closed his cell phone. He looked up and noticed Jacob.

"Hey, James. I would ask you how it's going, but by your facial expressions, I think I know the answer to that."

James shook his head and growled. "That obvious?"

"You could say that."

"What happened at the meeting today?"

Jacob wanted to forget everything that had happened, but James wasn't going to allow that. "Basically, the attorney said it could be my word against Doctor Young's. If he doesn't back me on this, I could lose my job and my license."

"I was talking to Nate. He wouldn't tell me anything about your meeting today. I told him I wanted to be sitting next to you in the preliminary hearing. He said no. The state is only going after you since you did the cutting."

Jacob shook his head. "I appreciate you wanting to stick up for me, but this is my problem, not yours."

"Regardless, I was on the call, too. If anything, we should both be in front of the state, not just you."

Jacob smiled - something he hadn't done in a few days. "I appreciate that, brother. I've got this."

The station tones interrupted their conversation. "Medic-57, we have an unconscious male at 2147 Sunset Street, room twenty-three. We're receiving reports he isn't breathing."

"Can't put my bags down and we're running already. I'll go drop them inside while you get us en-route," Jacob said. He walked into the station and James trotted toward the ambulance.

Jacob climbed into the passenger seat—it was James' turn to drive. They alternated on who took the call and who drove. They devised a plan that whoever rode in the passenger seat, was in charge of the call. Jacob loved swapping calls. It meant one person wasn't stuck writing all of the reports.

Jacob stared out the window, oblivious to his surroundings, while James raced to the call. He pulled the ambulance into the parking lot.

"Medic-57, to dispatch. We're on scene," Jacob said.

They were on the lower east side of town where crime and drugs cursed the community. The hotel appeared unlivable. Several people walked out of their hotel rooms and watched the emergency crews. This was a daily occurrence for them and was something they'd become accustomed to. Jacob noticed dirty, barefoot children running around the neighborhood.

A firefighter approached Jacob as he climbed out of the ambulance. He was young and obviously a rookie.

"He's not breathing, but he has a pulse," the firefighter said wide eyed.

James and Jacob met at the back of their ambulance. Grabbing their jump bag, they ran toward the hotel room on the second floor.

Couldn't be on the first floor. That would be too easy.

Running up the stairs, the firefighter fell down striking his chin on the concrete step. He sprang up, red-faced, and continued up the stairs. Jacob couldn't help but laugh.

This kid reminds me a lot of me not to long ago.

Once they reached the door, there were two other firefighters in the room kneeling down next to a man on the floor. He was dressed in a navy blue pin stripe suit, profusely sweaty with one sleeve rolled up above his elbow. Jacob noticed he had a tourniquet wrapped round his arm and a needle sticking out of the bend in his elbow. A firefighter assisted his breathing with a bag valve mask hooked to a portable oxygen tank sitting on the floor.

"Someone found him lying on the floor and called 911," the fighter said.

"Do you know anything about him?" James asked.

"Besides the fact he isn't breathing? No."

Jacob retrieved the glucometer from their jump bag. Even though he was sure what the problem was, he still had to rule out the possibility of it being a diabetic issue. He stabbed the end of the man's finger and placed a drop of blood on the strip. It read one-hundred seventeen, which was normal. James placed the cardiac monitor on the man and ran a strip. His heart rate was forty-six.

Jacob retrieved the IV kit out of their bag and prepared the man's arm to start an IV.

"You need to bag him faster. His heart rate is dropping," James told the firefighter.

He squeezed the bag quicker.

James looked at the cardiac monitor, his heart rate increased and that bought them a few minutes.

Jacob slid the needle into his arm and blood flashed into the chamber. He was in the vein. He connected a saline lock onto the catheter and flushed it. "Give me the Narcan."

"Why don't we just intubate him?" James asked.

"Narcan will work just fine. We don't need to be that invasive," Jacob said. He purged the air out of the syringe, screwed it onto the saline lock, and then slowly dispersed the drug. If it was pushed too fast, the patient would vomit. After pushing in one milligram, he followed it up with a saline bolus. A moment later, the man's eyes flickered to life. He reached up and pushed the bag valve mask away from his face.

"Wha...what happened?"

"Sir, what's your name? Do you know where you are?" Jacob

asked.

He turned his head from side to side, seeing the paramedics and firefighters around him. The man sat up with the needle still in his arm and pulled it out. Blood flowed from the puncture wound. "Who are you people? What are you doing here?"

Jacob kneeled down next to him. "Sir, we were called because the maids found you not breathing. We're paramedics. What did you take?"

The man hung his head. "I've never done this before. This was a big mistake. I've been under a lot of stress and wanted to feel good for a little while. A friend gave me some heroin and said it would take all of my worries away. I'm so sorry."

"Sir, I hope you realize that if we hadn't been called, you'd be dead right now. You weren't breathing. We gave you a medication that stopped the effects of the drug. We're going to have to take you to the hospital. It isn't going to last long," Jacob said. He grabbed a small stack of gauze and taped it over the man's leaking wound from where he injected the heroin.

The man's mouth hung open. "Hospital? Is that necessary?"

"Yes. Why don't you come with us so we can make sure you're going to be okay?"

The man stood up tried to push his way past the men. "I don't need to go to the hospital. I'm feeling fine."

James stepped in front of him and placed a hand on his shoulder. "Sir, do you realize we just saved your life? You had a matter of minutes before you would've died. This isn't a joking matter. We're not judging you. No one in this room is judging you, but you need to go to the hospital. If you don't, you could die. Is that what you want?"

The man shook his head. A deep sigh slipped through his lips. "Okay, I'll go with you."

James let go of his shoulder. "That's a good choice. Follow me down to our ambulance and we can get you going."

The man complied and followed James out of the hotel room.

Jacob retrieved all of their gear. "Thank you guys for your help. You all did a great job," he said to the firefighters.

They smiled and followed Jacob down the stairs. Several people in the hotel were standing outside watching them or looking out of their windows.

Don't worry. We'll be back later for another one of you.

Jacob opened the side door of the ambulance and placed the equipment bags on the floor. The man climbed in, sat on the cot, and James obtained his vital signs. A small part of Jacob felt sorry for the man. He was looking for an escape from reality that almost cost him his life.

Jacob looked over at James. "I've got this. You go ahead and drive."

James smiled. "Copy that." He stepped out of the back of the ambulance and walked around to the driver's seat. "Medic-57, to dispatch."

"Go ahead, Medic-57."

"We'll be en-route to the hospital."

"Dispatch copies."

James returned the microphone to the rocker, shifted the ambulance into drive, and drove toward the hospital.

The patient sat back on the cot and conversed with Jacob. Part of his job was not only to tend to the physical needs, but also their emotional ones as well.

"You feeling okay, sir?" Jacob asked.

The man looked forward. "Yeah."

Jacob rested his elbows on his knees, leaning toward the patient. "I know you're embarrassed. It's okay. We all make mistakes."

"It was a mistake that almost cost me my life."

"The important thing is that you learn from it."

The man hung his head. "I know."

"It's obvious this isn't the normal lifestyle for you. Why did you choose that part of town to go to?"

"I didn't want to risk anyone seeing me."

Jacob leaned back against the seat. "I understand. I know life can be tough sometimes, but try not to do this again because next time, you may not be so lucky."

"You don't have to worry about that."

A few minutes later, they arrived at the hospital. James wrote the mileage on a piece of paper. "Medic-57, to dispatch. We're out at Magic County Hospital."

"Dispatch copies."

Jacob patted the man on the shoulder and then got out of the truck. He looked to the sky and relished the warmth of the sunshine on his face as they pushed the cot toward the entrance. There was a slight breeze and birds were flying in a playful manner.

The emergency room was busy. There were several nurses and doctors standing around the nurses' station in the middle of the ER, talking. The rooms surrounded the main desk. No matter where you sat at the desk, you could see every room. There were sixteen rooms, a lot less than Jacob was accustomed to.

"Whatcha got?" a nurse asked from behind the desk.

"Heroin overdose. We administered Narcan and his vital signs are stable," Jacob answered.

She shook her head. "Room twelve. A nurse will be with you in a few minutes." She glanced around the emergency room. "As you can see, we're pretty busy."

The men pushed the cot toward room twelve. James stopped in front of it. "Sir, if we let you down, do you think you can walk?"

"Yeah. I can do that."

They lowered the cot and James followed him into the room. Jacob retrieved a fresh set of linens and reassembled the cot. He looked around, watching the hustle and bustle around him.

A nurse caught his attention. She hung on the arm of a man in a white lab coat and laughed as he spoke—he must've been a doctor. Jacob set the sheets down, walked over, and stood directly behind her. The doctor's attention shifted to him.

"I...um...I have to pee," Jacob said.

The nurse stiffened and swung around toward Jacob. Her eyes widened and her mouth dropped open. After a moment, she jumped into his arms and flung her arms around his neck. The man in the lab coat looked displeased.

"Oh my God. Jacob! Is it you?"

Several of the other nurses and doctors took notice and stared at them.

"Yes, it is." He was gasping for air. "Bridge, I can't breathe."

She continued squeezing him tight. After a few moments, she let go of him and stood back. Looking around the emergency room, seeing everyone was watching her, she smoothed out her scrub top.

The man beside her glared. "Are you going to introduce me to your friend?"

Bridge's body stiffened. "This is Jacob. He's a friend of mine that I met when I was travel nursing in Arizona." She looked up at Jacob. "This is my...friend...Doctor Young."

Doctor Young glared at her. Bridge hung her head and then looked nervously around the emergency room. He stepped forward and held out his hand. "Nice to meet you."

Jacob returned the gesture and shook his hand. Young gave his hand a death grip.

"Are you the same Jacob that I talked through field C-section?"

Jacob stared at him for a moment before answering. "Yes, that was me."

Bridge looked shocked. "That was you, Jacob?"

"Unfortunately, it was."

Doctor Young released Jacob's hand, walked over, and placed an arm around Bridge. "It's great to meet one of my Bridge's friends."

My Bridge? Who does this guy think he is?

"She's an amazing woman. You're one lucky guy," Jacob said never taking his eyes off Bridge.

She stared at the floor.

"Doctor Jones is on line two for you," a nurse said to Doctor Young from the main desk.

His eyes narrowed. "Well, duty calls. It was nice to meet you, Jacob. Good work on that call, by the way." He turned toward Bridge and placed his hands on both of her shoulders. "I'll see you for lunch?"

"Sure."

He leaned down, kissed her on the forehead, and then walked over to take his call. Jacob stared at Bridge for a moment, walked over to his cot, and then walked out of the emergency room. Bridge ran after him. She grabbed his arm and spun him around.

"I'm sorry about that, Jacob. He can be a little possessive at times."

Jacob wanted nothing more than to take Bridge into his arms and kiss her, but that wasn't an option. "You seem happy. That's all that matters, right?"

"Don't be like that. What are you doing here? How long have you been here? Why haven't you tried getting in touch with me?"

There were a thousand things he wanted to say to her, but didn't know where to start. "I tried. No one would give me your number. I got here a few weeks ago, but it doesn't matter now anyway."

"Don't be this way, Jacob. I won't allow you to make me feel guilty for dating someone. I told you in Arizona I didn't want anything serious because I wasn't staying there."

Little did she know she was the reason he left the desert, coupled with the fact of what had happened with Becca, but he wasn't going to tell her that. "Look, I'm happy for you. You're a wonderful woman, but I think you could've done better."

Bridge's eyes narrowed. "You don't know him. How dare you say that?"

Jacob's shoulders slumped. "Bridge, he is in control of my life right now. I did that field C-section under his direction. State EMS is going after my license. They're going to subpoena him to testify. If he denies ever giving me the order, I'm screwed!"

"He won't do that. I'll talk to him."

"By the looks of it, he doesn't care for me right now. I wouldn't be surprised if he denied it."

Bridge crossed her arms over her chest. "I said I would talk to him."

James walked out of the emergency room. He stopped and stared quizzically at the two. "Everything okay?"

Bridge turned toward James. "Yeah, everything is great." She stomped back toward the ambulance entrance.

Jacob chased after Bridge, but noticed Young standing at the sliding glass doors glaring at him; he stopped. A feeling of helplessness grabbed him like a pair of hands and squeezed the last bit of air out of his lungs.

FIVE

JACOB PREPARED FOR his initial hearing with State EMS. Mr. Burgess, his attorney, called him and briefed him on the meeting. He stood in front of the mirror trying to convince himself everything was going to work out. His cell phone vibrated across the counter top.

"Hello?"

"Hey, Jacob. How's it going?" James asked.

Jacob sighed. "Good, for now. I'm about to leave for the hearing and I'm nervous."

"I don't blame ya. Stand by your decision and make sure they understand that without you, that baby would've died."

If only it were that easy.

"I'm going to try. I'm worried that Doctor Young is going to hold onto his little grudge that he has with me."

"Grudge?"

"You remember that nurse I was talking to the other day at the hospital?"

"You mean Bridgette?"

"Yeah. We met when she worked down in Phoenix. I was instantly attracted to her, for obvious reasons."

"She's a gorgeous woman."

"We went out a few times and I think there was a little spark. She backed off because she didn't want anything serious and then her contract ended and she had to come back to Idaho. The other day when I saw her, Doctor Young didn't look too pleased that his woman was hugging on another guy."

The phone was silent for a moment. "Well, you can't blame him. I'm sure you wouldn't have been thrilled either if the tables had been turned."

James had a point. Jacob hadn't thought of it that way. "You're right. Anyway, now he has control over my career."

"Don't stress over it. I'm sure he's professional enough not to do that."

"I hope you're right. I need to get going."

"Good luck, buddy."

Jacob walked into his bedroom and threw his phone on the bed. He finished getting dressed, but couldn't shake his trepidation. All Doctor Young had to do was deny giving Jacob the order to perform the field C-section and his career would be over. He pushed down a knot that had formed in his throat. After he finished getting dressed, Jacob walked to his front door and peered out of the window to see if any media were perched on his lawn and thankfully, no one was there. He walked out of his house, got into his truck, and headed toward the State EMS office. There was no avoiding this hearing. Still, he didn't think he had done anything wrong, and he was sticking to his guns. He only hoped that the committee members had a heart and could look past the protocols.

Jacob pulled into the parking lot filled with media vehicles from the various news stations. He clenched his trembling hands together as he glanced over and noticed Nate conversing with Mr. Burgess. Moments later, the media spotted him and rushed toward his truck. Nate and Mr. Burgess took notice and ran toward him. The media surrounded his truck, taking pictures, and asking questions. Mr. Burgess pulled Jacob through the parking lot with the media following closely behind like vultures circling their prey. Nate held the crowd back as they neared the building and then once inside, he pulled the doors shut with a firm click.

"This is crazy," Jacob said shaking his head.

Nate nodded. "The word must've gotten out."

Mr. Burgess smoothed out the sleeves of his suit coat. "This could be in our favor. It's obvious the public has heard about you saving the baby. That should play on the decision of the committee. They don't want to become 'public enemy number one,' and Lord knows we can use all of the help we can get."

Jacob turned around and noticed Young approaching them and Bridge was with him. He held her hand with a smirk on his face.

"I'm glad you could make it, Doctor Young," Mr. Burgess said.

"It's my pleasure. I'll do anything I can to help. This is my fiancé, Bridgette Nelson."

Fiancé? When did that happen?

Jacob was shocked. Bridge wouldn't look up at him; she stared at the floor.

"It's a pleasure to meet you, Bridgette." Mr. Burgess shook her hand.

Bridgette looked embarrassed. "Nice to meet you, too."

Tension loomed in the air as Doctor Young grinned at Jacob.

A door behind them opened and a woman stepped out. "I'm looking for Jacob Myers."

"I'm Jacob."

"We're ready for you," she said holding the door open.

Mr. Burgess' cell phone rang. "Excuse me for just a moment." He opened his phone and stepped a few feet away.

Jacob walked through the door. Nate, Doctor Young, and Bridge followed closely behind. They entered a large conference room with an elevated bench at the end of the room. There were three men and two women perched behind it. Jacob walked to the front of the room and sat down at a small table. Nate, Doctor Young, and Bridge sat down behind him. Mr. Burgess burst through the doors, walked hurriedly toward Jacob, and took a seat next to him.

Jacob leaned in close to Mr. Burgess, whispering. "Anything you need to tell me about?"

"Not right now." Mr. Burgess shifted in his seat, grabbed his brief case, and pulled out a file full of paperwork.

Jacob shifted nervously in his seat and focused his attention on the panel of members in front of him. His heart raced. This was it: the decisive moment when he would find out his fate. Sweat beaded on his forehead.

"I'd like to call this hearing to order. Is Jacob Myers present?" a gray-haired man asked.

"Yes. I'm Jacob Myers."

The man looked grimly at Jacob and nodded, acknowledging him. "Is his counsel present?"

"Yes, Mr. Chairman. Mr. Burgess, attorney at law, present."

"Very well. This isn't an official hearing, merely a committee review to determine if the state wishes to suspend Mr. Myers' paramedic license and file criminal charges with the district attorney."

"Criminal charges? That's insane. I saved a baby's life," Jacob blurted out.

Mr. Burgess grabbed Jacob's arm. "You need to shut up and let me do the talking. The only time you speak is if they ask you a question. Do you understand?"

Jacob tried to regain his composure. "Yes."

The members of the committee quietly spoke amongst themselves. "Can we continue counselor?"

"Yes, Mr. Chairman. My apologies."

"The reason we're here today is due to Jacob Myers performing a procedure that isn't approved by the state for paramedics." The Chairman flipped through several pieces of paper. "Mr. Myers performed a field C-section on a woman that was in cardiac arrest. Is that correct?"

"Yes, Mr. Chairman," Mr. Burgess replied.

Jacob's anger grew by the minute.

"Mr. Myers, do you understand what you did was wrong and not approved by the state?" the Chairman asked.

Mr. Burgess nodded to him.

"I understand it's not approved, but I think you all are overlooking the fact that if I hadn't done it, the baby would've died. I won't admit that I was wrong."

The chairman set down the stack of papers. "No one is questioning the fact that you saved the baby's life. We're merely stating that you performed a skill outside of the scope of practice approved by the state for paramedics."

"I performed it under the medical direction of Doctor Young at Magic County Hospital," Jacob said. His voice grew louder as his agitation peaked.

"Mr. Chairman, if I may?" Mr. Burgess asked.

"Go ahead."

He stood. "We realize that field C-sections aren't approved by the state. My client realized that this was a life and death situation, so he did as protocol stated and called for medical direction. Under direct online medical supervision, he performed a procedure that saved a life that would've been lost had he not done it."

"I understand that. The fact remains that he did a procedure not approved by the state. Bottom line." The chairman leaned forward on the bench. "I empathize with him. I do. The fact remains, he isn't trained for this."

Jacob sank back in his seat. It was apparent the committee had already made up their minds. He felt like he was drowning in a sea of despair with no chance of surviving.

"Mr. Chairman, Doctor Young is here and would like to be heard."

The chairman looked at the other members of the panel. They nodded in agreement. "That's fine. We'll hear what he has to say."

Mr. Burgess looked behind him and beckoned the doctor.

Young patted Bridge's hand, stood up, and approached the table.

Jacob's heart thumped against his chest. Would this man help him or nail him to the wall?

"For the record, state your name for the committee," the chairman said.

"Doctor Ed Young. I'm an emergency room physician at Magic County Hospital."

"Go ahead, Doctor Young."

The clock on the wall ticked the seconds away as Jacob held his breath.

"The paramedic, Jacob, called me from the scene of the accident. During extrication, the pregnant female went into cardiac arrest. Jacob followed protocol and called for online medical direction. I was on duty that day. In traumatic arrest, a victim has a ninety-nine percent mortality rate. I gave him online orders and talked him through the C-section. If anyone should be in trouble, it should be me."

Jacob felt the muscles of his jaw relax. He had a new respect for the doctor and was relieved the man had a deeper character than he had given him credit for having.

Each member of the panel looked at one another. "I understand that you gave him the order, doctor. The fact remains he isn't approved to perform such a procedure," the chairman said.

Jacob glared at the members of the committee. His life was spinning carelessly out of control in front of his eyes. Even with Doctor Young testifying for him, it appeared the committee was going to persecute his decision.

"I understand and respect what you're saying, Mr. Chairman, but you're ignoring the fact that the paramedics are under our control. He did followed my orders. I think it's preposterous that his career is hanging in the balance."

The chairman grabbed a large three-ring binder. "Doctor Young, I would like for you to come and grab these state approved protocols."

Doctor Young approached the bench, grabbed the binder, and then stood next to Mr. Burgess.

"If you would, please open the section that has the field C-section protocol," the chairman said.

Doctor Young opened the binder and flipped through the pages. A few moments later, he closed the binder. "It's not in here."

The chairman leaned back in his seat. "Exactly my point."

Mr. Burgess bolted up from his chair. "Mr. Chairman, we realize that there isn't such a protocol. You've made that abundantly clear. If the committee doesn't mind, I'd like to call one more person that's here to speak on Jacob's behalf."

The chairman had a puzzled look on his face. He looked at the other members of the committee. Each of them gave an approving nod. "That would be fine. Go ahead and call your next witness."

Doctor Young placed the binder down on the table and returned to his seat. Mr. Burgess walked back to the doors and opened them. Jacob turned around in his seat. A man walked through the door holding an infant in his arms and stood next to the table where Jacob was sitting. Mr. Burgess returned to his seat.

"Identify yourself for this committee, please sir," the chairman said.

He stood in front of the committee gently rocking the baby. "My name is Dale Blakenship. This is my son, Jacob Blakenship. I'm here today to tell you that if it wasn't for paramedic Jacob Myers, my son would've died, too." Tears welled up in his eyes.

The committee all looked at one another. "We understand this, sir. The fact remains that Jacob practiced medicine outside of his scope of practice. That cannot, and will not, be tolerated. We're sorry for your loss, sir," the chairman said.

Dale approached the committee, still holding his son. "Look at him. Look at my son. If it wasn't for Jacob, he would be dead. Can you understand that? Tell me, do you all have kids?"

The committee all looked at one another shocked by his question. Several of them nodded.

"Tell me this. What would you all do if the shoe was on *your* foot and you found out a paramedic didn't do something to save them? Would you be devastated? Would you be angry? Would your life be changed forever?" Dale grew louder. "You can't fault this man for following his heart or the orders given by the doctor. How do you put the price of a human life on a piece of paper? Because of him, my son is alive today. He shouldn't be persecuted; he should be considered a hero!"

The committee whispered amongst themselves.

Jacob was speechless and Mr. Burgess studied the members.

"Sir, you don't understand. The paramedics...."

"The paramedics saved my baby's life and that's all that matters!" He stepped closer to the bench. "I promise you this. If you formally charge Jacob and take away his license, I will go outside and speak to the media. I will tell them that you've punished him for saving my son's life. I'm quite confident that the community will side with me. You're all elected officials. I'm sure it will be virtually impossible to be re-elected when I'm done with you." He turned around and walked over to the table where Jacob was sitting. "I thank you sir, for saving my son's life." Tears streamed down his cheeks.

He walked out of the door and the room became eerily silent. The committee looked at one another. The chairman quietly conversed with the other members and said, "We'll need you all to leave the room so we can deliberate and make a decision. Once we're done, we'll call you back in."

Jacob and Mr. Burgess walked out of the room. Doctor Young, Bridge, and Nate followed closely behind.

"What do you think is going to happen?" Jacob asked.

"I don't know. It's hard to say. They have every right to suspend your paramedic license and file charges with the district attorney, but I think Dale's testimony helped you," Mr. Burgess said.

Jacob looked around, but Dale was gone. He wanted a chance to thank him. "Mr. Burgess, regardless of what happens, thank you."

"It's my pleasure," Mr. Burgess said, patting Jacob on the shoulder.

A few minutes later, a woman came out of the room. "We're ready for you to come back inside."

Jacob looked at Nate and Mr. Burgess nervously. The moment had come to find out his fate. He looked over and noticed Doctor Young kissing Bridge. She noticed Jacob and pulled away. Jacob pushed the scene to the back of his mind. He couldn't worry about that right now. He had to keep his mind clear. They all reentered the room. Jacob and Mr. Burgess returned to their seats at the table.

The chairman cleared his throat and looked down at a stack of papers he was holding. "We don't condone what you have done, Mr. Myers. It's a blatant violation of the state approved protocols."

Jacob sat straight in his seat, staring at the chairman.

Why is he dragging this out? Just say it already!

"It's the official decision of this committee that we will not be suspending your paramedic license, nor will we be filing charges with the district attorney." He put down the stack of papers and leaned forward in his seat with his elbows resting on the bench. "However, we will file an official complaint against your license and place it in your file. If you so much as sneeze too hard, we won't hesitate to suspend your license and prohibit you from ever practicing medicine again as long as you live. This is the committee's official decision. This matter is closed."

Jacob leaped out of his seat. He grabbed Mr. Burgess' hand and shook it. "I can't thank you enough. You have no idea how happy I am."

"It's my pleasure, Jacob. I agree one-hundred percent with what you did. If it were my child, I would expect you to do the same thing."

Jacob looked behind him; Bridge was smiling. Doctor Young stared forward. The weight lifted from Jacob's shoulders. He walked toward the doctor and held out his hand. "Thank you for everything you've done. I appreciate it."

Doctor Young turned toward Bridge. "Can you give us a moment, dear? I need to speak to Jacob."

"Um...sure." She glanced at Jacob with a weak smile and left the room.

Ed Young watched as Bridge walked away. He turned his attention back to Jacob. "Listen to me. The only reason I did this was to keep Bridge happy. I don't like you. I don't like the way you look at her. If it was my choice, I would've hung you out to dry," he said sternly. "You stay away from her. She's with me now. If you haven't noticed, we got engaged last night. Stay *away* from her!" He stomped out of the room.

Nate walked over to Jacob. "Is everything okay?"

Jacob stared as Young left. "Yeah. We're good."

"You got very lucky on this one. You might want to think twice about ever doing something like this again," Nate said.

Jacob thought for a moment. If the same call happened again, would he do the same thing? "You know, Nate, I would do it again in a heartbeat. If they take my paramedic license, I could live with that, but I couldn't live with myself knowing I had let someone die just because it isn't in the rule book."

SIX

JACOB ARRIVED AT the station earlier than normal. He wanted time to tell James everything. He pulled into his favorite parking spot and grabbed his bag out of the back of his truck. Nate stood stiffly with his arms crossed over his chest standing next to his partner.

"What did I do wrong now?" Jacob asked.

Nate shook his head. "My phone hasn't stopped blowing up since your little gutting you did."

Jacob dropped his bag on the ground. "Gutting? How about we call it what it was; a lifesaving procedure?"

Nate's brow furrowed. "I bet you think you're the best paramedic in the field now, don't you? Hero paramedic saves the day. You're anything but a hero. Granted, you saved the baby's life, but have you thought about what could've happened had the result ended differently? You didn't think about that, did you?"

Things could've gone bad, but they didn't. "I will apologize for the grief you've had to endure, but I won't apologize for saving that baby's life."

The two men stared each other down.

James stepped between them. "Guys, this matter is closed. Why don't we follow suit and move on?"

Nate stepped backward while shaking his head. "You've caused me a lot of stress. I understand why you did what you did, but it hasn't made my life any easier. You need to think about all the implications before you do anything like this in the future." Nate walked past them, got into his command truck, and sped out of the parking lot with tires squealing.

Jacob and James watched Nate race down the street.

"He can be a jerk sometimes. Ignore him. He's dealing with a lot right now."

Jacob bent down and picked up his bag. "I guess. I thought maybe he would ride this media circus and take credit for one of his paramedics saving a baby's life. Guess I was wrong."

As Jacob walked toward the ambulance bay, the station tones sounded.

"Medic-57, we have a one vehicle traffic accident on Rosewood Avenue, one-half mile south of Glennwood Street."

"No rest for the weary," Jacob said. He walked inside of the bay, threw down his bag, and climbed into the passenger side of the ambulance.

James joined him. "Medic-57, we'll be en-route. Do we have a patient count?"

"One patient. He ran off the road and crashed into a tree. Injuries are unknown at this time. Police are on scene and fire department has been notified."

James pulled out into traffic and the early morning commuters yielded the right of way to them. Each driver stared, trying to catch a glimpse of them as they passed by. The sun was shining with a backdrop of a clear blue sky. There was something about the warm air, blue skies, and the sunshine that catapulted Jacob into a good mood. After a few miles, they approached the vehicle that had barreled into a tree.

"Medic-57, to dispatch," James said.

"Go ahead, Medic-57."

"We're on scene of a one vehicle accident with major damage. More report to follow."

"Dispatch copies."

The two men got out of the ambulance and donned their reflective vests. There were two police cars and a fire engine on scene. The front of the SUV wrapped around the Oak tree; the windshield was shattered. Jacob looked back and saw several wavy skid marks on the pavement. There were two firefighters and two police officers standing next to the vehicle, leaning in through the window and talking to the patient.

Jacob walked up behind the firefighters and James spoke to another police officer. "What do ya got?"

"Thirty-two year old male patient that lost control of his vehicle and struck this tree. He's apparently been drinking," the firefighter answered.

Jacob stiffened. He had no tolerance for drunk drivers. For a brief moment, the pictures of Stitch and the small child being run over by a drunk in front of him flashed through his mind. His pulse throbbed in his ears. He squeezed in between the two firefighters.

"Sir, are you hurting anywhere?" Jacob asked.

"Huh? What?" the man answered.

"I asked if you're hurting anywhere."

The man swayed back and forth in his seat. His seatbelt strapped across his chest. He looked as though he was having difficulty focusing. He squinted his eyes.

"No, mate."

Jacob noticed an empty Vodka bottle lying on the floorboard. The strong odor of the alcohol floated through the air. He walked around to the passenger side and picked up the bottle.

"Hey, that's mine!" the man yelled. He reached toward Jacob and tried to snatch the bottle from his hand.

"You can't have it. That's what caused you to wreck in the first place," Jacob said.

The man leaned against the door. "You're a funny guy. I like you." He reached up for Jacob's face.

The firefighters laughed until Jacob glared at them. He backed up out of reach of the man. "What's your name, sir?"

"Too many questions. I need a nap," the man said as he laid his head down against the door and closed his eyes.

The firefighters and the police officers laughed.

Jacob's frustration grew. "We need to get him out of the vehicle. Think you can take the time to do your job?"

The men stopped laughing and shot dirty looks at Jacob. One of the firefighters reached down and pulled on the door handle—it was stuck. The other firefighters joined him and together they pulled on the door until it sprang open.

James overheard what Jacob said and walked over to him. "You were a little rough on them, don't you think?"

Jacob was a stubborn man and didn't like to admit when he was wrong, but he was. He grabbed the shoulders of the two firefighters. "I'm sorry, guys. I was out of line. I recently had a bad experience with a drunk driver. I shouldn't have taken that out on you."

They smiled. "No problem. We understand."

The two firefighters walked over and retrieved the cot from the back of their ambulance. Jacob knelt down next to the man.

"Wake up, sleeping beauty. We're going to take you to the hospital," he said shaking the man's shoulder.

"What? Where am I?" he asked slurring his words.

"You were in an accident. We're taking you to the hospital. You hurting anywhere?"

"What? I don't want to go to the hospital," the man answered. He pushed Jacob's hand away.

One of the police officers walked over next to Jacob. "Sir, I think you need to go."

"Are you deaf? I don't want to go!"

"If you don't go with the paramedics, I'm going to place you under arrest and take you to jail for suspicion of DWI."

The man focused his eyes on the officer. "Now that you mention it, my knee hurts. I better go with them."

"Wise choice," the officer said, grinning.

The firefighters returned with the cot and lowered it. Jacob cleared his c-spine, and, helped the man to his feet.

"Ouch, easy. My knee hurts," the man said, limping toward the waiting cot and then he sat down.

Jacob and James lifted the cot and pushed him toward the ambulance. Jacob was having a difficult time treating the man with any kind of respect. He knew he had to because the man was a human being who made a bad choice, but he couldn't help feeling angry with the drunk driver.

One of the firefighters sprinted up to them. "Do you guys need us? We were toned out to a structure fire."

Jacob looked up and saw the man had already laid his head back and was fast asleep. "No, we're good. You guys be careful."

He nodded and ran to his fire truck. The police officers jumped into their cars and sped away from the scene with their tires squealing. James and Jacob lifted the man into the back of the ambulance and locked the cot in place. James jumped up into the back of their truck.

The man opened his eyes and looked around. "Where did the police run off to?"

"They had to go on a house fire. Sir, what's your name?" James asked him.

"I don't want to go to the hospital," the man growled. He tugged on the seatbelts.

Jacob stepped up to the end of the cot. "Sir, you need to go. Let's just run you up there and get you checked out."

"I said I don't want to go! Let me out of here!"

Jacob stood outside the ambulance at the foot of the cot. "Sir, you need to go and get checked out by the doctor. It's better to be safe since you've been drinking. The alcohol could mask serious symptoms."

The man's eyes narrowed and his body stiffened. He reared back his legs and kicked Jacob in the face. Jacob toppled backwards and landed flat on his back on the asphalt. James sat next to the man with his mouth gaping open.

Jacob lay on his back for a moment, trying to shake the cobwebs out of his head. Everything was spinning and his ears felt like they were filling with a warm liquid. When opened his eyes, he saw three of James swaying in front of him. After a few moments, Jacob picked himself up off the ground. His head pounded and the spinning became worse.

James pushed down on the man's chest forcing him against the cot. "Listen, you jerk. You just assaulted a health care provider. That's a felony in this state. I suggest you sit back, shut up, and let us take you to the hospital before things get ugly."

The man raised his hands up in the air, surrendering. "Okay, take it easy. I'll go."

James shifted his attention to Jacob. "Are you okay?"

Jacob took a moment to steady himself. "Yeah. I'm fine."

Jacob approached the back of the ambulance and James laughed.

"What's so funny?" Jacob asked angrily.

"It says *Nike* on your forehead."

He reached up and touched his forehead. He could feel indentations. Jacob stumbled around to the driver's side of the ambulance and leaned down looking in the side view mirror. *Nike* was stamped vertically on his forehead. His head began to swim again; he grabbed the ambulance to steady himself. He walked to the back of the truck.

"You don't hit paramedics, you idiot. We're here to help you. Now we're going to file charges against you. What do you think about that?" James said.

"That wouldn't be wise. I'm not the kind of guy you mess with," the man slurred.

Jacob held onto the back of the ambulance. It felt as though someone was trying to drive a wedge between his eyes. He scrunched his eyes closed trying to push the pain away. The urge to vomit was overwhelming.

"You don't look too steady on your feet," James said to his partner.

Jacob squinted his eyes shut trying to clear the blurry vision, but it didn't help. "Yeah. I'm fine. You ready to go?"

"You sure you're okay to drive? Maybe I should."

Jacob's stubbornness kicked in. He wasn't going to show weakness and let the drunken patient know how hurt he was. "No. I'll be fine." He looked at the man sitting on the cot. "It wouldn't be wise for me to be in the back with him right now."

The man laughed.

Jacob slammed the doors to the ambulance shut and staggered to the driver's side. He climbed into the driver's seat and shut the door.

"Medic-57 to dispatch."

"Go ahead."

"We'll be en-route to the hospital."

"Dispatch copies."

Jacob shifted the ambulance into drive. He saw three of everything. He reached up and placed his hand over his right eye and it helped. Normally, Jacob would've felt foolish for doing it, but now it was a necessity to be able to drive.

A car full of teenagers drove next to him.

"Are you a pirate? You taking an eye test or something?" one of the teenagers yelled out of the window.

Jacob ignored their comments and sped forward. A short time later, they arrived at the hospital. He put the ambulance into park and removed his hand from over his eye.

"Medic-57 to dispatch."

"Go ahead."

"We've arrived at Magic County Hospital. Can you dispatch an officer to the emergency room please? We need to file an assault report."

"Dispatch copies."

Jacob climbed out and fell against the ambulance. Once he was able to gain his bearings, he walked to the back of the truck. He opened the doors and the man on the cot instantly made eye contact with him.

"That was a mistake. I heard what you said on the radio." He glared at Jacob.

"I'm not the idiot that drove drunk and assaulted a health care worker. It's a felony and I'm going to press charges. You're going to learn one way or another," Jacob growled. He had enough. Too many times, he heard about health care workers assaulted, and nothing was ever done about it.

James climbed out of the back of the ambulance and looked over at Jacob. "You don't look so good. I think we should have you checked out while we're here."

"I don't need it. I'll be fine."

"Fine? Then why did you have to drive covering one of your eyes? Don't be so stubborn and get checked out."

Jacob hated it when someone called him stubborn. He was raised to be tough and not to complain; that's exactly what he was doing now.

James pulled the cot out of the ambulance and they pushed the man through the entrance and into the emergency room. Jacob looked around. From what he could tell, they were busy. His nausea grew and a cold sweat trickled down the back of his neck.

"I need to sit down," Jacob said as he collapsed face first onto the floor unconscious. A hollow thud from his head striking the floor echoed through the emergency room.

Doctor Young ordered a stat head CT. James helped two nurses move him to a stretcher and then they pushed him toward radiology. Ten minutes later the nurses returned with Jacob and moved him to an empty room.

Jacob opened his eyes. Bridge stared down at him with a worried look on her face. Doctor Young stood next to her with his arm draped around her shoulders.

James walked into the room and stood next to his bed. "I called Nate. He's on his way down here."

Jacob reached up and touched his head; it was pounding. "What happened?"

"You passed smooth out, brother," James said.

Jacob looked to where the voice was coming from—it was James standing at the door. "I passed out?"

"Yes, you did. Landed flat on your face on the floor."

Jacob reached up and touched his nose. Pain jolted throughout his face. "The last thing I remember was feeling like I needed to sit down."

Doctor Young had his arm around Bridge, caressing her shoulder. "Your CT was clear. You don't have any signs of bleeding on your brain. Looks like you just have a serious concussion. I'm going to admit you for a twenty-four hour observation."

"I'm fine. I don't need that. I want to get back to work." Jacob tried to sit up, but succumbed to dizziness, and fell back against the bed. His temples pounded and his stomach churned, threatening to empty its contents.

Bridge placed her hand on his chest and pushed him down. "Don't be so foolish, Jacob. Now isn't the time to be stubborn. Do as the doctor told you and lie back." She kept her hand on his chest, lightly patting him.

Doctor Young frowned.

Nate walked into the room and looked down at Jacob. "You okay?"

"Yeah. My head and nose are killing me. Other than that, I'm fine."

Nate turned toward James. "What happened?"

"A drunk driver we loaded into the ambulance kicked him in the face."

"Where was law enforcement?"

"A structure fire kicked out over the radio. We cleared them and the fire department. He had passed out and we told them we could handle it from there."

Nate's brow wrinkled. "I need to speak to you outside, now!"

James nodded, weakly smiled at his partner, and stepped outside of the room. Jacob could hear Nate yelling at him. He wanted to run to his partner's defense, but his body wouldn't allow it. He closed his eyes, hoping the swimming would go away. At least the nausea had subsided.

"I'll be back later to check on you," Bridge caressed his cheek and left the room.

Young stood over Jacob glaring at him. "I'm going to go write your admittance orders. If you need anything, ask the nurses." He turned and stormed out of the room.

Nate blamed James for Jacob getting hurt. His yelling resonated through the emergency room. Jacob tried to sit up, but his head pounded more forcefully. He fell back against the pillow and closed his eyes. In the distance, he could hear Young berating Bridge. It was frustrating listening to two people he cared about being scolded and there was nothing he could do about it.

Jacob staggered out of bed and steadied himself against the counter, watching Ed Young speak to Bridge.

"What is your problem? Why are you acting this way?" Ed asked.

"You're unbelievable. He's my friend. You need to accept that and quit trying to show ownership every time you're around him. I'm not a piece of property," Bridge yelled.

Ed reached over and tried to hold onto Bridge's shoulder, but she pushed him away. "Honey, you need to calm down. You're being irrational and embarrassing me."

"Don't you honey me. I'm being irrational? You're the irrational one. What has gotten into you lately? You've become jealous and possessive. I don't like it. If things don't change...."

Doctor Young stiffened. "Then what? What are you going to do?"

Bridge folded her arms across her chest. "If things don't change, you're going to push me away. I will not be treated like a piece of property."

Doctor Young crossed his arms over his chest. His jaw tense. "You need to figure out where your priorities are or you might lose me!" He stomped out of the emergency room.

Bridge walked over to the charge nurse.

"Everything okay, Bridge?"

"I need a few minutes. I'm going for a walk. Is that okay?"

"Sure thing, dear. Take all of the time you need. We have a float nurse that can take over your rooms until you get back."

"Thank you." Bridge walked toward the ambulance entrance and out of the emergency room.

Jacob climbed back into the bed. He felt like someone was striking him in the back of his head with a sledgehammer. His vision blurred and he couldn't focus.

A few minutes later, James walked back into Jacob's room. "How ya feeling, bud?"

"Like I just did eight rounds with the heavyweight champion of the world. Can you turn that light off? It's killing me."

James strolled over and flipped the light switch off. "That better?"

"Yeah. Thanks."

Now with the light off, Jacob was able to open his eyes. His head didn't hurt as much if he didn't move. "I'm sorry about Nate chewing you out. It's just as much my fault as yours."

James laughed. "It's not a big deal. It's his job to keep us safe."

"I didn't think he cared much about me. Guess I was wrong."

"You have to understand that he was under a lot of pressure from our call with the baby. You can't hold that against him. He's a fair man. I know you're new here, but he has brought this department out of the stone ages."

Nate walked back into Jacob's room. "I just spoke with the police officers. They're arresting the man you two brought in. He's going to be charged with DWI and assaulting a health care provider." He looked back and forth between James and Jacob. "The next time you two decide to clear law enforcement before the scene is completely safe, I'm going to fire both of you. Is that clear?"

"Yes, sir," James answered.

"You got it, boss," Jacob said.

A few moments later, two officers walked past Jacob's room with the man they transported in handcuffs. He was kicking at them and trying to pull his arms away. He stopped in front of Jacob's room.

"You're going to pay for this. Watch your back!" the man screamed.

Nate pointed toward the ambulance entrance. "Get him out of here."

The two officers dragged the man away. He continued to scream profanities as they went.

James shook his head and turned toward Jacob. "You're a popular man. This is the second time this week someone has threatened you."

Nate looked at the two men with confusion on his face.

"Guess I have that effect on people," Jacob said.

SEVEN

JACOB STOOD AT the sink brushing his teeth and a light knock on the door caught his attention. He glanced over his shoulder and smiled.

"Are you sure it's okay that you're here with me right now?" Jacob asked.

Bridge's smile vanished. "He doesn't own me, even though he thinks he does." She crossed her arms and leaned against the doorway.

Desperately trying to hide his true feelings, he turned his back toward her.

"Why won't you look at me, Jacob? I miss the guy that fumbled his words around me."

Jacob shoved his phone is his pocket. "I'm still the same guy. You're the one that has changed."

Bridge walked briskly across the room, grabbed Jacob by his arm, and turned him around to face her.

"Look at me, damn it! I will not let...."

Jacob dropped his wallet, threw his arms around her waist, and pulled her close to him. He planted his lips against hers. At first, Bridge tried to push him away, but within moments, she melted into him. Bridge put her arms around his neck and kissed him. After a few moments, Jacob released her lips and looked into her eyes. She had a hypnotic gaze. She released her hold on him and took a few steps back.

"I've wanted to do that for a long time," Jacob said.

"I...I can't do this. This is wrong. It shouldn't have happened." She shook her head and left the room.

Jacob was shocked. He was consumed by a mixture of emotions—

satisfaction and anger. He pulled his cell phone out of his pocket and dialed James. After a few rings, he answered.

"Hello?"

"Hey, James. I've been discharged from the hospital. Can you come pick me up?"

"Sure thing, buddy. I'll be there in ten minutes."

"Thanks." Jacob shut his phone, put it in his front pocket, and walked out of his room. He waved at the nurses as he approached the elevator. Reaching to push the button, he had a flashback of the last time he left the hospital as a patient. This time he didn't have any difficulties commanding his body. A slight grin crossed his face. The elevator doors opened, he stepped inside, and pushed the button for the first floor. Descending to the ground floor, the memory of Bridge's lips pressed against his lingered. He knew that he should feel guilty about it, but he didn't.

The elevator doors opened and he decided to walk through the emergency room, maybe have a chance to see Bridge once again. He rounded the corner and caught a glimpse of Bridge standing at the nurse's station. He confidently walked toward her. She rifled through a stack of papers and didn't notice he was there.

"Bridge, we need to talk," Jacob said.

She looked up at him, shocked. "What are you doing here?" She scanned the emergency room.

"You can't ignore what happened."

She leaned toward him with her hands on the desk. "Nothing happened!"

"What are you two talking about?" Doctor Young asked.

Jacob broke the gaze he had on Bridge and looked over at the doctor. "Just arguing who was better at starting IV's. She fails to realize how awesome I am."

"Is that so? Guess you weren't awesome enough to dodge the foot of a drunk," Young laughed.

Jacob fought off the urge to tell him that he had kissed Bridge. He knew it would be more trouble than it was worth and he would most likely lose any chances to be with her. "You got me on that one, doc."

The doc had a pleased look on his face. He put an arm around Bridge and pulled her close to him. She stared at the desk, not making eye contact with either of them.

"How are you feeling?" Young asked Jacob.

"A little bit of a headache, but I'll be fine. Thank you for taking care of me. I appreciate it." Jacob extended his hand toward him.

The doctor hesitated, and then returned the gesture.

"It's not a problem. Glad I could help," he said as he firmly gripped Jacob's hand.

Jacob's hand turned numb. He pulled it away. "Well, I should be going. You two have a great night."

Doctor Young had a smirk across his face as Jacob walked away. He stopped out of their view and looked back.

Bridge pulled away from Ed. "Is it necessary to flaunt our relationship in front of him every time you see him?"

"Why are you defending him?"

They stood staring at one another.

"You're unbelievable. I don't want to talk to you right now." Bridge tried to walk by, but he grabbed her arm.

His eyes narrowed and stared at Bridge. "Don't walk away from me when I'm talking to you. We're not finished here!"

Bridge ripped her arm out of his grip and looked him square in the eyes. "Don't you ever touch me like that again. If you do...."

"What? What are you going to do?"

Bridge shook her head and walked out of the ambulance entrance.

"Go ahead. Run to him. I know that's what you want to do anyway." Young shouted.

You're making this too easy, doc. Jacob thought.

EIGHT

ONCE JACOB AND James checked off their ambulance, they did the weekly disinfecting of the patient compartment. Jacob didn't share his partner's germ-a-phobia tendencies. They were exposed to contagious illnesses on a daily basis and he felt there wasn't enough disinfectant in the world to protect them.

"You feeling okay?" James asked.

"Yeah. The headaches are getting better, but I'm constantly nauseated. That was one hell of a kick that man caught me with."

James laughed.

"What's so funny?"

"I'm sorry, man, but that Nike imprint on your forehead was hilarious."

Jacob didn't find it amusing. What really angered him was the fact he let his guard down enough for the man to assault him. "That's messed up that you find humor in my pain."

"Oh, don't be so sensitive. You have to admit if the shoe was on the other foot, or in this case, on a different forehead, you'd find it funny, too."

Jacob thought about it for a few minutes. James had a point, but he wasn't going to give him the satisfaction of knowing he did.

"You hungry?"

"Yes. Want to go grab a bite to eat?" James asked.

"Where should we go?"

"There's a donut shop a few blocks from here." James patted his stomach and said, "I have a figure to work on."

Jacob put his rag down and peeled off his gloves. "I'm driving."

James climbed into the passenger side, grabbed his cell phone, and scrolled through his messages as Jacob pulled into traffic. The bright blue sky and slight breeze lightened Jacob's mood. He couldn't explain it, but he felt more at home in Boise than he did in Phoenix. He pulled into the donut shop and backed into a parking spot. The two men strolled across the parking lot. Jacob peered over his shoulder and noticed a man sitting in a white Mercedes with dark tinted windows staring at him. He glanced through the windshield and noticed it was Doctor Young.

"What are you looking at?" James asked.

"Nothing important. Let's go." He picked up the pace and so did James. Jacob burst into a sprint. They ran stride for stride. Jacob reached for the door, but tripped over the curb, and landed face first on the ground.

James burst into laughter.

Jacob glared at him. He looked around to see if anyone noticed and then walked inside.

James walked in behind him, still laughing. The patrons in the donut shop looked to see what the commotion was all about. Jacob felt foolish and approached the counter brushing his uniform off.

"You sure are clumsy," James said.

"Some friend you are. That makes two times you've laughed at me when I was hurt. With friends like you who need enemies?"

James walked up behind him and put a hand on his shoulder. "It's sexy when you're angry."

Jacob hung his head and started laughing. He couldn't stay angry with James for very long. The two men approached the counter.

"What can I get you guys?" the young woman behind the counter asked.

Jacob studied the brightly lit menu. His stomach wanted something, anything to fill the void. Everything on the menu looked good and he couldn't decide on what to get.

"Since you're so indecisive, I'll go ahead and order." James pushed past Jacob. "I'll take a half dozen of glazed donuts and a large milk."

"I'll have the same."

They paid for their food and walked across the lobby to an empty table. Jacob tore into his donuts and James laughed.

"What?" Jacob asked with a mouthful of food.

"Where are your manners?"

"At your mom's house. I left them with her this morning," Jacob grinned.

James stopped laughing. "That ain't right. Why you have to bring my mom into this?"

"Now who's sensitive?" Jacob asked, laughing.

They sat at their table eating and looking around at the people in the donut shop. There hadn't been any radio traffic since they arrived. A calm before the storm—Jacob thought.

After finishing their meals, they walked out of the donut shop back toward their ambulance. Jacob noticed that Doctor Young was still sitting in his car and staring at him. He squealed his tires as he sped out of the parking lot into traffic and narrowly missed striking a truck.

James shook his head. "What an idiot."

"You can say that again," Jacob offered. He walked over to the driver's side of the ambulance and stepped in a large puddle of fluid on the ground by his door. "Damn it."

"What's wrong now?"

"I hate it when people have leaks from their cars in the parking lot. I had to step in it, too."

James laughed. "It's not your day, is it?"

"Apparently not."

Jacob scuffed his feet back and forth trying to get the remnants of the fluid off the bottom of his boots and leaving wet streaks on the asphalt. He slowly approached the road and traffic wasn't coming. He pushed the gas pedal down and sped out of the parking lot.

"I don't feel like going back to the station. What do you say we drive around doing some area familiarization?" Jacob asked.

"Sounds good to me, amigo."

Driving down the four-lane road, each man was in a world of his own. Jacob flashed back to kissing Bridge. It was a dream come true, even though he felt a small amount of guilt. He never wanted to be the "other man," but he fell victim to the tenacious attraction he had for Bridge. He could still feel the touch of her soft lips pressed against his. The unit tone blaring over the radio broke the silence in the ambulance.

"Medic-57, we have an emergency call at 1215 Lewis Street. You have a sixty-three year old female with right sided deficits. Family believes she's suffering from a stroke."

James grabbed the microphone. "Medic-57, copies. Show us en-route." He calmly replaced the microphone into the rocker.

Jacob flipped on the lights and sirens and pressed the gas pedal to the floor. Driving code three was his favorite thing to do, next to saving someone's life. The feeling was exhilarating, racing past cars that yielded the right of way to them. It gave him a sense of power and control.

"A mile from here you're going to take a right hand turn. The address is a few blocks down Lewis Street," James said.

Jacob rushed past vehicles at a high rate of speed. It was vitally important that they got the patient to the hospital as quickly as possible. There was a three-hour window from onset of symptoms that if the patient didn't receive the proper treatment, they could suffer irreversible deficits.

They approached the intersection of Lewis Street. Jacob glanced, noticed there weren't any cars occupying the lanes, and grinned from ear to ear.

"What?" James asked.

Jacob turned hard to the right. He looked over and noticed James holding on for dear life. He slightly turned to the left just before he decided to yank the wheel.

"What the hell? Slow down, Jacob."

In mid turn, Jacob felt the back of the ambulance sliding hard to the left. He turned the wheel to the right trying to correct it and pressed down on the brakes. The pedal limply flopped to the floor. He pumped the brake pedal and there wasn't any resistance.

"We have no brakes!" Jacob shouted.

James' eyes were wide and his knuckles were white from the grip he had on the door handle. Jacob continued to pump the brakes, but the pedal limply fell to the floor. He jumped the curb into a small patch of grass adjacent to a line of oak trees. He turned the wheel to the right and the back end of the ambulance swung around. They spun in circles out of control. Jacob looked up and noticed they were heading straight into the tree line.

"Hold on," Jacob screamed.

The front of the ambulance narrowly missed the trees as the back end swung around and smashed into a large oak tree. The ambulance swayed back and forth as it came to a rest. Jacob's head hit the door jamb and a small trickle of blood slid down his cheek. He looked over and saw James holding his face with both of his hands.

Jacob reached over and shook his shoulder. "Hey, are you okay?"

James shook his head and started laughing. He dropped his hands and looked at Jacob still laughing. "Yeah. I'm fine. What in the hell was that all about?"

"We didn't have any brakes. I pumped the pedal and it flopped around under my feet. I was trying to scare you."

"Mission accomplished." James reached down and grabbed the radio. "Medic-57 to dispatch."

"Go ahead, Medic-57."

"We've been in an accident on the corner of Lewis Street and Baker Avenue. Dispatch another unit to this call."

"Are you all okay? Do we need to send the fire department and another ambulance to your location? Was anyone else involved?"

"No, we're fine. We were the only unit involved. Notify Nate and send us a wrecker, please."

"Dispatch copies."

Jacob's trembling hands gripped the steering wheel. He was certain they were going to need the Jaws of Life to release his grip.

"Have fun explaining this one to Nate," James said, laughing.

NINE

JACOB AND JAMES sat in Nate's office, waiting for him to finish up with his phone call. They nervously looked at one another as Nate glared at them.

"I see. That makes no sense. I understand. How long before the ambulance will be back in service? That's not long. Okay, sounds good. Thank you." Nate slammed the phone down. He leaned back in his seat; his arms perched behind his head as he rocked back and forth without breaking eye contact with Jacob.

Jacob leaned forward resting his elbows on his knees. "Before you say anything boss, I wanted to say…."

"Do me a favor and don't bore me with your excuses. I wanted you both to know your brake lines were cut."

Jacob looked over at James.

"Apparently someone was trying to hurt one of you, if not both of you."

Jacob was confused. Who would…wait a minute. Doctor Young was in the parking lot before they left. Could it be him? No. Maybe?

Nate leaned forward resting his elbows on his desk. "Can either of you think of anyone that would do this?"

A lump formed in Jacob's throat. "No."

James sat in his seat shaking his head. "No, me either."

Nate examined Jacob. "Why do I get the feeling there's something you aren't telling me?"

Jacob had his suspicions, but didn't dare voice them. The last thing he wanted to do was falsely accuse someone without any proof. It would hurt him professionally. "I don't know, boss. I don't have anything for you."

Nate stared at him. "As far as you driving erratically, I'm not going to discipline you. I would be a liar if I told you I had never done the same thing. Luckily for you, the accident wasn't your fault. The police are going to investigate it. I'll need an incident report from both of you." He opened a drawer and pulled two pieces of paper. He leaned across his desk and handed it to Jacob.

"When do you need it by?" Jacob asked.

"Fill it out and drop it in the box at your station. The courier will bring it to me with your paperwork. That will be all, gentlemen." Nate turned in his chair and pecked at the keys on his computer.

Jacob and James walked out the office.

Jacob felt relieved. He was certain Nate was going to drop the hammer on him. Since he began working at Magic County EMS, he had been in the director's office more than he had since he started his career. Just when he would begin to feel comfortable, reality would slap him across the face, reminding him he still had much to learn. Regardless, he dodged a bullet. Since his field C-section it felt as if he had a bull's eye on his back.

Jacob read a book while James drove the ambulance. He was unusually quiet and couldn't stop thinking about who cut the brake line on their ambulance. He had his suspicions, but without solid proof, he wasn't going to make any unfounded accusations.

"It's a beautiful day out today, don't you think?" James asked.

"Yeah."

James looked over at Jacob. "What's on your mind?"

Jacob closed his book and placed it on the dash. "Nothing. Just not in a sociable mood I guess."

"That's unusual for you. Whatever we say in this ambulance stays in this ambulance. You know the rules."

Jacob sat back in his seat and sighed. "Just wondering who cut our brake lines."

James turned his focus on the road. "I don't know, man. It's scary if you think about it. You have any idea?"

Jacob thought he did, but wasn't going to say anything. He was still feeling out James to figure out how much he could trust him. "Nope. Hopefully it was an isolated incident."

"Yeah. Me too."

James stopped at a red light.

They sat idling at the stop light when screeching tires approaching in the eastbound lanes across from the passenger side of their ambulance caught their attention. Both men looked over and saw a small pick-up truck swerve to avoid a stopped car in front of them, clip the back end of the car, flip over it and sailed through the air in front of them. The truck landed upside down in the middle of the intersection and skidded on its top until it slammed into the front of another vehicle.

Jacob looked over at James. "Did that just happen?"

James flipped on the lights and navigated their ambulance over next to the truck. He retrieved the microphone. "Medic-57, to dispatch."

"Go ahead, Medic-57."

"We just witnessed a vehicle roll over at the intersection of Maple and Stone. Dispatch fire department to our location. Stand by for further scene size up." He threw the microphone down, opened his door, and put his reflective vest on.

Jacob followed suit and exited the ambulance. Several people had stepped out of their vehicles and were approaching the truck. The smell of burnt rubber and anti-freeze lingered in the air.

A woman stood next to the truck with her hands over her mouth.

"Ma'am, step back please," James said to her as he approached, but she did not move. "Ma'am, please. It's too dangerous for you to be here."

The woman blankly stared at James. "Are they dead?"

James' frustration level overflowed. "I don't know. If you would please move I could find out. Now kindly step away from the vehicle," he barked.

She slowly backed away from the truck.

Jacob went to the other side of the truck and knelt. The top of the truck was crushed and he could not see inside of it.

"Got anything, Jacob?"

"No, I can't see inside. When is the fire department going to be here?"

"They're on their way," James offered.

"Hello? Can you hear me?" Jacob asked anxiously, but silence commanded inside the truck.

James ran around to the front of the truck. He knelt down on the ground still unable to see anything through the windshield.

There was movement inside the truck. A kicking sound coming from the back of the truck caught James and Jacob's attention. Both men got up and ran around to the back of the truck in time to see the back window crashing to the ground. A Hispanic man crawled out on his stomach across the hot asphalt. Once he was clear of the truck, he sat down, pulled a pack of cigarettes out of his pocket with trembling hands, and lit one.

"Sir, put that out," James said, concerned about gasoline on the asphalt. "You don't want to catch on fire, do you?"

The man took a long drag off it and blew the smoke into the air. He looked James square in the eyes. "No habla ingles," he said and shrugged his shoulders.

James shook his head.

Jacob knelt down next to him. "Sir, we're the paramedics, not the police. Are you hurt anywhere?"

The man took another drag off his cigarette and blew the smoke in Jacob's face. "No habla ingles."

Jacob coughed and fanned the smoke around his face. "That wasn't nice."

The man shrugged his shoulders.

Two police cars and a fire truck approached the scene. The man's attention shifted over to the direction of the sirens. His face went blank. James got up and strolled over to one of the arriving police units. He spoke for a few moments with the officer and then they walked back to where the man was sitting.

The officer stood over him. "You got a driver's license?"

"No habla inglés."

"Just great," the officer said. "Does anyone speak Spanish?" He looked around to the curious onlookers, but no one answered.

The man smiled until the officer turned back around. He reached up and grabbed his neck. "Senor, mucho dolor."

James stood next to the officer shaking his head.

"What do you want to do?" Jacob asked.

James let out a sigh. "I guess we'll board him up in full c-spine." He knelt down next to the man. "Do you want to go to the hospital?" he asked in his best Spanish accent.

Jacob laughed.

James glared at him. Jacob cleared his throat and looked around ignoring him.

The man continued to hold his neck. "Mucho dolor, senor."

Jacob went back to the ambulance and retrieved the equipment they needed to place the man on the full spinal immobilization. Once secured to the backboard, with the assistance of a few firefighters, they moved him over to their cot. The firefighters loaded him into the back of the ambulance. Jacob climbed in with him.

"My turn to take a call. Let's get going to the hospital," Jacob said.

James smiled. "It's about time you did some work." He shut the back doors to the ambulance and climbed into the driver's seat.

Jacob grabbed a blood pressure cuff, a stethoscope, and took the man's vital signs. He leaned over to where the man could see him from the backboard. "Sir, I'm going to start an IV. I know you don't understand what I'm saying. This is going to hurt a little bit. Please try not to move, okay?"

The man sighed and his face grew stiff. "No habla ingles, senor."

Communicating with the man proved to be difficult. All of his years in Phoenix, and he couldn't speak a single word of Spanish.

I should've learned it while I had the chance.

Jacob prepared the equipment he needed to start the IV. The road they were traveling was quite bumpy and he had a difficult time steadying the man's hand. He moved with the swaying ambulance. He located a vein in the back of his hand. In between bumps, he plunged the needle into the skin.

"Ouch! That freaking hurt!" the man screamed. "Are you using a dull needle or what?"

Jacob looked at him, baffled. "I thought you couldn't speak English?"

"Of course I can speak English, you idiot. I just didn't want to tell the cops I didn't have a driver's license. Stop digging."

Jacob glanced toward the front of the ambulance and noticed James picked up the radio microphone, and began quietly talking, but Jacob couldn't hear what he was saying.

"Sit still and I'll have this IV done in a minute." He repositioned the needle, got a flash of blood in the chamber and advanced the catheter until it was flush with his skin. He placed a saline lock on it and then taped it down. "All done."

The man rubbed the back of his hand. "Is this your first day?"

"Nope. It's my second," Jacob chided.

The man refused to talk to Jacob for the remainder of the transport and he could care less. They arrived at the hospital. James walked around to the back of the ambulance and opened the doors. They pulled the cot out. The man looked up and noticed two police officers standing over him.

"You're not getting off this easy. Do you habla that, amigo?" the officer asked him, smiling.

TEN

JACOB TOSSED AND turned the entire night. His mind kept racing, thinking about their accident, but more so the feel of Bridge's lips pressed against his. He wanted her and he had to have her. Every muscle in his body tingled as she stood draped in his arms.

Then there was the good doctor, Ed Young. The man helped him keep his paramedic license, but he had what Jacob wanted, Bridge. Though she was denying the chemistry that bound them, he was sure Bridge had feelings for him too. His life became confusing. That seemed to be the pattern that he was trapped in lately. For every correct turn he made, he would make a drastic U-turn.

Not too long ago, he was making critical mistakes in his career. He had now swapped them for life mistakes. Why couldn't he get everything on track at the same time? Why did everything he do have to be a monumental mistake? Though he hadn't thought much of it lately, he still didn't believe God existed. How could he? He witnessed pain and misery in his career, and now his personal life was in peril.

Jacob sat up in his bed, trying to shake the doubt that clouded his mind. He sat on the edge looking down at the floor. Part of him felt guilty for kissing Bridge and the other part of him yearned for her that much more.

After a quick shower, Jacob sat down in his recliner, and stared at his cell phone. The urge to call the emergency room to see if Bridge was working overwhelmed him. He could be crossing a thin line of professionalism by pursuing her, but he didn't care because she was worth the risk. Each time he got the nerve to call, he dropped the phone in his lap. Without thinking about it any longer, he picked up his cell phone and dialed the number. After it rang a few times he was about to hang it up.

"Emergency room," a woman answered.

"Um…uh…is Bridge working?"

"Hold please."

Piano music filled his head and he pushed down the urge to hang up.

A moment later, the music abruptly ended. "ER. This is Bridgette."

His heart skipped a beat. Hearing her voice astounded him. "Um, hi Bridge. Are you busy?"

She sighed. "Kind of. What's up?"

Jacob searched his mind for the right words. "I, um, we need to talk in person."

Silence resonated on the other end of the phone.

"Bridge?"

"Yeah. I'm here."

"We need to talk."

"I don't think it's a good idea."

"All I want is five minutes. Can you indulge me for that long, at least?" Jacob pleaded.

Bridge sighed. "Yeah. I guess I can do that. I get off work at seven. Ed is working the night shift, so I guess tonight would work."

Jacob jumped up from his recliner and danced around his house. "That would be great. Where do you want to meet?"

She was silent for a moment. "I don't want to go anywhere too public. This town is much smaller. Meet me at Grayson Park. You know where that is?"

"Yeah. I'll be there at seven." Jacob didn't have a clue where the park was, but he wasn't going to push his luck and have Bridge change her mind.

"I'll be there a little after seven. I have to go," Bridge said and hung up the phone.

Jacob stood in the middle of his living room glowing with excitement. This was his chance to plead his case with her. There would be no interruptions by Doctor Ed Young since he would be working.

He rushed into his bedroom and looked at the clothes strung all over the floor. Jacob had no problem washing and drying his clothes, but putting them away was another story. He picked up pieces of clothing and threw them everywhere in his room. He had to find the right outfit to wear. This was his one chance to have alone time with Bridge without the fear of Ed imposing his ownership in front of him.

Jacob could tell it was beginning to wear on her. She was an independent woman who didn't like to feel owned and Jacob wouldn't treat her that way. If she were with him, he would cherish her and treat her like a queen. Ed's loss would be his gain.

Jacob arrived at the park thirty minutes early. He paced back and forth in the park trying to wrap his mind around what he was going to say. Grayson Park was on the outskirts of Boise, away from the busy hustle and bustle of city life. A river flowed on the eastern side of the park. Lush green trees of various sizes and shapes lined the greenbelt. There were children's playground toys scattered in the sand. Being later in the evening, there weren't many people occupying the park, which meant more privacy for him and Bridge.

His legs grew tired from pacing. He sat down on a bench next to a set of monkey bars. The sun had begun its descent below the horizon and a dull orange glow encompassed the sky. The light poles in the park flickered to life.

A few moments later, Jacob saw a set of headlights approaching through the parking lot. He felt nauseated. The car parked directly across from where he was sitting. The urge to run over to her and take her into his arms was overwhelming, but he knew that wouldn't be a wise choice.

Bridge got out and strolled across the sand where the monkey bars were. Her body language was stiff. She looked at the ground as she walked toward Jacob. Unsure of what to do, he tapped his feet on the ground. The nausea became more prominent with each step she took. Vomiting was a definite possibility.

Bridge stood in front of him, still looking at the ground.

"Hey," Jacob said.

"Hey. I shouldn't be here. This is wrong."

Jacob sighed. "Why don't you sit down?"

Bridge looked up from the ground. Jacob could see the fear in her eyes. She weakly smiled and sat down next to him. He shifted toward her, and she scooted a few inches away from him. He had never seen her act this way before. It tugged at his heart seeing her afraid.

What has he done to you?

"Thank you for coming to talk with me."

Bridge continued to look at the ground. "Sure. No problem."

There were a thousand things Jacob wanted to say, but couldn't find the right words. His heart sank for her. The reason she was feeling this way was because of him.

"Bridge, I know you're engaged, but you can't deny the kiss. I felt the way you embraced it. I know you have feelings for me. Why can't you admit it?"

Bridge's shoulders slumped. "It was a mistake and I got caught up in the moment. That won't happen again," she said softly.

Jacob's frustration began to rise. He leaned closer to Bridge, but she withdrew.

"I know you feel something for me. Why can't you admit it?"

Bridge stiffened and sat up straight. "How dare you. Who do you think you are, telling me how I feel? You don't know me. My life was uncomplicated until you showed up. Now Ed is constantly badgering me about you. We have done nothing but fight since you showed up. Why in the hell did you come here anyway?" Bridge shouted.

Jacob told Bridge everything that had happened with Becca. The anger etched in her face quickly replaced with sorrow. The more he told her, the more she began to soften toward him.

"Oh my. I had no idea. I'm so sorry, Jacob. I can't imagine what you must've gone through."

Memories of that fateful night flooded Jacob's mind as if it happened yesterday. "It's okay. You didn't know. I couldn't stay there any longer. I had no ties to family, so I moved here."

"Why Boise? Why here?"

"Because...."

The sound of squealing tires speeding through the parking lot caught their attention.

"Oh, God. It's Ed," Bridge groaned.

She bolted up from the bench and trotted toward her car. Jacob sat on the bench watching her. The car sped toward Bridge's car, slammed on its brakes, and skidded to a stop before striking her car. Ed jumped out of his car wearing scrubs and stomped toward Bridge. She stopped and hung her head. He stood inches from her and yelled at her, but Jacob couldn't make out what he was saying. Bridge didn't saying anything. Ed pointed a finger at her and was yelling, but Bridge didn't defend herself.

As Jacob stared at them, his anger brewed.

How dare you treat her this way? She doesn't deserve it.

Ed continued to barrage her with vulgar words. He grabbed her by both of her arms and shook her. Jacob had enough. He jumped up from the bench and sprinted toward them through the grass. He jumped over a railroad tie and ran through a large sandbox. Sand kicked up as his feet stomped onto the ground.

"Hey. Get your damn hands off of her!" Jacob screamed.

Ed ignored him and continued to curse and shake Bridge, but still she said nothing.

Why is she letting him do this to her? What kind of control does he have over her?

Jacob ran up to them and grabbed Ed by one of his arms. "I said, let...."

Ed reached across and punched Jacob in the nose with his right hand. Lightning flashed in Jacob's head and he toppled backwards. The back of his head bounced off the asphalt and a hollow thud echoed through the air. Pain coursed through his face. His head swam with dizziness and his vision became blurry.

Bridge ran toward Jacob. "Are you crazy? What the hell is wrong with you?"

Ed grabbed her arm and stopped her. "Get in your car and leave, now!" he shouted while pointing a finger in her face.

Bridge stood in front of him wide eyed and petrified. Her lips quivered. She looked over at Jacob and a tear streamed down her cheek. She looked back at Ed, flung her arm free of his grip, and ran toward her car. She got into it and sped toward the street.

Jacob, lying flat on his back, looked up at Ed as he watched Bridge leave. He walked over and knelt down next to Jacob.

"You stay away from her. She's mine. Do you hear me?"

Jacob's vision was blurry and blood was running out of his nose. A metallic taste invaded his mouth and excruciating pain pulsated throughout his face.

He nodded. "Yeah."

A grin crossed Ed's face. "I heard about your little accident the other day. It would be a shame if something like that were to happen again, don't you agree?"

Jacob's vision was still blurry. He tried to lift his head off the ground, but dizziness prohibited that from happening.

Ed stood glaring down at Jacob. "You're pathetic. I don't know what she sees in you. You can't give her the life I can. You're just an ambulance driver. Remember that."

Ed shook his head and laughed. He got into his car and sped through the parking lot.

Jacob took in a few deep breaths trying to fight off the dizziness. *What have I done?*

ELEVEN

JACOB FELT FOOLISH. Beaten up by Ed Young was a low point in his life, especially in front of Bridge. Once he arrived at the station, Jacob did everything he could to avoid James. Recounting the events from the night before to his partner was something he'd rather not do.

While James was busy cooking breakfast, Jacob slipped by him and into his bedroom. He set his bag down on his bed and then stood in front of the mirror inspecting his face. There was a small cut on the bridge of his nose and his left eye was black. The longer he studied his face, the more the anger within him brewed. Jacob was certain he still had lingering effects from his concussion and that's why he couldn't get up to defend himself.

Why does she put up with the way he treats her? She's better than that.

A knock on the door interrupted Jacob's thoughts. James stood at the door holding a plate of food. "Hey, man, are you…what happened to you?"

He knew that he would eventually have to explain what happened, but he didn't want to. "It's nothing."

James stared at him in bewilderment. "Bull crap nothing happened. Have you seen your face?"

Of course, I have.

"It's nothing. I don't want to talk about it, okay?"

"Look, what goes on in your personal life is your business. I like to think we're not just work partners, but also friends."

Jacob sat down on his bed. "I had a little run in with someone."

"I'd say you did. Tell me what happened," James said, sitting down next to Jacob.

"I got into it with Doctor Young."

Confusion crossed James' face. "Doctor Young? The same doctor that works in the ER?"

"Yeah."

"Why? Where? What happened?"

There was no hiding it any longer. He had to tell James. Otherwise, he would look stupid if he only gave half the story. For the next thirty minutes, he explained everything to James. How he knew Bridge from Arizona and about the altercation he had the night before. James sat on the bed next to Jacob, looking on with wise eyes.

"It's a messed up situation," Jacob said.

"You can say that again. You think Doctor Young is the one who cut our brake lines?"

"Yeah. It makes sense. He was there in the parking lot while we were inside."

"Why didn't you tell me all of this sooner?"

Jacob chose not to tell him the truth. He was afraid it might offend him. "Don't have the proof."

The two men sat in silence for a moment. James was still holding the plate of food.

"Here take this. It's probably already cold." James handed the plate to Jacob and then left his room. Jacob got up and walked into the kitchen. After the plate finished warming up in the microwave, he took it out and devoured the contents.

James was in the back of the ambulance doing the morning check off. Jacob joined him.

James zipped the jump bag closed. He sat staring at the ground. "Man, you need to tell me these things. In the truck, we have to have each other's back. I know you're still fairly new in the field. I thought maybe you'd learned that by now."

Jacob knew he'd disappointed James, but he had trust issues. "I'm sorry. It won't happen again."

"It's okay. You've been through a lot in your life. Just remember, I will always have your back."

"I appreciate that."

The tones blared over the radio. "Medic-57, we have a mobile home fire with possible entrapment at 410 East Lowry. Fire department has been notified."

"I'm glad we got a call. Thought we were about to start hugging each other," James said, laughing.

Jacob smiled. "Not on your luckiest day, amigo."

The two men exited the back of the ambulance. James jumped into the passenger seat while Jacob got into the driver's seat.

James grabbed the microphone. "Medic-57 is en-route."

"Dispatch copies. Reports are there is a woman trapped inside. The other occupants have exited safely."

Jacob turned on the lights and the sirens. Traffic was light as he entered the two-lane road. His stomach turned into knots. This would be his first burn victim. When Jacob was doing his burn rotations during Paramedic School, a doctor once told him that a burn victim's best day was the day they were burned. After completing that rotation, it made sense to him. Each day the patients had to have the burnt area scrubbed with small wire brushes. It was horrific. They adequately sedated them before putting them through the grueling procedure, but it was still quite painful.

They were the first arriving unit on scene. Thick black smoke billowed out of the doublewide trailer. Two small children were in the yard. A little girl, who looked to be ten years old, paced back and forth frantically screaming.

"Mommy, where are you? Someone please help my mommy!"

A little boy, who appeared to be around seven years old, knelt down drawing in the dirt with a stick. He didn't look upset. Both children didn't appear injured. Thank God, Jacob thought.

"Medic-57, we're on scene. What is the ETA of the fire department?" James asked.

"We'll check and advise."

James and Jacob exited their ambulance and ran into the front yard. The little girl noticed them and ran toward Jacob and he knelt down eye level with her. "Is someone still inside?"

The little girl's body shook. "Yes. My mommy is. Get her out...please!"

The boy continued playing with a stick, drawing in the dirt. "Mom's inside," he nonchalantly said.

"Dispatch to Medic-57."

James grabbed his radio. "Go ahead dispatch."

"Fire department ETA is ten minutes."

James looked over at Jacob. "Whoever is in that house doesn't have ten minutes."

A blood-curdling scream came from inside of the trailer. It forced the hair on the back of Jacob's neck to stand up. The little girl turned and tried to run toward her home, but James grabbed her and pulled her back.

"Mommy!" the little girl screamed. She pulled at James' arms trying to escape from his grip.

"That's my mommy. She must be coming outside. She takes forever in her wheelchair," the little boy said.

"Wheelchair?" Jacob asked him.

"Yeah. She sits in a wheelchair," the boy answered.

Neighbors congregated in the street, softly talking to one another. In the distance, the faint sound of sirens were approaching the scene. The shrill screams of the woman inside echoed through the neighborhood. Jacob left the boy's side and tried to get close to the trailer. The heat formed an invisible wall that prohibited him from getting close. He felt helpless. The flames shot out of the door. The glass in a window shattered and flames danced out of it. The woman screamed in agony.

"Aren't you going to do something? Help her!" a man yelled from the street.

There was nothing they could do. Without the proper fireproof attire, it would be suicide to run into the burning trailer. The crowd grew in numbers and two police cars arrived on scene. One of the officers ran toward the crowd trying to get them back on the other side of the street. The other officer ran up to Jacob and James.

"Is there someone still inside of there?" the officer asked.

"Oh God! Help me!" a woman screamed from inside of the trailer.

The police officer tried to run up to the trailer, but couldn't get close enough. A moment later, a fire engine arrived. James told the officer to take the children away from the yard. He ran up to the firefighters. "There's a woman still inside. The kids said she is in a wheelchair. We tried to get close to the door, but couldn't. It's too damn hot."

The four firefighters donned their self-contained breathing apparatus. Two of them grabbed a fire hose, charged the line with water, and ran toward the burning trailer. There were several loud cracks and pops of glass and wood as the flames grew in size. The four men gathered at the door. Two men entered while the other two were crouched at the door spraying water inside. A few moments later, they exited with a woman in a wheelchair. They carried her down the steps toward James and Jacob.

James got the attention of one of the firefighters. "Come help me grab our cot and gear." The two men ran toward the ambulance.

Every inch of the woman's skin was charred. Her hair had melted to her scalp and her breathing was labored.

Jacob knelt down in front of her. "Ma'am, are you able to talk?"

She shook her head.

James and the firefighter returned with the cot.

"We need to get her in the back of the ambulance. She's in bad shape," Jacob said.

Flames danced and consumed the trailer house behind them. Two more fire engines arrived on the scene. Several firefighters worked at pulling the equipment off their trucks to battle the blaze.

Jacob positioned himself behind the woman. James and a firefighter each grabbed one of the woman's legs. In unison, they lifted her out of the wheelchair and moved her over to the awaiting cot. The skin from her legs sloughed off exposing pink tissue. They lifted the cot and raced toward the ambulance. Jacob ran around to the side door, climbed in, and sat down on the captain's seat behind the head of the cot. James and the firefighter joined him in the back of the ambulance.

"We'll need to get a helicopter. Can you do that for me?" Jacob asked a firefighter that stood at the side door.

"Sure thing." He stepped away from the ambulance and talked on his radio.

James grabbed a pair of trauma shears. "I need to cut your clothes off, ma'am."

She nodded. Her difficulty breathing became worse. She was audibly wheezing and with each passing moment, her breaths became shorter and more labored. James began to cut the burnt clothes off her. The clothing had melted in several places, into her skin. He strategically cut around those areas. Jacob grabbed an oxygen mask and placed it over the woman's face. She panicked and reached up trying to rip it away.

Jacob leaned in close to her. "Leave that alone, ma'am. It's oxygen. You need that right now."

Still struggling to breathe, she withdrew her hand.

Once James had the remnants of her clothing removed, he searched for an area of skin that wasn't burnt for an IV site. On her left arm, there was a small patch of skin undamaged from the fire in the inside bend of her elbow. He grabbed an alcohol prep and cleansed the area.

Looking over his shoulder at a firefighter he said, "Spike two bags of saline for me using the blood tubing. We need to start bolusing her with a lot of fluid."

The firefighter grabbed the tubing, two bags of saline, and assembled them.

"I'm going to start an IV, ma'am. Try not to move," James instructed.

She nodded.

James slid the needle into her arm, got a flash of blood in the chamber, advanced the catheter, and then secured the tubing into it. He reached up and loosened the clamp to the tubing. Fluid quickly dripped in the chamber. He taped it down to her arm. The tape had difficulty sticking to her charred skin. James wrapped Kerlex around the IV site to help hold it securely in place.

Jacob placed the patches for the cardiac monitor onto the woman and a rapid heart rate scrolled across the screen. "We need to knock her down and intubate her. If we wait much longer, her airway will be too swollen to pass a tube through."

James agreed. He retrieved the medication bag from their jump kit.

"Helicopter will be here in ten minutes. We're going to use the empty field across the street for the landing zone," the firefighter said through the side door of the ambulance.

"Sounds good." Jacob leaned down close to the woman's ear. "Ma'am, we are going to give you some medicine and put you to sleep. We need to insert a tube into your trachea and breathe for you. I promise you won't feel a thing."

She nodded and a tear trickled out of the corner of her eye down her charred cheek.

Jacob grabbed the intubation kit and began to assemble the necessary equipment. This was going to be Jacob's first rapid sequence intubation. His hands trembled.

We are about to take away her breathing. I hope I can get the tube in.

James prepared several different medications. He glanced over at Jacob. "You ready?"

"Yeah," Jacob nervously answered.

James pushed the first drug, Etomidate. It would put her into a hypnotic state so she wouldn't remember the procedure they were about to perform. A firefighter placed the bag valve mask over her face and began pushing oxygen into her lungs.

A few minutes later, James grabbed the Succinylcholine and inserted the needle into the IV tubing. "Here we go," James said. He quickly pushed the drug into the tubing.

In a few seconds, her breathing would stop, and he was responsible for getting the tube inserted. If he proved to be unsuccessful, she could die. The muscles in her face twitched. Once they stopped, it was time for him to get her intubated. Jacob inserted the laryngoscope into her mouth. Her tongue had swollen, making it difficult for him to see anything. He repositioned the blade and still wasn't able to see her vocal cords.

"Everything is swollen," Jacob said.

"Can you see her vocal cords?" James asked.

"No." Jacob's anxiety rose like a thermometer on a hot summer day. The tissue in her airway had started to swell. He bit down on his bottom lip trying to calm his nerves. Perspiration beaded on his brow. He didn't want to fail at getting an airway, but if it took much longer, he was going to have to hand it over to James.

"Her heart rate is starting to drop. You need to hurry up," James ordered.

Jacob sucked in a deep breath trying to control his emotions. The precious seconds were ticking away. He pushed the blade of the laryngoscope in a little deeper and lifted with every bit of strength he had. Her swollen and blackened vocal cords appeared.

"I see them. They're covered in soot," Jacob said.

James glanced at the cardiac monitor. "Her heart rate is at fifty. Get her tubed, now."

Jacob manipulated the tube and was able to slide it past her vocal cords. He inflated the cuff, pulled out the stylette, and attached the BVM to the end of the tube. With each squeeze of the bag, Jacob watched the heart rate on the monitor, but it slowed to forty beats.

Come on! I'm in!

After a few moments, the heart rate slowly increased. Fifty…sixty…seventy…eighty…one-hundred. A sigh of relief slipped through Jacob's lips. He looked over at James to see an approving smile. It felt like the weight of the world was lifted from his shoulders. With the tube secured, James listened to her lung sounds. The concerned look faded into relaxation.

"Tube's in place. Good job."

With a sense of accomplishment, Jacob was able to relax. He completed his first RSI. It was different in a cardiac arrest. They weren't breathing to begin with. Even though her breathing was extremely labored, at least she was breathing before they gave her medications to stop it.

The back doors to the ambulance opened up; the flight crew had arrived. Jacob was so focused on getting the woman intubated that he didn't hear the helicopter land. They assisted the crew with moving the woman over to the flight cot. After a brief report, she was loaded into the helicopter and airborne toward the burn center.

Jacob stood at the back of the ambulance looking at the mess they had created. There was equipment and trash all over the floor. The stench of burnt flesh wafted through the air. He choked down a knot that formed in his throat. A few moments ago, it was uncontrolled chaos, but now it was eerily quiet.

James stood beside him and placed a hand on his shoulder. "Good job, partner. You just got your first rapid sequence intubation."

The adrenaline from the call slowly wore off. He looked over his shoulder and saw one of the police officers talking to the small children and his heart sank for them. The little girl was still visibly upset. The little boy on the other hand, appeared oblivious to how seriously injured his mother was. The officer was consoling the little girl who continued to weep while her little brother drew in the dirt with a stick.

Jacob walked over to them and knelt down on one knee. "You guys okay?"

The little girl looked at him with tears streaming down her cheeks. "Is my mommy going to be okay?" she asked in a cracked voice.

"Right now she's doing okay, sweetie. The doctors are going to take real good care of her," Jacob answered.

"Mom isn't hurt. She's fine," the little boy said.

"It's your fault. Mom is hurt because of you," the little girl screamed at her brother.

Jacob looked confused. "What do you mean, sweetie?"

She turned toward Jacob. "I told him not to do it. He doesn't listen. Mom is going to be so mad," she yelled.

"I didn't do nothing," the little boy answered.

Jacob was dumbfounded by how the little boy didn't care about anything that had just occurred. "What happened?"

"He was playing with fire. He caught his pillow on fire and then threw it in the closet. Mommy was in her bedroom in the back of the trailer. I told him not to do it. He never listens to me."

"Mom is fine," the little boy said.

Jacob looked over at the police officer and shook his head. "What happens now?"

"CPS will take them until we can contact a next of kin. How are things looking?"

Jacob shook his head, trying not to let the children know their mother probably wasn't going to make it. He reached over and patted the little girl on the back. "They're going to take good care of your mommy, I promise."

She looked up at Jacob and her eyes welled up with tears.

Jacob stood and walked back to the ambulance. James was busy placing the trash in the biohazard bags.

"I feel so bad for those kids. The little boy is oblivious. He started the fire."

"Yeah. I heard." James grabbed trash and shoved it into the bio bags.

"That poor woman wheeled herself through the fire. I can't imagine how horrible that must've been," Jacob said.

"Me either."

A burn victim's best day is the day they get burned.

TWELVE

JACOB'S CONFIDENCE SOARED during his few well-deserved days off. Calls of that type reminded him why he had become a paramedic. Still young in his career, each shift he learned how to be more proficient in his skills. Despite the gloomy atmosphere outside, his confidence perched itself on cloud nine. Most days the sun shone and the birds were whistling their praises as they flew freely around, but that wasn't the case today. Clouds hung low in the humid air and rain drizzled, blanketing everything in its path.

Jacob's cell phone rang. He looked at the screen and noticed Nate's number. He considered not answering.

Now what did I do?

"Hello?"

"Hey, Jacob. You got a minute?"

"Yeah. What's up?"

"I wanted to give you a follow-up on your burn victim from yesterday."

"Okay."

"There's no easy way to say this, but she died early this morning. I'm sorry."

Jacob's elated mood tumbled down like the Berlin Wall. All of their efforts proved worthless. He knew her injuries weren't conducive for life, but it still bothered him that she passed away.

"I understand. Thanks for calling." Jacob hung up his phone. He plopped down in his recliner and thought about how sorry he felt for her children. They lost their mother and that wasn't right. How her son acted bothered him even more. The oblivious child didn't realize he killed his mother by playing with fire. Anger and sadness swarmed his mind.

We did everything we could. What could we have done differently?

A knock on his front door distracted his thoughts. He wasn't in a social mood and flung open the door. "What?" he growled.

Bridge stood in front of him with red, puffy eyes.

"Hi," she whispered.

Bridge shocked Jacob showing up at his house. He felt foolish for answering the door the way he did. He walked past her and out to his driveway, looking to see if Ed had followed her.

Bridge turned around and watched him.

Ed wasn't there. Jacob returned to his doorway. "What are you doing here? You shouldn't be here." He stepped back inside the house and started to close the door. Bridge held out her hand, stopping it.

"Ed doesn't know where I am. You don't have to worry about him showing up here." A despondent look crossed her face.

He hated seeing her upset. "Come in," he offered as he stepped to the side allowing, her into his house.

Bridge walked by him and stood just inside of the door. Jacob plopped into his recliner. It disheartened him seeing the most beautiful woman he knew standing before him a mere shell of her normal self.

Jacob rocked in his recliner. "What brings you here?"

"I'm sorry."

"Sorry for what?" Jacob knew what she meant, but he wanted to hear her say it.

"I'm sorry for Ed behaving the way he did. It's uncalled for."

Jacob had a thousand things he wanted to say. He wanted to be mean and malicious, but he couldn't. He would have rather pull her into his arms and planted his lips on hers. "Want to sit down?"

Bridge nodded and sat on the far end of the couch away from Jacob.

He noticed the distance between them. "What brings you here?"

She hung her head.

Jacob wanted to walk over, put his arm around her, and tell her everything would work out, but he couldn't.

"I wanted to say I'm sorry. I feel horrible," Bridge said as she gazed at the floor.

"Nothing for you to apologize about. Stuff happens. I'm more worried about you."

"I'm fine."

"You don't act like it." Jacob shifted in his recliner toward her. "You can look at me, you know."

Bridge glanced at Jacob. A tear ran down her cheek. "I shouldn't be here." She walked toward the front door.

Jacob sprung from his chair and stood in front of her, blocking her exit. She stared at the floor, and began to cry. Jacob grabbed her and pulled her into his arms. The warmth of her body sent shivers down his spine.

"I don't know what to do. He's never acted like this before," Bridge said, sobbing.

"It's okay. You're going to be all right." He stroked the back of her head, running his fingers over her hair.

Bridge pulled back from him. "I feel so stupid. I shouldn't be crying like this in front of you." She dried her eyes. "I'm scared. He's changed, and now I'm more of a possession to him."

"Why don't you break it off? It's only going to get worse. You deserve better than this, Bridge."

She continued to dry her eyes. "You don't understand. I can't."

"Why not?" Jacob's irritation rose.

"You won't understand."

"Then explain it to me."

Bridge looked off to the side. Her facial expressions morphed from sadness to anger. "He can give me a life I could never have without him."

Jacob took a few steps back. "Since when did you become the materialistic type?"

Bridge crossed her arms over her chest and glared at him. "You don't know anything about me. Don't sit here and judge me."

Jacob fought off the urge to fire back at her. "I'm not judging you, Bridge. I feel like you deserve better than the way he's treating you, is all."

A car honking broke the tension between them and Bridge's face turned pale. Jacob looked out of the window of the front door and saw Ed Young.

Jacob said, "Stay here."

"Who is it?"

"Don't worry about it. No matter what happens, you stay right here."

Bridge nodded.

Jacob walked through the door and slammed it shut. Anger brewed within him and he had enough. He approached Ed's car and slammed his fists into the window.

Ed rolled it down.

"What the hell do you want?" Jacob growled.

"Is my fiancé here?" Ed asked with a smirk across his face.

"It's none of your damn business. You need to leave." Jacob's lips were quivering.

Ed looked over at his driveway and pointed. "I see her car right there. Tell her to come outside."

"You don't tell me what to do. This is *my* house. In fact, why don't you step out and let's have a little chat." Jacob's fists were balled up and he took a few steps back.

Ed laughed. "Didn't you get enough the other night? I won't be as forgiving this time."

"I said get out. You won't be sucker punching me this time."

Ed shook his head. "You're not worth my time. Tell my woman to come out here. We need to talk."

"Are you deaf? It's none of your business if she's here or not. Get out of your car, before I drag you through your window." The veins on Jacob's forehead were pulsating.

Ed exhaled lightly. "I'm trying hard to be the grown-up here. You're testing my patience."

Jacob wanted nothing more than to beat him to a bloody pulp. His anger peaked and he couldn't control it any longer. He reared back and kicked Ed's car door several times. With each blow, the depth of the dents increased.

"I said get out of your car. Be a man for the first time in your life."

Ed's eyes narrowed and he looked down at the door. "You just made the biggest mistake of your life, boy. You have no clue who you're messing with. This isn't over. Not even close." Ed slammed down the gas pedal and sped down the street.

Jacob stood with his fists clinched and overflowing with anger. He turned around. Bridge stood outside his front door shaking her head. She rushed toward her car and Jacob ran over to stop her.

"Wait. Don't leave," Jacob pleaded with her. He reached out to grab her arm, but she pushed him away.

"I shouldn't have come here. Things are worse now. Thank you," Bridge shouted. She climbed inside her car and slammed the door shut.

Jacob tapped on her window. "Bridge, please don't leave. I'm sorry. I want to protect you."

"Protect me? I don't need your protection," she screamed from behind her window. She put her car in reverse, squealed out of the driveway, and flew down the road.

I keep making things worse. What am I going to do now?

THIRTEEN

JACOB AND JAMES arrived at Midway Middle School as requested by Nate for career day. They had to answer a barrage of questions by curious teenagers about what paramedics did during their shift. Jacob enjoyed sharing his career experiences, but James, not so much. The two men arrived at the school a few minutes early and got out of the ambulance. Several kids were running around in the courtyard chasing each other. Jacob felt envious of the kids and their carefree lives. James reluctantly followed behind his partner.

As they entered into the main office, flashbacks of his school days flooded Jacob's mind. On more than one occasion, he had to visit the principal's office. There were several teachers and office staff busy answering the phones and dealing with the students standing at the main desk.

Jacob glanced over his shoulder and noticed two boys that were sitting at opposite ends of a bench. One boy had a black eye, while the other had a busted lip. They glared at one another and Jacob couldn't help but smile.

"Can I help you gentlemen?" an elderly woman asked, looking over glasses that sat on the end of her nose.

"We're here for career day," Jacob answered.

She smiled. "You two drew the short straw, eh?"

James rolled his eyes. "We sure did."

Jacob elbowed James. Education and public relations events were a part of their job. It gave him a sense of accomplishment giving back to the community they served.

"You'll be speaking with the eighth graders. We felt the older kids would be more suited to hear your stories. There are several different speakers talking about their professions in different rooms. You will have Carl in the class with you. He's a funeral home owner."

"Sounds good. Which way do we go?" Jacob asked.

"Take a left out of this office and you'll see a classroom on the right side down the hall with a sign that says *Paramedics.*"

"Thank you," Jacob said.

"Have fun boys. Try not to scare the kids too much, okay?"

James rolled his eyes again. The two walked out of the office and made their way toward the classroom dodging two boys chasing one another down the hall.

"Great. Not only do we have to talk to a bunch of snot nosed kids that could care less what we have to say, but we also have to share a room with a funeral director. Could this day get any better?" James sneered.

"You need to cheer up. This isn't that bad. Don't you want to be able to share some of your experiences with others that may give them some insight on becoming a paramedic?"

"Seriously? Did you ever pay attention to anyone that came to your classroom when you were in school?"

Jacob thought about it for a moment. "No. I guess you have a point. Let's make the best of it, okay?"

"If you say...." James stopped and stared in front of him. His mouth dropped open.

Jacob looked to see what had him distracted. A young woman he assumed to be the teacher stood outside the classroom door. She was five-foot-two, had long brown hair, a slender figure, and pouty lips. She looked over and saw the two men staring at her. Smiling, she walked toward them.

She approached Jacob holding out her hand toward him. "Hi. I'm Annabelle. I'm a teacher here at the school. No one told me the paramedics were going to be such handsome men."

Jacob reached out and shook her hand. "I'm...I'm Jacob. Nice to meet you."

James pushed by Jacob. "Hello, young lady. My name is James. I'm so glad to be here. I can't wait to share my experiences of saving people's lives with the bright minds of tomorrow."

A few minutes ago, you were complaining about having to do this detail.

She released Jacob's hand and reached out for James' hand. "We're glad to have you here. The kids will be excited I'm sure. I know I am,"

Annabelle said smiling at James.

Jacob's frustration went into overdrive. *Sure, now that there's a pretty woman you're going to act like you're excited to be here?*

"Right this way, gentlemen," Annabelle said as she turned and walked into the classroom.

James smiled. "I'm glad we came. This may not be too bad after all." He slugged Jacob on the arm.

Jacob shook his head. "Whatever you say, amigo."

They walked into a classroom full of children and half of the kids looked as if they could care less who was there. James walked to the front of the room and cleared his throat. Carl sat in the back of the room and didn't appear impressed. He shook his head and continued to read a newspaper.

"Class, these two men are paramedics. I expect you to give them your undivided attention." She walked over and sat down on a stool to the side of the room. "The room is yours."

"Hey kids, my name is James. I'm a paramedic. Do you all know what it is we do?"

"My dad said you eat a lot of donuts and drive around all day," a boy from the back of the room answered. A few of the kids laughed.

"No. That would be cops. Just look at how their bellies hang over their belts."

The room erupted into laughter.

"Quiet down kids," Annabelle said with a smile.

James stuck his chest out. "We go out and render medical attention to anyone that calls 911. Our calls range from sick people, to someone having a heart attack, to a bad vehicle accident. We never know what we're going to come across when we're on duty. That's half the excitement."

A girl in the front row raised her hand.

James pointed at her. "You have a question?"

"Do you see dead people?"

"No. We save lives. The funeral home director gets to see them," James boasted.

More kids laughed. Carl's brow furrowed and he shook his head.

Another girl in the front row raised her hand. "What kind of hours do you work?"

"Twenty-four hour shifts. We have a station that we stay at that is what we call *home away from home.*"

"I bet it's cool getting to drive fast," a boy said.

James smirked. "It is until your partner crashes the ambulance."

Jacob stiffened.

"You crashed?" the same boy asked.

"I didn't, but my partner here did," James answered, pointing at Jacob.

The kids whispered amongst themselves.

"What happened?"

"He tried to scare me and lost control of the ambulance."

Now you're just showing off.

Annabelle stared curiously at Jacob and he felt uncomfortable.

"Don't worry, kids. No one was injured. It goes to show you that even the best drivers can wreck. Lesson to be learned; don't try to scare someone when you're behind the wheel, because it doesn't end well," James said smiling, at Jacob.

Annabelle stood and walked over next to James. "Okay, kids, that's enough questions for now. Let's give Carl a chance to talk about his job."

James walked to the back of the room and stood next to Carl. Jacob joined him.

Carl stood and smiled at the men.

"Pay attention class," Annabelle said. "Carl will tell you about what he does. Let's act like the young adults you are and keep your questions appropriate." She nodded at Carl and then returned to her seat.

Carl cleared his throat. "I'm a funeral home director and I help families in their time of need." He looked over toward James and Jacob. "Unlike these guys, I don't get time off. I'm on call twenty-four hours a day and seven days a week. I don't have the luxury of getting to sleep because I'm usually busy."

Jacob glared at him. He couldn't decide who angered him more, James or Carl.

"I go to where someone has passed away, bring them back to the funeral home, and prepare their bodies for their funeral."

Silence rolled through the room and every child stared at him.

Jacob leaned close to James. "It doesn't take a brain surgeon to pick up stiffs," he whispered. James nodded his head.

A little girl in the front row slowly raised her hand.

"Yes?" Carl asked.

"Do…do you touch them?"

Carl chuckled. "Yes, I do. I have to make them look presentable for their families."

"I heard you cut their throats and suck their blood out," a boy blurted out.

Carl laughed. "No. That's not true. I do have to replace their blood with a chemical that helps preserve their bodies, but I don't suck their blood out. Do I look like a vampire?"

Kid's laugher rolled through the room. Anabelle held a single finger over her mouth toward the children.

In the back corner of the room, a little girl hung her head and tears were streaming down her cheeks. A look of concern crossed Annabelle's face. She rushed over and knelt down next to the girl. She quietly spoke to her while the rest of the class were looking over their shoulders watching them. Annabelle guided her out the classroom. Silence drifted through the room. After a few minutes, she returned.

"Okay, class. We've run out of time. Let us thank these men for taking time out of their busy schedules to come speak with you all. Let's give them a round of applause," she said and clapped her hands.

The kids sat in their seats, confused.

Annabelle's brow furrowed. "Class?"

Scattered claps echoed through the room. The sound of a bell coming from a speaker in the front of the class interrupted them.

"I will see you all tomorrow. Don't forget to do your homework."

The kids gathered their things and walked toward the door leading to the hall. A petite girl with brown hair in pigtails approached Jacob holding a notebook and a pencil.

"I'm writing a paper on becoming a paramedic. I have a question, and I want you to be honest with me, okay?"

"Sure," Jacob answered. He looked over his shoulder and stuck his tongue out at James.

"What's the worst thing you've ever seen? Be honest."

Jacob felt uncomfortable. He had seen things that he didn't want to tell to an adult, much less a kid. He tapped his foot on the ground avoiding eye contact with the little girl. She sighed loudly and Annabelle curiously looked at him.

"Um…let me see," Jacob said.

"Be honest," she sternly said as she awaited his reply.

"A woman burned from her head down to her toes in a house fire," Jacob answered.

The girl's eyes widened and Jacob regretted being so honest.

"Um…thank you." She turned and walked away.

Some things are left better unsaid.

FOURTEEN

"YOU GRAB THE c-spine stuff and I'll get the jump bag. This looks pretty bad." Jacob picked up the microphone. "Medic-57 to dispatch. We're on scene. We have one small compact car on its roof with a patient ejected."

He threw down the microphone and jumped out of the ambulance. James joined him and grabbed their equipment. They were in a busy intersection known for hellacious accidents. Jacob's adrenaline worked overtime coursing through his veins. He sucked in a deep breath and slowly exhaled, attempting to control his nerves.

A young man lie face down in the middle of the road. They were the first arriving unit on scene. In the distance, Jacob could hear the sirens of the incoming fire engine approaching. There were no other vehicles involved that Jacob noticed.

James pressed two fingers on the side of the man's neck. "He's got a pulse. His breathing is shallow and irregular."

Jacob set the jump bag down. He looked inside of the car, it was empty. He checked the perimeter of the vehicle looking for a possible patient that may have been ejected, but he didn't find anyone. Several cars stopped. People got out and walked toward the wreckage.

"Did anyone see anything?" James asked.

No one answered.

"Anyone? Did any of you see the accident?"

A woman stepped forward. "Yeah. I did."

"What happened?"

"He drove erratic, hit the back corner of another vehicle, and then went airborne. The car rolled several times. I didn't see him get thrown

97

out though," she said as her trembling hands covered her mouth.

A fire engine arrived. Four firefighters exited their truck and ran toward the scene.

"What do you need?" one of the firefighters asked.

"Get him on the board," James ordered.

The man was face down on the asphalt, and blood flowed out of several lacerations on his face. His facial structures were barely recognizable. Both of his arms had deep abrasions and he wasn't moving. His clothes were tattered with rips and holes and the smell of alcohol encompassed him. James reached down and secured a cervical collar around his neck and Jacob placed the backboard behind him.

One of the firefighters grabbed his neck. "On my count, we're going to log roll him onto the backboard. One-two-three."

The men rolled him over on his back and onto the long spinal board. James reached down and shifted his hips to center him on the board. Jacob pulled out his trauma sheers and began to cut away his torn white tee shirt and blue jeans. Blood spattered the front of the shirt and his jeans had several rips in the legs.

A man in dark blue dress pants and a pinstriped shirt with suspenders ran up and stood over the man on the backboard. "I'm a cardio-thoracic surgeon. I need to assess this patient."

Jacob looked up at him. "What's your name?"

"Doctor Griffin. I work at Magic County Hospital," he said as he knelt down at the head of the man.

"We appreciate you stopping doctor, but we have things under control."

Doctor Griffin reached down and pushed on the man's chest. "I think he needs his chest decompressed. He may have a tension pneumothorax. Give me a needle," he instructed.

Jacob rolled his eyes. "Like I said, we appreciate you stopping, but we'll take it from here."

He shook his head. "I'm a doctor. You need to do as I tell you or I'll be forced to call your supervisor."

James reached over and pushed his hands away from the patient. "You heard my partner. We don't need you here. Now kindly leave, please."

"What's your name?" the doctor shouted.

"James."

"I'm going to hold you personally responsible for prohibiting me from doing my job if you don't do what I'm telling you to do."

James stood up. "Are you willing to ride in with this patient and take over his care all the way to the hospital?"

"You paramedics are all alike. You think you know everything," he said through a clenched jaw.

"It's an easy question, doctor. Are you?"

The doctor shook his head and walked away. It amazed Jacob how James handled the doctor. He wouldn't have been able to talk to him like that.

Once secured to the backboard, the firefighters picked the injured man up and moved him to the cot. "What's going on?" the man asked, looking around.

"You were in an accident." James answered. "Are you hurting anywhere?"

The man's eyes closed and he stopped breathing.

James raked his knuckles across the man's sternum. "Sir? Can you hear me?"

His eyes flickered to life. "Ouch. That freaking hurts. Stop!" the man screamed. He reached up and pushed James' hand away.

"What's your name?" James asked.

"Danie...." He stopped breathing again.

Jacob looked over at James with a concerned look on his face. "This isn't good."

James brushed his knuckles across the man's sternum.

"Ouch. Stop doing that!"

"What's your name?" James asked again.

"Da...." His eyes shut and he stopped breathing.

"We need to get him in the truck now," James ordered.

They pushed him to the ambulance and loaded him inside. James sat down at the captain's seat next to his head. "We need to RSI him. You had the last tube. This one is mine," James barked.

Jacob offered no resistance. This would be the first time he pushed the medications and nervousness crept into his body.

James pulled out the equipment he needed to intubate the man. He handed an oropharyngeal airway to one of the firefighters. "Put this in his mouth and start bagging him."

The firefighter slid the OPA into the man's mouth and he gagged. He pulled it out. Once he hooked the BVM up to the oxygen, he began to assist his ventilations. Jacob grabbed everything he needed to start an IV. The man had an enormous vein in his forearm.

This should be easy.

After wiping his skin with an alcohol prep, he slid the large bore needle into his arm and blood flashed into the chamber. He taped the IV down, hooked an IV line into it, and ran the fluid wide open. Saline dripped in rapid succession into the chamber.

"You remember what drugs we need to give?" James asked.

Jacob's mind went blank. It wasn't the time for him to forget the medications and dosages he needed to administer.

James shook his head. "You need to remember this stuff. I won't always be here to help you."

This isn't fair. I've never had to push medications to paralyze someone. Hell, we hardly ever pushed medications in Arizona.

Jacob stared at him blankly.

James sighed. "We need Lidocaine, Versed and Succynocholine....in that order."

Jacob knew what all of the drugs were for, except Versed. With James already irritated at him, he didn't dare ask. Grabbing the medication box, he pulled out each of the drugs they needed. Once the syringes were filled with the medications, he sat them down on the bench seat.

"What are you waiting for? Start pushing the drugs," James snapped.

Jacob reached down and grabbed the Lidocaine. He dispersed the liquid into the IV line. The firefighter continued to ventilate the man.

James sat ready to slide the tube into the man's throat, but only when the medications were all administered. "Let's go. We need to get him tubed."

Jacob pushed the next medication. The man's face twitched and he stopped breathing.

James slid the laryngoscope blade into his mouth. His eyes narrowed he bit down on his bottom lip. With each tug of the laryngoscope, frustration washed over his face.

"I can't see anything. His epiglottis is anterior."

"You want me to take a look?" Jacob asked.

"No. Not yet."

Beads of sweat formed on James' forehead.

Jacob glanced at the cardiac monitor. "His heart rate is starting to drop. You need to stop so we can bag him.

James let out a sigh. He removed the laryngoscope and the steel blade clanked against the man's front teeth. The firefighter resumed ventilating him with the BVM. After a minute, his heart rate increased.

"I can see the tip of his epiglottis, but it's anterior." James appeared in deep thought. "I'm going to look again. We may need to take his c-collar off."

Jacob stiffened. Flashes of the call on the river rushed through his mind where Charles had removed the C-collar and the woman ended up paralyzed as a result. He wasn't going to allow that to happen. He'd learned from that call to do the procedures the proper way. If they didn't, they could cause the patient permanent damage.

"We can't do that. I've seen what can happen if we take it off."

"We may not have a choice."

Jacob's stomach tensed.

James picked up the laryngoscope. "I'm going to take another look. If I can't get it this time, your turn, Jacob."

The firefighter squeezed the BVM a few quick bursts and then moved out of James' way. Determination crossed his face. He slid the laryngoscope back in the man's mouth. He pushed the blade in deeper and the man began to gag. James removed the blade.

The man coughed a few times and then took in several deep breaths. "Please don't do that again," he pleaded.

James glared at Jacob. "Did you push the Versed?"

Jacob glanced on the seat next to him. He grabbed the vial and turned the label toward him. Versed stretched across the white label; he forgot. "No."

James's eyes narrowed. "Do you know what you've done?"

Jacob shrugged his shoulders.

"The Versed would keep him from remembering anything we just did; it's an amnesiac. He felt every bit of pain that I caused during the intubation."

Jacob knew he screwed up. With the anxiety of being responsible for pushing the medications, coupled with James's insistence of him working faster, he forgot to push the drug that wouldn't allow the man to remember the brutal procedure. His chest tightened, making it difficult to breathe. Flashes of the days he used to screw up on a regular basis scrolled through his mind.

"Why did you do that? Who are you? Where am I? What happened?" the man asked. He pulled at the spider straps attempting to take them off.

James reached down and grasped the man's hand. "Sir, don't do that. You were involved in an accident. You rolled your car several times."

"I don't remember anything."

"What's your name?"

"Daniel."

"Are you hurting anywhere?"

Daniel laughed. "Nah, man, I'm feeling pretty good right now." He reached up to his neck. "Why is my throat so sore?"

Jacob sat on the bench seat staring at the floor.

"You weren't breathing right, so we gave you some medicine to allow us to put a tube in your trachea to breathe for you," James answered.

"I'm breathing fine," Daniel said.

"When we found you sir, you weren't," Jacob barked. The frustration he felt poured over toward Daniel. It would be easy to push his shortcomings onto the man since he drove drunk, but it wouldn't take away the monumental mistake he made with the medication.

James glared at Jacob. "I think he's doing fine now. Get in the front and drive us to the hospital."

Jacob hung his head, got up, and exited the back of the ambulance.

"You need me for anything?" the firefighter asked.

"No. We're good. Thanks for your help," James answered.

The firefighter shook his head and climbed out of the ambulance.

"Medic-57, to dispatch," Jacob announced.

"Go ahead, Medic-57."

"We'll be en-route to Magic County Hospital."

"Dispatch copies."

Guilt consumed Jacob. Part of him didn't feel sorry for the man since he drove drunk, but it baffled him how he wouldn't breathe without stimulation. After the failed intubation attempt, he breathed normally without any difficulties. Why did that happen?

Jacob could hear James asking Daniel several questions and he answered them without difficulty. He still didn't remember driving his car, or the accident, but he *did* remember James digging in his throat. At a small level, he empathized with the man. He couldn't imagine having someone perform that procedure on him. As he passed cars on the way to the hospital, his guilt peaked. Because of the seriousness of the mistake, he could be suspended or lose his job. If that happened, his world would topple down.

Jacob pulled into the parking lot of the hospital. He dreaded having to face James. Moreover, he feared facing Nate. There wasn't any way possible he wouldn't hear about his enormous mistake.

After informing the dispatcher of their arrival at the hospital, Jacob climbed out of the ambulance, walked to the back of the truck, and stood staring at the doors. He reached up for the handle, but hesitated. He began feeling like a rookie all over again, making stupid mistakes. He was still a new paramedic, but there was no excuse. Right drug, right dose, right route, right patient, and right time. *Right drug and time* echoed through his head. He opened the doors to the back of the ambulance. James glared at him. He felt like a scolded child. James climbed out of the back of the ambulance. They pulled the man out of the truck and pushed him toward the ambulance entrance.

"I can't hide this," James said.

"I know."

The walk through the parking lot didn't seem long enough. The closer to the doors they were, the more nauseated Jacob felt. The emergency room buzzed with chaos and there weren't many empty rooms.

Jacob glanced over at the nurse's station and noticed Bridge speaking with another nurse. The sight of her still astounded him. An eerie feeling crept up his spine. He looked over his shoulder and saw Ed staring at him. His eyes were filled with hate and discontent, but Jacob didn't care. He had bigger problems to contend with now.

"What do you boys have?" the charge nurse asked.

"Male patient possibly ejected from a roll-over accident," James answered.

"Possibly ejected?"

"He doesn't remember the accident. We found him lying on the road when we arrived."

She tapped a finger on her chin while she studied the room assignment board. "Take him to trauma-two. Bridgette will be in shortly to take report from you."

Bridge? Please dear God, any nurse but Bridge.

They pushed their cot to trauma-two. Once inside, James unbuckled the seat belts and they lowered the cot. "Keep your arms across your chest, Daniel. Don't reach out for anything. If you do, you may cause us to drop you."

"Okay."

They lifted him off the cot and set him down on the awaiting bed. Jacob noticed James glaring at him.

Doctor Young stormed into the room. He looked down his nose at Jacob, not losing eye contact. "What did you bring in?"

James stepped forward. "This is Daniel...."

Doctor Young glanced at James. "I'm not talking to you. I'm talking to Jacob."

"He's *my* patient. If you want to know..."

"I assume you're not listening to me. I asked Jacob," Young said as his eyes narrowed.

"Like my partner said, he is his patient. Direct all of your questions to him," Jacob growled.

"Did I ask you for your opinion?" Doctor Young spouted back.

"We found Daniel intoxicated and he rolled his car, possibly ejected. We found him face down on the ground next to his car," James said. Tension hovered in the room like a dark storm cloud about to unleash its fury. "We attempted to RSI him, but were unsuccessful." His face remained stiff and expressionless.

Here we go.

Young approached Daniel. "I'm going to be your doctor, sir. Where are you hurting?"

Daniel giggled. "I'm not feeling much of anything right now. My throat is sore though," he said, grabbing to his neck.

Doctor Young approached Jacob and stood inches from his face. "Why in the hell did you try to RSI this man? Doesn't look like he needed that."

The emergency room became quiet. Nurses behind their desk stopped what they were doing and stared into the trauma room.

"He didn't breathe without painful stimulation. I attempted to RSI him, but I wasn't successful. I forgot to give him some Versed before I attempted the intubation. I take full responsibility for it."

Jacob couldn't believe his ears. He made the monumental mistake. *Why is he taking the blame? I'm the one that screwed up.*

Doctor Young turned his attention toward Jacob and grabbed his arm. "Come with me. I need to speak to you outside." He pulled Jacob out of the room and stopped just outside of the door.

"I *know* you did it. I've known James for years and he wouldn't make that kind of mistake. I'm going to *ruin* you for this."

Jacob stared coldly into his eyes. "You heard James. He did it."

"No, he didn't." The doctor crossed his arms over his chest. "What were you doing during all of this? You expect me to believe that James administered the drugs and attempted the intubation?"

"I had other things to do," Jacob fired back.

Bridge ran up and got in between the battling men. "What's going on?"

"Your dear friend Jacob forgot to push Versed on an attempted RSI. For some reason James is taking the blame for it."

Every person in the emergency room focused on them.

"If James said he did it then he did," Bridge said, looking into Doctor Young's eyes.

His bottom lip quivered. "Why are you always defending him? Is there something going on between you two?"

A knot the size of a softball formed in Jacob's throat.

"Are you serious right now?" Bridge asked with her arms across her chest.

"How many times have I caught you running to him? Every time I turn around you're with him. What else am I supposed to think?"

"You're *unbelievable,*" Bridge growled.

Ed grabbed one of Bridge's arms. "Baby, this isn't the time or the place."

Bridge pulled her arm free and pushed him in the chest. "Don't touch me. Don't *ever* touch me again. I don't deserve to be treated this way. At first your jealousy amused me, but you've gone too far this time." She reached down, wiggled the engagement ring off her finger, and then threw it at Doctor Young's chest. "It's over. I don't want to marry you any longer."

Jacob and James stared at one another with their mouths drooped open, not speaking.

"You're making a huge mistake. I can have any woman I want."

"You can have them because you'll never have me again." Bridge pushed past him and stomped out of the emergency room.

Young stared at Jacob with hate-filled eyes.

"Sucks to be you," Jacob said with a grin.

FIFTEEN

JACOB STRETCHED OUT on his couch aimlessly flipping through the channels on his TV. He didn't pay attention to the images that scrolled across the screen—he thought about Bridge. Seeing her break up with the doc made him happy. The image of her throwing her ring at him elicited a smile on his face. A knock on the front door interrupted his daydreaming. He dropped the remote on the floor and leisurely strolled across the living room. Seeing Bridge standing in his doorway surprised him. She stood in front of him, sniffling, with tears streaming down her cheeks.

"Can I come in?" she asked with a quivering voice.

Her unannounced visit shocked Jacob. He stepped to the side and she walked past him. He took a few steps onto his porch and scanned the neighborhood; no sight of Ed Young. He walked back inside and closed the front door. Bridge sat down on his couch with her elbows resting on her knees, rocking back and forth. He walked over to his recliner and sat down.

"What's going on, Bridge?"

She continued rocking. "I don't know why I'm here. I had no one else to talk to. I'm sorry."

Jacob wanted to grab her and hold her in his arms. Seeing her so upset broke his heart. "It's okay. I'm glad you came by. How are you doing?"

She looked up at him and her eyes narrowed. "How does it look like I'm doing? I'm falling apart, Jacob."

The tone in her voice made him feel uncomfortable. "I know you feel this way now, but I think you made the right choice. He wasn't right for you and he didn't deserve you."

Bridge's eyes welled up with tears and she held her hands over her eyes as she wept. Jacob sat down next to her. She scooted away from him to the other end of the couch. He fought the urge to wrap his arms around her and comfort her.

She dried her eyes. "I made a mistake coming here," she said as she stood.

Jacob jumped to his feet. "Please don't go. Stay."

Bridge looked at him curiously.

"Um...I have to pee," Jacob said.

Bridge chuckled. "You can be such a dork sometimes."

"I resemble that remark."

"Yes, you do."

Jacob felt a sense of accomplishment making her laugh. "Have you eaten? You look famished."

"I am kind of hungry," Bridge said. She walked into his kitchen and opened the door to his refrigerator. "I see your eating habits haven't changed."

Jacob walked into the kitchen and leaned against the wall. "You know me. I hate to cook for myself. Feel like pizza? My treat."

Bridge closed the refrigerator door. "Sure."

Jacob walked back into the living room and retrieved his phone. "Want anything in particular?"

"Whatever you want is fine with me."

Jacob called in their order and Bridge sat down on the couch looking at the floor. She grabbed the remote and flipped through the channels. Jacob didn't mind. Neither of them spoke while awaiting their food. He enjoyed her company, even though they weren't talking. There were so many things he wanted to say, and ask, but he chose not to push it.

A short time later, Jacob heard a knock on the front door. He got up from his recliner and opened it. A white BMW parked across the street grabbed his attention. The window rolled down and Doctor Young glared at him.

Jacob smiled.

She's here with me now. I win. You lose.

He paid the delivery boy for the food. Glancing across the street, he smiled, waved, and then walked back inside of his house locking the door behind him.

"Who were you waving at?"

"My neighbor across the street. Just being friendly." He hated being dishonest with her, but he knew it would bother her if she knew who he waved at. He walked into the dining room and put the pizza down on the table.

Bridge walked into the kitchen. "I'll get some plates. Do you have anything to drink?"

"Sodas are in the fridge."

She returned a few moments later and Jacob smiled at her.

"What?"

"Nothing. Just glad you're here."

Bridge placed a plate and a soda in front of Jacob. "Don't think anything of it. We're just friends. I'm using you for some free food and mildly entertaining company." She had a grin on her face.

"Mildly?"

"You can be fun to be around, at times. Don't let it get to your head." She grabbed two pieces of pizza and put them on Jacob's plate.

He tried hiding the pleasure on his face. She grabbed two pieces for herself. Sitting down, she held her hand out to Jacob.

"Why are you looking at me so weird? Don't you pray before you eat?" Bridge asked.

Jacob didn't pray—ever. Not to ruin the mood, he reached over and grasped her hand. The touch of her skin sent electricity through his body. His thumb traced over the knuckles on her hand.

"Well?" Bridge asked looking into his eyes.

"Well what?"

"You're the man of the house. Aren't you going to pray?"

"I am?"

"It *is* your house and *you're* a man, aren't you?"

Jacob chuckled. "I guess I am. I'm not good at praying. Why don't you do it?"

Bridge hung her head and then glanced back at Jacob. "God isn't going to grade you on how well you pray. Just bow your head and say what comes to mind."

Jacob felt butterflies forming in his stomach. Did holding her hand cause that, or because he acted like a fool? He grinned. "Rub a dub dub. Thanks for the grub. Yay God." He looked up and Bridge stared at him. .

Bridge's mouth hung open. "What was *that?*"

"A prayer we used to say in Cub Scouts," Jacob boasted.

She shook her head and pulled her hand away from him.

"Something wrong?"

Bridge reached down and grabbed a piece of her pizza. "No. Just not a prayer I expected is all. You were in the Cub Scouts?"

"Yeah. They kicked me out though."

"What for?" she asked with a mouth full of food.

"I got caught eating brownies."

Bridge laughed and started choking.

Jacob reached across and patted her on the back. "You okay? I can do mouth to mouth on you if you'd like."

Bridge held up her hand, waving a finger back and forth. After a few minutes, she stopped coughing and devoured her food. Jacob told her more about some of the calls he'd been on the past few months and she appeared genuinely interested. Once they finished eating, she got up and cleared off the table.

"You don't have to do that. I can clean up later."

She put her hands on her hips. "I told you long ago my parents raised me to be a proper lady. Now go get in your recliner and allow me to be a hospitable woman."

Jacob knew this was an argument he couldn't win. He grabbed a white napkin and waved it in the air, Bridge smiled. He walked into the living room and flipped through the channels on his TV. A short time later, she joined him.

"All done."

"Why thank you, ma'am. I appreciate your hospitality," Jacob said in a southern drawl.

"You never cease to amaze me, Mr. Myers. Well, I should be going. I have a lot to do today and I've taken up enough of your time."

Jacob sat forward in his recliner. "You have to go so soon?" *Please don't go! I want to spend more time with you.*

"Yeah, I do. I haven't done any laundry yet, and I have to work tomorrow."

Jacob's shoulders sank. "Well, if you must. Thank you for coming over. If you ever need anything, don't hesitate to ask."

"I know."

"Allow me to walk you to the door."

She smiled approvingly. "Such a gentleman."

He walked her to the front door. They stood looking at one another. Jacob wanted to kiss her, but he knew the timing wasn't right since she had just broken things off with Doctor Young. Holding out her arms, Jacob leaned in for a hug. At first, she lightly held her arms around his neck. He stepped closer to her.

"Thank you," she whispered into his ear.

"Anytime."

The smell of her hair astounded him. He squeezed tighter and she pulled him closer to her. A flood of euphoria washed over his body as he held her in his arms. She leaned back and they stared into one another's eyes. He fought the urge to kiss her, the insatiable need to feel her lips pressed against his. He leaned in, but she pulled out of his arms.

"I'm sorry," she said.

Jacob felt embarrassed, yet he still yearned to have her in his arms. "Don't be. I shouldn't have...."

Bridge opened the front door and stopped... staring across the street. Jacob walked up behind her to see what she was looking at. Ed Young glared at them both. His eyes narrowed. The engine roared to life and his car squealed down the street.

She watched as he drove away. "He followed me. Who knows how long he's been watching your house," she said with a quiver in her voice.

He placed a hand on her shoulder, but she pulled away. "Maybe I should follow you home."

Spinning around, she faced him. "Why do men always think they have to protect us? I'm a big girl, and I can take care of myself."

"I'm not saying...."

"I have to go." She turned and stomped toward her car.

He walked out and stopped a few feet away from the front door. Bridge got into her car and sped down the street in the opposite direction that Doctor Young had traveled.

Jacob felt disappointed as he watched her leave. *Two steps forward and then six steps back.*

Jacob sat in his recliner for several hours after Bridge left. He stared at the television with his mind wandering. He knew Doctor Young was outside his house, but didn't care. He could've told her, but chose not to in fear it would ruin their afternoon.

Unable to sit still, he decided to go for a drive and clear his head. He got dressed, grabbed his keys, and headed out of the front door. A bright orange glow encompassed the horizon from the setting sun. He put his favorite CD on and cranked the volume up. The upbeat tempo thumped through the speakers.

For an hour, Jacob drove up and down the bare main streets of downtown Boise. He decided to exchange the city streets for a more scenic route and drove down the two-lane highway adjacent to the river. The once orange sky faded into black, speckled with bright stars.

The windows were up with the air conditioner pumping cool air into the cab. The river flowed a short distance below the curvy road. A steep mountain towered on the inside of the road. On the passenger side, a dented guardrail from multiple collisions protected vehicles from driving into the river.

Music pulsed through the speakers, lightening his mood. As he navigated the road, tapping on his steering wheel to the beat of the music, he noticed a set of headlights approaching behind him, but thought nothing of it.

Jacob continued to drive down the road when he noticed the headlights were directly behind him with the high beams on. He flipped the rearview mirror up. The car behind him slammed into the back of his truck. The steering wheel jerked hard to the right and he had to tighten his grip on it so he didn't lose control. He flipped down the rearview mirror and the car still had its high beams on. He began to slow down, attempting to pull over once again, and caught another impact from the car behind him. It became increasingly difficult to keep his truck on the road. He slammed the gas pedal to the floor trying to create distance between him and the car. He looked in the rearview mirror and the car quickly caught up to him. His truck had a V8 engine, but he wouldn't be able to outrun the sports car. Fear ran through his body. He felt the steering wheel bending under his forceful grip. The curves became sharper. He watched the side of the road looking for a safe place to pull over. The car gained ground on him and pulled up next to him. Jacob looked over, but couldn't see through the tinted windows of the white car.

Pressing down on the gas pedal, the car next to him kept pace. It slammed into him and he nearly lost control. Realizing he couldn't outrun the car, Jacob slammed his truck into the car. The sound of grinding metal echoed over the music in his truck, but it barely budged. He glanced up and noticed a ninety-degree turn in the road going to the left. He pressed the accelerator to the floor. He followed the turn of the road and the car slammed into his door sending him toward the guardrail. The front of his truck burst through the guardrail and the hood buckled from the force. His truck rolled down a small embankment and he landed in the river. Water splashed up over his truck impeding his vision through the starred windshield and he began to sink. Water flowed into the cab. Jacob unfastened his seat belt and tried to open the door, but it wouldn't budge. He scooted across the cab and tried to open the passenger door. It didn't budge. Jacob's truck had lost power and he couldn't roll down the window. Terror overwhelmed him. It would be a matter of minutes before the entire cab filled with water.

Remembering he had a box of spark plugs in the glove compartment, he retrieved the box with trembling hands. He pulled the box out, ripped it open, and pulled out a spark plug. The truck settled on the bottom of the river. The cab had filled with water up to his chest. He took the spark plug and began hitting the window. After the fifth time of striking it, the window shattered and water flooded into the cab. Once on his knees on the seat, Jacob took a deep breath, and then pulled himself through the opened window. The dark water clouded his sense of direction.

Jacob exhaled and swam in the direction he felt the bubbles traveling. Pulling with his arms, kicking his legs, he swam as hard and fast as he could. His muscles burned with each stroke. He reached the surface just as the last breath escaped his lungs. The cool air hit his face and he inhaled deeply, sucking in water and fatigue set in. Jacob rolled over to his back and swam for the shore.

After a few minutes of doing the backstroke, his legs were able to reach the ground on the bottom of the river. With the last ounce of energy he had, Jacob reached the shore and then collapsed face down on the grass. Breathing deeply, his heart thumped in his chest. Fatigue and numbness set in. He heard a car door open and then shut. He pulled himself up to his knees and looked toward the roadway just in time to see the white car speed away.

SIXTEEN

THE NEXT MORNING, Jacob got ready for work early and decided to go to the police station to file a report. Luckily, a woman drove up on the accident and allowed Jacob to use her cell phone. He called James to pick him up. The tow-truck driver, who happened to be a diver, swam under water and hooked up chains onto the truck. He loaded it onto the flatbed truck and towed it to an automotive shop near Jacob's house.

He pulled up in front of the police station and a shiver jolted down his spine. His last experience with the police turned out to be disastrous. From time to time, he thought about Becca, but he shook off the horrible thoughts that flooded his mind and walked toward the doors.

The sun shone in the crystal blue sky, but his mood resembled that of a horrendous storm. He couldn't figure out why someone would try to kill him.

A portly officer sat behind the main desk devouring a double cheeseburger. Mustard trickled down from the corner of his mouth. By the looks of his waistline, Jacob could tell he'd consumed several of the heart attack specials in his lifetime.

Jacob approached the desk and cleared his throat. The officer never looked up.

"Yeah. What do you want?" the officer asked while chewing a mouthful of food.

"I need to file a police report. I believe someone is trying to kill me."

"Oh yeah?" The officer had more interest in contributing to heart disease than dealing with Jacob. "You'll find a detective back there in the squad room," he said, pointing at a hallway behind him.

"Thank you."

Jacob walked down the hall toward the squad room. The walls were covered with photos of various police officers with each one having a gold plate underneath them. Jacob stopped to read about a few of the officers who lost their lives in the line of duty. He approached the squad room and it resembled the one where he had seen Becca looking at him through her icy eyes. There were several officers working at their desks. Jacob wasn't sure who to speak to, so he walked up to the first desk he saw.

A man in a designer suit looked up at him. "Can I help you?"

"I need to speak to a detective. I think someone is trying to kill me," Jacob answered.

"What makes you think that?"

"Can I sit down?"

He smiled. "Sure. Where are my manners?" The man stood and reached out to shake his hand. "I'm Detective Morrison."

Jacob shook his hand and sat down.

Morrison leaned back in his chair, rocking back and forth. "What makes you think someone is trying to kill you?"

Jacob sighed. "The brake lines on our ambulance were cut, causing us to wreck a few days ago. Last night, someone ran me off the road into the river."

The detective tapped his chin with a finger. "Hmm. Interesting. Any idea who it is?"

Jacob stiffened. He had his suspicions, but didn't have any tangible proof. "Doctor Young," he blurted out.

Detective Morrison stopped rocking. He laughed. *"The* Doctor Young that works at the hospital?"

"Yes." Jacob sat in anticipation of how the detective would react. He'd become accustomed to law enforcement not believing him. They hadn't in Arizona, so why should Idaho be any different?

Morrison sat forward in his chair and leaned on his desk. "I doubt that. You must be mistaken."

Jacob's jaw tensed. "I saw him at the donut shop where we stopped to eat, and I'm pretty sure I saw his car at the river as it drove off."

"Pretty sure? You realize this is a serious accusation. You're talking about a well-respected doctor. If you're wrong, you could be held legally liable."

"All I know is someone is trying to kill me. Are you going to do something about it?"

Detective Morrison smirked. "I'll look into it."

Jacob looked at his watch. "I have to go. I'm on duty today. Thank you for your time." He shook hands with the detective.

On his way to the station, Jacob couldn't shake the feeling that the detective didn't take him seriously. He wasn't completely sure himself. Could it be a coincidence that Doctor Young happened to be at the donut shop, and what appeared to be his car at the accident scene? Jacob wasn't certain.

He arrived at the station, but didn't see James' truck. A young man eagerly walked out of the station toward him.

"Hi. My name is Bishop. I'm a reserve EMT-Basic working with you today," he said holding out his hand toward Jacob.

Jacob looked at him confused. "Where's James?"

"He had a family emergency."

Jacob shook his hand. "That's unusual having a basic work on the truck. We're usually double paramedic."

"Guess they couldn't find another paramedic to work. Are you that hard to get along with?" he asked, laughing.

Jacob rolled his eyes and walked past Bishop into the station. He put his personal belongings into his room and walked back into the day room.

"I hope I didn't offend you. I like to joke around," Bishop said.

Jacob felt foolish. Bishop had no clue what he'd been going through. "I'm sorry. I have a lot on my mind. I shouldn't have been so rude."

"It's okay. I understand."

If you did, you wouldn't be here now. I'm being hunted by someone trying to kill me. You could get hurt, too.

Jacob walked toward the ambulance bay. "Let's go check off the truck."

For the next thirty minutes, they inventoried the equipment. Jacob wasn't in a sociable mood, so he didn't say much. Bishop's eager attitude made it obvious he was a new EMT. He wore a neatly pressed uniform, freshly shaven face, and a shine on his boots that could blind someone.

"How long have you been in the field?" Jacob asked.

Bishop grinned from ear to ear. "This is my second shift, ever. We don't get many as reserves. I'm thinking about applying for paramedic school this fall."

Great! I'm working with a brand new guy. Could this day get any worse?

"Can I give you some friendly advice?"

Bishop closed the equipment bag. "Sure. I'd love to hear anything you have to offer."

"Get a job working full time on an ambulance for a few years before you attempt going to paramedic school. You'll need the experience if you want to become a good paramedic. You can mess up on your advanced skills, but if you have a solid foundation of basic skills, you won't kill anyone." That was the best advice he could give anyone, especially if they thought about going to paramedic school without any experience.

The station tones blared over the speakers and interrupted their conversation.

"Medic-57, we have a non-emergent transfer at 1120 Brown Road at the urgent clinic. You have a six-year old male patient not feeling well."

A smile crossed over Bishop's face. He jumped up, rushed out of the back of the ambulance, and ran to the driver's seat.

Jacob shook his head and laughed. It wasn't long ago that he'd been the same way. His partner's eagerness felt refreshing. It helped him remember why he chose a job in the medical field.

Bishop started the ambulance, flipped on the lights, and looked around for his partner.

Jacob climbed into the passenger side. "A little eager, are ya?" he asked as he reached over and turned off the emergency lights.

Bishop frowned. "Why did you do that?"

"This call is non-emergent, which means code one—no lights or sirens." He grabbed the microphone. "Dispatch, Medic-57 is en-route."

"Dispatch copies. You have a six-year old male patient not feeling well. Doctor on scene is requesting transport to the emergency room."

Bishop's shoulders slumped. He put the ambulance into drive and then pulled out of the bay.

When they arrived at the doctor's office, Bishop hopped out of the ambulance and ran toward the front door.

Jacob smiled. "Hey."

Bishop stopped and turned around. "Yeah?"

"Do you plan on carrying the kid? Think we might need our equipment bag?"

He nodded and ran toward the back of the ambulance. Jacob couldn't suppress his laughter. He remembered his first call at the river when he did the same exact thing and Stitch stopped him. He missed him dearly. A day didn't go by that he didn't think of Stitch. There were so many things he wished he could say to his friend. Stitch played a big part in getting Jacob into EMS, and he knew that he'd be proud of how far he'd come in his career.

The men walked toward the back door of the doctor's office with a fully loaded cot. Jacob, having the highest certification on the ambulance, meant he had to take all the calls.

An elderly woman opened the door and smiled. "Hello, boys. Right this way." She held the door open while they pushed their cot past her.

Jacob noticed everyone in the office appeared calm. That's a good sign. Walking into a room full of frantic medical personnel wasn't a good thing. She led them to one of the exam rooms a short distance away. A man paced back and forth outside of the door with a concerned look on his face.

"How are you doing, sir?"

He sighed. "I've been better. You're here for my son."

The elderly woman walked around the corner holding an envelope. "Here's his paperwork. The doctor wants him taken to Magic County ER."

Jacob faced Bishop. "Go inside and get a set of vital signs."

Bishop nodded and walked inside of the room with their equipment bag.

"What's his diagnosis?" Jacob asked.

"Dehydration. He's had nausea and vomiting for the past four days. I looked for an IV, but didn't see anything. I figured I would wait for the professionals," she said, smiling.

"Ma'am, flattery will get you everywhere with me." Jacob walked into the room. A pale-skinned boy with sandy blonde hair and deep blue eyes lay flat on the exam table. His sunken eyes and dry lips grabbed Jacob's attention. It wasn't a good sign seeing a child of his age so still. A woman sat next to the exam table holding his hand with tears streaming down her cheeks. She looked up at Jacob when he entered the room.

"Hello, ma'am. I'm a paramedic and I'll be taking your son to the hospital. Can you tell me when this all started?" Jacob asked.

She wiped the tears from her cheeks. "He had been complaining of belly pain for several days. Four days ago, he started throwing up all of the time. We took him to the emergency room, but we ended up sitting in the waiting room for over eight hours. His belly felt better so we left."

Jacob turned toward the little boy while Bishop checked his blood pressure. "How ya feeling, bud?"

He turned his head toward Jacob. "I don't feel so good. My belly hurts."

"Can you show me where?"

He pointed to the middle of his stomach. "Right here."

Jacob palpated his stomach. His eyes narrowed as he felt a hard mass in the center of his abdomen. It could've been any number of things and he ran the possible diagnoses through his mind. He looked back down at the small boy and couldn't shake the feeling in his gut that the child was critically ill.

Bishop deflated the blood pressure cuff and pulled the stethoscope out of his ears. "His pressure is 86/50 and his heart rate is 132 beats per minute."

"Do you feel like you need to throw up?" Jacob asked the little boy.

"Not right…." He stopped talking. Blankly looking at Jacob, both of the boy's pupils were completely dilated.

"Go get the doctor." Jacob shook the little boy's shoulder. "Can you hear me, buddy?"

The woman stood, tears flowing like a river down her face. "What's going on?"

The man standing outside burst through the door. "What's the matter with my son?"

Jacob didn't know what to tell him—he wasn't sure himself. He grabbed the boy's wrist. A strong pulse beat rapidly under his fingers. He glanced up and noticed his chest rise and fall, another good sign. *What's going on with this kid? I'm stumped!*

A few moments later, the doctor walked into the room. "What's wrong?"

"While I spoke to him I watched his pupils dilate. He stopped responding to me."

The doctor walked over and examined the boy's eyes.

The boy blinked. "I don't feel so good. I want my mommy," he said, reaching for her.

The woman pulled her son into her arms and she wept.

"You need to get going," the doctor said as he left the room.

Jacob couldn't agree more. He needed an IV before they left in case the child's condition worsened. Pediatric patients terrified him, especially critically sick ones.

"Someone tell me what the hell is going on with my son!"

Jacob told Bishop to get an IV set up. "Sir, I'm not sure what's wrong with your son. What I *do* know is we need to get an IV in him. Without that, I can't help him. Once I get that started, we'll go to the hospital."

The man's upper lip quivered. "Do whatever you think you need to."

Jacob grabbed a tourniquet. "Okay, buddy. I'm going to put this rubber band around your arm. I need to give you a little shot. Can you be a big boy for me?"

The boy nodded.

Jacob pulled the tourniquet around his arm, wiped it with an alcohol prep, and then searched for a vein, but he couldn't find one. Nervousness crept through his body. He desperately needed an IV. He looked up and the boy stared at the ceiling. His pupils dilated again.

"We need to get going." Jacob threw the IV supplies into the jump bag. "Get the cot, Bishop."

The child's mother cried out, "Is he going to be okay?"

"We're going to do everything we can to help him, ma'am," Jacob reassured her.

Jacob and Bishop rushed the boy toward their ambulance. The boy's parents followed closely behind. As they loaded him into the ambulance, the boy's eyes flickered to life and he reached out for his parents.

"Can I ride with him?" his mother asked, sobbing.

"It would be better if you followed behind, ma'am. We're going to drive with the lights and sirens on, so don't try to keep up. A police officer will still give you a ticket if you speed." Jacob said. His partner didn't need a frantic parent sitting next to him adding to his stress. He remembered when that happened to him when he worked as an EMT. He wouldn't allow that unwarranted stress to be shoved down his partner's throat. His co-worker needed to concentrate on transporting them safely to the hospital.

"Daddy loves you, buddy. We'll be right behind you," the man said, reaching out for his son.

Jacob jumped into the back of the ambulance. "Code three, Bishop. Drive fast, but don't kill me."

Bishop slammed the doors shut, ran to the front of the ambulance, and jumped into the driver's seat. "Medic-57, to dispatch."

"Go ahead, Medic-57,"

"We're en-route to Magic Valley, code three." Bishop turned on the emergency lights, flipped on the sirens, and squealed out of the parking lot.

Jacob grabbed the rails on the ceiling of the ambulance. "This isn't a damn race. Back it off a little."

The little boy remained motionless, oblivious to his surroundings, and that worried Jacob. Children his age normally would be asking hundreds of questions. After placing the cardiac monitor onto the boy's chest, he looked again for a vein to start an IV, but he still couldn't find one.

"How far out are we from the hospital?"

"Ten minutes," Bishop answered.

Ten minutes? This kid doesn't have *two minutes.*

Jacob learned early on to trust his gut feeling. Right now, his gut said the child was in danger.

Bishop navigated the traffic with ease. Looking out the back window, Jacob didn't see the little boy's parents any longer. He grabbed a non-rebreather mask hooked to high flow oxygen and placed it on him—he didn't know what else he could do. Without IV access, Jacob felt like his hands were tied. He needed James now more than ever.

A few minutes later, Bishop pulled into the ambulance parking at the hospital.

Jacob flung the doors open and jumped out of the back once it stopped moving. As Bishop ran around to help him, Jacob noticed the little boy wasn't breathing. He pressed his fingers against the boy's neck and didn't feel a pulse.

"Get him in the ER, *now,*" Jacob screamed. He ran around to the side of the cot and began to compress the boy's chest. They rushed through the doors and into the emergency room.

"He's in cardiac arrest," Jacob yelled. For a brief moment, the staff looked stunned. A few nurses ran from behind the main desk.

"Trauma-one," yelled a nurse.

Still compressing his chest, Jacob looked at the doctor desk. Doctor Young wasn't there. He sighed with relief. Once in the room, they moved the little boy over to the awaiting bed. A nurse took over compressions. Jacob stepped back. He ran his fingers through his sweat saturated hair.

A doctor ran into the room. "What happened?"

Jacob gave him a quick report on what had transpired. Stepping back, the team went to work on the child. Bishop stepped in and took over compressions. Everything moved in fast forward. Two more nurses joined in and went to work. Tears welled up in his eyes. Emotions were crashing over him like a large tidal wave. He turned and walked out to the ambulance bay. Sitting down on the bumper of the ambulance, Jacob wept. In his mind, he felt as if he had failed the little boy and his parents. He wasn't able to do anything to help the child. Wasn't that his job, to save lives?

The doors to the emergency room opened and Bridge walked toward him. He tried to dry his eyes and choke down his tears.

Bridge knelt down in front of him and held his hands. "Are you okay?"

Jacob turned his head and wiped the tears away. "Yeah. I'm fine."

"Why are you so stubborn? It's okay if you cry. It shows you're still human."

"I'm sorry. Guys don't cry."

"A real man cries. It's okay."

Jacob couldn't hold it back any longer and burst into tears, again. Bridge pulled him into her arms while he wept. A few minutes later, the doctor walked outside and shook his head.

"I'm sorry. We did everything we could. He's gone."

Jacob felt overwhelmed with guilt. If he'd known the parents wouldn't see their child alive again, he would've allowed them to ride in the ambulance. How could he face them? How could he keep going in this job? More than ever, he doubted his ability to do the job.

SEVENTEEN

THE RED NUMBERS of the digital clock showed four o'clock in the afternoon and Jacob hadn't gotten out of bed yet—he didn't see the point. He felt responsible for the death of the little boy. Six years old was far too young to die. He ran the call repeatedly in his head wondering if he'd done everything he could. Death played a major role in his job. When an adult died, he could accept that since they'd lived their lives, but when a child died, he had trouble accepting that. They weren't supposed to die that young.

His cell phone rang several times throughout the day, but he ignored the urge to answer it. He didn't want to speak to anyone. His questionable belief in God suffered a lethal blow.

As the sun set in the horizon, Jacob heard a knock on the front door. He couldn't muster the energy to answer it. He heard another forceful knock that shook the windows, but he chose to continue ignoring it. Just outside of his bedroom window, he could hear footsteps. He rolled over in his bed facing the window.

"Jacob? I know you're there. I saw the rental car in the driveway. Go answer your door," said Bridge.

Jacob sighed and pulled a pillow over his head. "Go away."

"Jacob Myers, get your butt out of bed and answer your damn door. I'm not leaving until you do."

Why is she so stubborn?

Jacob groaned, flung the blanket off him, slipped on a pair of shorts, and walked toward the front door. Bridge glared at him through the window. He opened the door.

"Hey."

"How long were you going to leave me out here knocking?"

Jacob walked over and plopped down in his recliner. Bridge walked inside and slammed the door shut. She stood in front of him.

"What?"

"I've been knocking on your door for the past fifteen minutes. You had me worried, so I came over to see how you were doing."

"I'm fine."

"It doesn't look like it. Have you been out of bed today?"

Jacob grabbed the remote control, but Bridge yanked it out of his hands and threw it onto the couch.

Jacob rolled his eyes.

She knelt down in front of him. "I know you're upset about that call. There's nothing you could've done differently. That kid was dead before you got to him."

"How do you know?"

The anger in her face succumbed to sympathy. "They did an autopsy on him this morning. He died from a severe infection, malnutrition, and dehydration."

Jacob's face stiffened. "The parents did it to him?"

"No. He had a case of intussusception."

Jacob looked at her bewildered. "What's that?"

"It's where the intestine telescopes inside of itself, cutting the rest of the body off from nutrition. After interviewing the parents, it turns out that he had this going on for well over a month. A large portion of his intestine had died. The combination of the infection and his body being starved killed him."

Guilt brewed deep inside of him, but knowing there wasn't anything he could have done differently to change the outcome, offered him some relief. Tears freely flowed down his face. Bridge leaned in close and took him into her arms. Jacob pulled her close and wept. He had a hard time allowing her to see him weak and vulnerable. His male ego slapped him in the face, but he didn't care.

She leaned back and wiped away Jacob's tears. Overcome with emotion, he pulled her close to him. He stared into her startled eyes and then plunged his lips onto hers. At first, Bridge tried to pull away, but stopped. Their lips found a rhythm. She placed a hand on the back of his head and reciprocated the gesture. The sweetness of her lips and feeling her breath on his cheek sent his world into a tailspin.

Pulling away from him, her eyes had a mixture of pleasure and fear. She wiped off her lips. "You need to get dressed. I'm not going to allow you to sit here sulking all day. Hurry up; I have plans for us today."

"Why are you fighting your feelings? I know you feel the same way as I do. I don't understand."

"I can't do this. I just ended a serious relationship. I'm trying hard to be your friend."

Jacob's shoulders slumped. "I can't do this either. I want something more. You should go."

She looked at him, shocked. "Are you serious?"

"Yeah."

"Fine. Guess I'll see you around." She turned and stormed toward the front door. She stopped and looked over her shoulder toward Jacob. "You're asking too much of me right now. I'll still be here when you're ready to be friends." She stomped out the door and slammed it behind her.

Jacob received a phone call from Nate, requesting him to come to his office. He ran several scenarios through his mind trying to figure out what Nate wanted. Once he arrived at the main station, he sat in the rental car for a few minutes collecting his thoughts. Uncertainty crept through his body. Shrugging off his insecurities, he got out of the car and walked toward Nate's office. Regardless of the reason, he would hold his head high, and stand by whatever decision he made that Nate questioned.

Nate pointed at a chair. "Have a seat."

"What's going on, boss? Did I do something wrong?"

Nate leaned back in his chair. "No. I'm just concerned about you. I've read your report on the pediatric code. From what I can gather, it was a rough call."

If he only knew.

"I'm fine."

"Jacob, there's nothing wrong with admitting the call rattled you. Hell, I would be in pieces right now. My job is to make sure you can continue to do your job."

He wanted to tell Nate how he felt, but his male ego reared its ugly head.   "I'm fine, honestly."

Nate rocked in his chair. "I'm not convinced. They're having a critical incident debriefing at the hospital today. I'm ordering you to attend."

Jacob exhaled. "It's not necessary."

Nate's face stiffened. "It's not an option. You will attend. If you don't, I won't allow you back on the ambulance until you do. I need to make sure you're mentally capable of handling the rigors of this job. Are we clear?"

"Crystal."

Nate leaned forward and rested his elbows on the desk. "It starts in thirty minutes. This is for your own good. Get going."

Jacob nodded and walked out of Nate's office.

I don't need to talk about my feelings to complete strangers. I'm fine.

Jacob arrived at Magic County Hospital. The receptionist gave him directions to the CISD meeting. Walking down the hall, he hid the guilt that consumed him. He felt envious of the people living in their pain-free existences. If others only knew the emotional scars his career left deep inside of him.

Standing outside of the door to the conference room, Jacob sucked in a deep breath. As he walked into the room, he recognized several nurses from the emergency room that night. Tears were flowing and he felt uncomfortable. The chairs were arranged in a circle with a table perched in the middle with several boxes of tissues on it. No one noticed that he walked into the room; they were too busy with their own grief. Jacob was angry with Nate. He didn't feel like he needed to be at the meeting, but if he didn't attend it he wouldn't be allowed back on the ambulance.

A few minutes later, a middle-aged man rushed into the room. He sat down at one of the empty seats. Everyone in attendance took notice of him. That made Jacob feel unimportant. They couldn't even nod or say hi to him when he walked into the room.

"Hey, guys. For those of you that don't know me, my name is David. I'm the regional coordinator for CISD." Everyone in the room stared at him as he spoke. He grabbed a file and briefly flipped through several pages. "I understand we had a pediatric arrest in the emergency room last night. Anyone want to start?"

Everyone looked inquisitively at one another, but no one answered.

David glanced at his watch. "I think we should be able to wrap this up in about twenty minutes. Someone please start."

A nurse grabbed a few tissues from the table and dabbed her eyes. "It was horrible. I've never felt so helpless in all of my life. Nothing we did seemed to help." She began to weep. "All I...all I could see was my son." She bowed her head and cried. Her head violently bobbed up and down. A woman next to her put an arm around her, and sympathetically rubbed her shoulder. The room grew silent as all eyes were upon her.

For the next several minutes, people shared their grief with the case. With each passing moment, Jacob became more open to the idea of sharing his feelings. At first, he felt going to the meeting would be useless and a waste of time. The more he listened to other people's grief, the more he realized he wasn't okay. The conversation lulled and Jacob mustered up the courage to speak. He cleared his throat. A hesitation still loomed in his mind, but he knew he needed to share his feelings. Otherwise, the call might cause damage he wouldn't be able to recover from.

"My name is Jacob, and I was the paramedic that...."

David interrupted him. "I'm sorry, but we've run out of time. I want to thank everyone for attending today. I hope this has helped." He gathered his paperwork and exited the room.

Jacob sat in his seat in utter disbelief. Everyone else had an opportunity to speak except for him. Once the room cleared, Jacob stared at the ceiling. He wanted to punch the wall, but he knew that would do more harm than good. He stood and walked out of the room toward his car.

I will never attend CISD again. What a joke.

EIGHTEEN

JACOB PULLED INTO the station parking lot to a welcome sight; James' truck. Images of the child's face from his previous call were burned into his mind and after attending the useless CISD, he couldn't wait to talk with James about it. He was a firm believer in talking with co-workers—there wasn't any better therapy than sharing his feelings with people who truly understood.

James met him in the parking lot with a concerned look on his face. "I heard about your call. How are you doing?"

Jacob groaned. "Okay, I guess. I can't get it out of my head."

"You won't be able to. That's something that will take time. I'm sorry I couldn't be there with you. My little boy wouldn't stop throwing up, so I had to call in sick. I'm sorry, brother," James said as he patted Jacob on the shoulder.

A blue Crown Victoria pulled into the parking lot behind them. Detective Morrison stepped out of the car.

"Do you know him?" James asked.

"Yeah. Can you give me a minute?"

"Sure." James turned and walked back into the station.

Jacob approached the detective. "What brings you here?"

He slid his hands into his pants pockets. "I spoke with a Detective Horowitz down in Phoenix today. What he had to say surprised me. Sounds like you had a little trouble with a woman named Becca."

That name sent shivers down Jacob's spine. "Yeah. I'm sure he didn't have anything nice to say about me. Why in the hell did you call down there? What's going on here has nothing to do with Phoenix."

Detective Morrison leaned against his car, crossing his arms over his chest. "A little defensive, aren't you? In my line of work that usually means you're trying to hide something."

The veins on Jacob's forehead pulsated. "I don't have a damn thing to hide. That crazy woman stalked me, falsely accused me of raping her, and then killed herself in front of me."

Detective Morrison chuckled. "We'll never know if that is true or not since she's dead."

Jacob's anger spread like a wildfire out of control. "Is there a point to you coming here, or did you just want to harass me?"

Morrison's body stiffened. "I'm not here to harass you. I wanted to let you know we questioned Doctor Young last night. He has an alibi the night you were run off the road. Now who's falsely accusing someone?"

Jacob shook his head. "Is that all?"

"For now."

Jacob turned and stomped across the asphalt toward the station. The echo of his boots resonated through the air. Slamming the door behind him, he went straight to his room and slammed the door shut. Becca was dead, but she still managed to mess with his life.

A few minutes later, James lightly knocked on his door.

Jacob opened it, still visibly upset. "Yeah?"

"You okay?"

"I'm fine." Jacob rushed past him and sat down on a couch in the day room.

"What's going on, man? You look upset."

"That detective is rude and out of line."

"Why did he come by here?"

Jacob's heart thumped forcefully in his chest. "I went to file a police report on the car that ran me into the river. I shared my suspicions with him."

James sat down in the recliner across from him. "Who's that?"

Jacob knew James would think he was crazy, but he trusted his partner. "Doctor Young."

James sat up straight. "The same Doctor Young you've been having trouble with?"

"Yeah."

"What makes you think that?"

"I saw his car at the donut shop the day our brake lines were cut. Once I pulled myself out of the river, I saw a car that looked exactly like his leaving the scene. I'm positive it's him."

James sat back, staring up at the ceiling. "Could just be coincidence. Have you thought about that?"

Jacob's shoulders dropped. His partner didn't believe him either. "I'm sure it's him. I can't prove it right now, but I will."

The two men sat in silence for a few minutes. Jacob's life had become an emotional roller coaster since he started a career in EMS. He missed his mundane office job, at times. Things were much simpler and uncomplicated. He missed living in the protective bubble of oblivion that insulated him from the real world. The station tones blaring over the speakers interrupted the silence.

"Medic-57, we have a call at 510 Driftwood Lane for an unknown medical."

Jacob jumped up from the couch and followed James into the bay. "Medic-57 is en-route," Jacob answered.

"Dispatch copies. We don't have any information. Fire and police have been dispatched."

Jacob stared out the window as they sped toward the residence, his mind spinning carelessly out of control. The only time he didn't have difficulty concentrating was when a patient in need of medical attention was in front of him. No one could penetrate his world.

James pulled up in front of the address. The fire department were walking around the house looking into windows and trying to find entry.

"Medic-57 is on scene."

"Dispatch copies."

The men exited their ambulance and walked toward the front of the house.

"What's going on?" James asked.

"We can hear a man moaning, but we can't get into the house. All of the doors and windows are locked up tight and we can't see anything inside either," a firefighter answered.

"Any idea on the police's ETA?" Jacob asked.

A police car sped around the corner and skidded to a halt next to the fire truck. Two police officers exited their car and walked toward the men.

"What's going on?" one of the officers asked.

"We need you guys to do a forcible entry," the firefighter answered.

"Check all of the doors and windows?"

"Yeah. They're all locked."

The officer walked past them onto the porch. He pulled out his flashlight and tapped it on the front door. "Police. Can you open the door?"

No answer—just moans.

He banged the front door harder. "Police. Open up," he commanded.

Again, no answer.

The officer turned toward the firefighters. "Can't you get an axe and bust in this door?"

"We're not allowed. Go ahead if you want to."

The officer shook his head. Sliding his flashlight back into his belt and he heaved his foot into the front door. It flung open, smashed against the wall, and splinters of wood flew through the air from the door jamb.

The officer and his partner drew their guns. "You guys stay out here. We're going to clear the house."

The two officers cautiously entered the house yelling "Police" every so often. After several minutes, the officers exited the house and holstered their guns. They were laughing. "The house is clear. You guys can go in. He's in the back bedroom."

Jacob glanced at James, shrugged his shoulders, and walked into the house. James and the firefighters walked closely behind him. Once inside, Jacob looked around the living room. Piles of pornography tapes and magazines cluttered the tables. Coming from the back of the house, he could hear a man moaning. The group of men continued to walk toward the back of the house. At the end of a hall, Jacob noticed a door slightly open. He pushed past the door, entered the room, and stopped. The men behind him stumbled into his back.

"What are you doing?" James asked. He peered over Jacob's shoulder. "Oh my."

A thin man weighing no more than a hundred pounds sat on a bedpost, naked. He weakly looked up. "Oh God, please help me. I'm stuck," he said, and then hung his head.

Jacob pushed down the urge to laugh. He approached the man. "Sir, how did…." He choked down laughter. "How did you get on there?"

The man moaned. "I don't think I can hold myself up much longer. Please, just get me off this. It hurts…ohhhh." The man sat with the bedpost stuck in his rectum, leaning over on his bent knees.

The man groaned.

They witnessed many different types of emergencies. At times, the crews may have found them humorous and had difficulty remaining professional.

"Um, think we can lift you off the post?" Jacob asked.

"Don't you think I've tried that already?" the man said, glaring at him.

Jacob turned toward James and the firefighters. "You guys have any ideas?"

They shrugged their shoulders and offered no advice.

Staring at the man, Jacob couldn't think of what to do. After a few moments, he had an idea. "Let's get two of you guys on each side of him and let's see if we can lift him off the post."

Two of the firefighters nodded and walked over to position themselves next to the man. They got on each side of him, placed his arms around their necks, and attempted to lift him up.

"Ouch…ouch…stop. Please stop," the man shouted.

The firefighters stopped.

"Let's get the saw. We'll cut the post below him," the firefighter captain suggested.

James walked outside to help him retrieve the saw. The two firefighters remained next to the man helping hold his weight up. A few minutes later, James and the captain returned with the saw. Once they had it ready, the captain placed the blade a foot below the man. Jacob took the blanket off the bed and wrapped it around the man's lap trying his best to protect his skin.

"Are you ready?" the captain asked.

"Ohhh…please hurry. I'm in so much pain."

The captain sprung the saw to life. Flipping down the visor on his helmet, be began to cut the bedpost, wood spitting in all directions.

"No. Stop!" screamed the man. "Ouch…it hurts too much. It's vibrating too hard."

The captain ignored his pleading and continued to cut. A few moments later, he cut through the post. The two firefighters that were helping hold him up, laid him down on his side on the bed. A sigh of relief slipped through the man's gritted teeth. Perspiration beaded on his forehead and his lips quivered.

"We need our cot," Jacob said.

The two firefighters nodded and left to retrieve the cot. Jacob stood next to the man, shaking his head.

Jacob knelt down on the floor in front of the man resting his elbows on his knees. "We're going to take you to the hospital."

"I don't want to go. I'll be fine. I can get it out by myself," the man answered.

"Sir, we need to take you to the hospital. I'm sure you may be able to get it out, but I'm concerned with what damage it caused your rectum. It's vascular in there and you could bleed to death."

"I could die from this?"

"Yes sir, you could. Allow us to take you to the hospital, please."

"Okay."

The two firefighters returned to the room with the cot. They lifted the man from the bed and placed him on it. Lying on his side was the only option for transport. James and Jacob pushed the cot to their awaiting ambulance. With each bump, the man bellowed in pain. Jacob had a difficult time suppressing his laughter, but he also felt sorry for the man. He couldn't imagine how humiliated the man felt.

They lifted the cot into the ambulance and Jacob jumped into the back. "I'll take this one," Jacob said, grinning.

James returned the gesture, closed the doors to the ambulance, and began joking with the firefighters. Jacob obtained a set of vital signs and started an IV in the man's arm.

James grabbed the microphone. "Medic-57 to dispatch."

"Go ahead, Medic-57."

"We're en-route to Magic County Hospital."

"Dispatch copies."

James shifted the ambulance into drive, and headed toward the hospital.

The man looked down, not making eye contact with Jacob. With each bump in the road, he winced in pain. Jacob felt bad for him, but he had to ask him why he slid a bedpost into his rectum. His curiosity got the best of him.

"So, mind telling me what happened?" Jacob asked.

"Do I have to?"

"I need to know for my report."

The man cringed in pain. "I don't want to talk about it."

Jacob sighed. People didn't understand that he had a job to do, and the nursing staff would be asking him how it happened. He wanted to push the issue, but Jacob felt the man wouldn't talk to him about it.

"On a scale of one to ten, what would you rate your pain?"

"Ten."

"Where are you hurting at?"

"My butt and my stomach."

Jacob retrieved the narcotic box and pulled out a vial of morphine. "Do you have any drug allergies?"

"No."

Jacob drew the medication into a syringe. He administered five milligrams of it into the IV and the man relaxed. He didn't utter another word for the remainder of the transport. A short time later, they arrived at the hospital. James opened up the back doors to the ambulance and Jacob stepped out, laughing. He noticed Doctor Young and Bridge in an intense argument by the ambulance entrance. It took everything within him to not run over and defend her, but they had a patient. Young saw Jacob approaching with his patient. Their eyes met and tension immediately filled the air. The doctor glared at Jacob with hate in his eyes. Bridge turned to see what he was looking at. She shook her head and then walked inside the emergency room behind Jacob.

"Whatcha got?" a nurse asked from behind the desk.

"Male patient with a bedpost stuck in his rectum," Jacob answered.

Her mouth dropped open. "Seriously?"

Jacob nodded.

"Trauma-one. I'll have a nurse in there shortly."

Jacob and James moved the man over to the hospital bed. The man didn't grimace in pain when they moved him. Jacob prided himself on not being judgmental, but situations such as this made it difficult not to.

Bridge walked into the room, her face peppered with anger. "What's going on?" she asked.

Jacob looked down at the man, who buried his face into the bed in shame.

"He wouldn't tell me what happened."

Bridge knelt down next to the bed. "Are you in pain?"

He lifted his face from the bed. Perspiration beaded on his forehead and his skin flushed. "No. I'm feeling okay right now. The medicine helped."

Doctor Young stormed into the room. "What's going on with this patient?"

Jacob's body stiffened. He sucked in a deep breath and let the air slowly escape through his lips. Young had the uncanny ability to bring out the worst in him. "Male patient with a bedpost lodged in his rectum. We cut it with a saw. While en-route, I started an IV and I gave him five milligrams of morphine for pain."

Young approached Jacob and stood inches from his face. "Since when do we give pain medications for undiagnosed abdominal pain?"

Jacob smirked. "I didn't need a CT machine to know what caused his pain."

"Since when did *you* become a doctor?"

Jacob stepped closer to him.

Bridge bolted across the room and got in between them. She turned toward Ed. "I'll take it from here. You can come in and do your assessment when I'm finished."

He turned his focus from Jacob to Bridge. "Since when do you...."

"Now, Ed," Bridge shouted.

His shoulders slumped. "Fine. Only because I have a more critical patient in another room."

"Hey, Bridge. I had fun the other night having dinner with you," Jacob chimed in.

Doctor Young tried to push past Bridge, but she held him off. Jacob smiled at him. He shook his head and then angrily left the room. Bridge turned around and glared at Jacob.

"What?"

"I don't need you egging him on. If that's how it's going to be, then we can't be friends," Bridge said.

Jacob felt like a scolded child. She was right. He took every opportunity to get under Ed's skin. Repeatedly, Ed flaunted their relationship in front of Jacob. *Turnabout is fair play,* Jacob thought.

James pushed the cot out of the room.

Jacob's male ego had complete control over him and he didn't care. "Can you sign my narcotics off, please?"

Bridge yanked the pen out of his hand and signed his paperwork.

"I hope you get to feeling better, sir," Jacob said to the man. He waved a hand in the air as he left the room and walked toward the ambulance entrance. Once outside, Young came up behind him. Jacob turned around.

"You're barking up the wrong tree, little man."

James saw the confrontation and walked toward his partner.

Jacob laughed. "Little man?"

Ed stepped up, inches from his face. "You heard me. I had to speak to the police yesterday. You think I'm trying to hurt you?"

"If the shoe fits, wear it," Jacob snapped back.

"If I wanted you dead, you'd be dead. As for your flagrant disregard of protocols, I'll be calling Nate tomorrow. You're finished. You have no idea who you're messing with."

Jacob's eyes narrowed and a smirk crossed his face. "I know exactly who you are. I'm not scared of you. Go ahead and hide behind the M.D. initials in your name. I'm not worried."

"Watch your back. Next time I won't stop beating you senseless." He turned and walked toward the doors.

"Hey doc," Jacob said.

"What?"

"Bridge did have a great time with me the other night. She's noticing how a real man treats a woman."

Doctor Young's face immersed in redness. He turned and walked inside. Jacob felt jubilant with his small victory. That feeling quickly subsided when he noticed Bridge standing in the hallway. She shook her head and walked back inside of the emergency room.

NINETEEN

THE NEXT MORNING, Jacob sprung out of bed, grabbed his cell phone, and called a local florist. Bridge worked the day shift and he wanted to surprise her with her favorite flowers - red roses. He feared that she would take it as another poke at Doctor Young, but that wasn't his intention.

Once his anger had subsided, he felt guilty for forcing Bridge into the middle of his testosterone feud with the doc. After placing the flower order, Jacob plopped back down onto his couch. Lying there, staring at the ceiling, he imagined the expression on Bridge's face when the flowers arrived. He only wished he could be there to see it. His cell phone ringing distracted his daydream.

Jacob flipped open his phone. "Hey, Dad."

"Hello son," Blake said.

The tone in his voice concerned Jacob. He sat up. "What's going on?"

His father didn't say anything.

"Dad?"

"Yeah, I'm here."

"What's going on?"

"I have some bad news."

"Yeah. Go on."

"I have leukemia," Blake said.

A knot the size of a softball formed in Jacob's throat. His worst fear came true. He and his father were close and he couldn't imagine life without him. Even though he'd been away from home for several years, he kept in touch regularly.

"Son, are you there?"

Jacob nodded his head, not realizing his father couldn't see him. "When did you find out?"

"A little while ago. I haven't been feeling well so I went to see my doctor. He ran some tests and they came back with the diagnosis of cancer."

Jacob cleared his throat. "What are they going to do?" he asked with a crackle in his voice.

"Nothing."

"What do you mean nothing?"

"I'm not going to let them treat me. If God decides it's my time, then it's my time."

Jacob's sadness turned to anger. "Dad, you have to go through treatment. I need you, we all need you."

"Son, don't you think if God decides it's time for me to come home, nothing is going to change that?"

Jacob respected his father, but he didn't agree with him this time. "Think of it this way, Dad. God put doctors on the Earth to do his will. Can you agree with that?"

No answer.

"Dad?"

"I'm here."

"Well?"

"Maybe. Son, I don't want to get sick, be miserable, and lose all my hair. If my time has come to leave this world, I don't want to suffer during that borrowed time," Blake said.

It infuriated Jacob how his father could be stubborn at times. A wave of nausea hit his stomach. "You need to keep an open mind about this and listen to what the doctor says. Have you told them your thoughts yet?"

"Yes. He said with aggressive treatment I would have a ninety percent chance of recovery."

"Those are great odds." Jacob had a glimmer of hope. He processed the fact that his dad had cancer, but he could live with those odds.

"Doctors don't know everything. Whatever God decides is inevitable. No doctor in the world can change that."

Jacob felt like reaching through the phone and strangling his dad. He had better luck arguing with a brick wall at times. "You need to take everything into consideration and not be so selfish."

"How am I being selfish?"

"You're only thinking about yourself right now. You have to think of your kids and your wife. What does she say about it?"

Blake's tone softened. "That I'm doing the treatment."

"There's your answer. I'm not trying to be mean Dad, but we all need you. If the doctors are confident they can cure you, then you need to do the treatment. I understand you don't want to be sick. I think that's a small price to pay for your life."

"We'll see. I haven't made any decisions yet."

"You need to make up your mind sooner rather than later. I'm only telling you this because I love you. We all love you."

"I know. I'm not feeling well right now. I'm going to go lay down. I'll call you later, son. I love you."

Jacob's eyes welled up with tears. "I love you too, Dad."

James had a narcotic order to fill at the hospital. Jacob scanned the emergency room looking for Bridge, but didn't see her anywhere. A crystal vase filled with bright red roses sat at the main nurse's desk. A few nurses were huddle together whispering and they smiled at him. Jacob nodded, pulled the card out of the envelope, and read it. He'd only wished he could've been there when the flowers arrived. It would've been gratifying seeing her facial expressions when they delivered them.

A few moments later, Bridge walked around the corner. She stopped and frowned. "What are you doing?"

"James had a narcotic order to fill. I'm just hanging out."

Bridge's brow furrowed. "You know what I mean. You just can't leave it alone, can you?"

Before Jacob arrived at the hospital, he expected Bridge to be surprised and thankful, but that wasn't the case. "I got you those flowers to apologize. I haven't been nice lately with this whole Doctor Young situation. I thought you'd be happy." Shaking his head, he turned and walked back toward the parking lot. Scurrying footsteps across the asphalt grabbed his attention.

"Jacob. Wait!"

He turned around. "Yeah?"

"I'm sorry. I love them. Can you ever forgive me?" Bridge asked, looking at him with sad puppy dog eyes.

"Hmm. I don't know."

She put her hands on her hips and tilted her head sideways. "I said I'm sorry."

Jacob tried to hide a smile. "Maybe if you'll go ice skating with me and then dinner."

Bridge stared at him in deep thought. "That's blackmail, you know."

"Yeah. You got a problem with that?"

"No."

"It's a date. Pick you up at six tomorrow night."

"What if I say no?"

"Won't matter." He turned around and walked toward the ambulance. "I'm taking you out, regardless."

Bridge watched him walk away, smiling.

The two men exited their ambulance. In front of them, a six-foot-six man weighing a good three-hundred pounds flung various police officers around like rag dolls. It didn't matter how many of them grabbed him; he out muscled them and tossed them to the ground.

"Holy crap, he's big!" Jacob said.

"Big isn't the word for it," James said, wide-eyed.

Jacob approached an officer. "What's going on?"

"He's freaking out. We've tried everything we can to calm him down, but nothing is working," the officer said out of breath.

"What do you want to do?" James asked.

Jacob rushed toward their ambulance. A few moments later, he returned with a syringe in his hand.

"What's that?" James asked.

"Haldol," Jacob answered and James smiled.

The man continued to fight all of the police officers. "You'll never take me alive," he screamed. He pushed an officer into his police car and glass flew into the air.

"Sir, you need to calm down," a portly officer stated.

Jacob sat back and waited for an opening. The man continued tossing officers through the air. He turned his back and Jacob jumped into action. He ran up behind the man, stabbed the needle into his shoulder, plunged its contents into him, and then ran away. The man spun around reaching for Jacob, but he stood safely behind a police car.

"How long is it going to take before that medicine works?" an officer asked.

"Five to ten minutes." Jacob grinned.

The man pushed officers down and swung at anyone within striking distance. His aggression began to slow. His arms swung wildly at officers without connecting. He staggered sideways and then caught his balance.

"Here we go," said Jacob.

The man's arms began swaying as a blank look washed across his face and he had difficulty keeping his legs under him. "Wha…what did you guys give me?" He staggered, words slurring, stumbling around and his legs gave way. His large body crashed to the ground and his head bounced on the asphalt.

"Whoa. That's crazy," an officer said.

Jacob and James walked over to the huge body lying on the ground in front of them. Jacob knelt down next to him. "He's breathing. I don't know how long it's going to keep him down, so we'd better get him on the cot and restrained."

"What did you give him?" an officer asked him.

"Haldol. It's a chemical restraint. Makes the patient sleepy," Jacob offered.

It took six people to pick the large man up from the ground. Once on the cot, they placed his hands and feet in leather restraints and pushed him toward their ambulance.

"What exactly happened?" Jacob asked.

"We were called for a man out of control. He plays football at the University as an offensive lineman. We couldn't get him under control. He babbled incoherently and didn't make any sense. Next thing we knew, he started beating the crap out of us," the officer said.

Jacob hopped into the back with the man. "Do you have any info on him?"

"Sure do. Here ya go," the officer said, fishing a card out of his pocket.

"Thank you."

"You okay with this?" James asked, standing at the opened back doors.

"I'm good. Let's get going."

James closed the doors, got into the front, and then drove toward the hospital.

The man continued to be in a drug-induced stupor and Jacob didn't mind at all. At times, he would have short periods of not breathing. Jacob would reach down, sternal rub him, and his breathing would resume. When they arrived at the hospital, James helped Jacob unload the large man. Veins bulged on their foreheads as they lifted him. Once in the emergency room, Jacob glanced over at the physician's desk and Doctor Young glared at him.

Great. Here we go again.

Bridge sat at the main desk. "What did ya bring me?"

"Combative patient. I had to give him Haldol. He beat on several police officers. We didn't have a choice."

A concerned look crossed her face. "Are you okay?"

Young sat at his desk shaking his head.

Jacob chuckled. "Yeah. I'm fine. He didn't get a hold of me, thankfully."

"Take him to trauma-two."

Jacob led the way pulling the cot. Bridge walked into the room. Following closely behind her were two male aides. "I figured you could use the help," she said.

They hoisted him onto the stretcher and Bridge tied the restraints to the hospital bed. "So what happened?"

"He went ballistic, beat on several officers, and then I gave him Haldol. Once it kicked in he dropped to the ground like a sack of potatoes."

"So, paramedic, mind explaining to me why you didn't place him in c-spine precautions when he fell and was unable to answer your questions? How do you know his neck and or back isn't broken?" Doctor Young asked from behind him.

Jacob's shoulders slumped. He glanced at Bridge and she glared at her ex-lover.

Jacob turned around. "He didn't have any obvious signs of injury so I chose to forgo it."

James stepped in between them. "It was my choice, doctor. I pulled seniority on the call."

Ed Young never broke eye contact with Jacob. "You're not going to protect him this time. He messed up and he knows it."

Bridge grabbed Ed's arm and pulled him outside of the room; she'd had enough.

Young pulled his arm free of Bridge's firm grip.

"What are you doing?" Bridge asked.

His eyes narrowed. "My job. He messed up on this call and I'm not comfortable with letting it go."

"This has nothing to do with how he treated the patient. You have it out for him and it's all about causing him problems."

The doctor just laughed. "You don't know me if you think I would let my personal opinions cloud my professional judgment."

"You're right; I don't know who you are. That's why I dumped you."

Ed Young stiffened. "I don't know what you see in him. I could've given you a great life and the world."

Bridge sighed. "You turned out not to be the man I thought you were. I don't want anything from you. I'll be damned if I sit back and watch you try to ruin Jacob professionally out of spite."

"There's nothing you can do to stop me. If I can't have you, no one will."

Bridge stood in front of him, eyes wide. She looked toward the room. "Jacob."

He stepped out. "Yeah?"

"We still on for our date tomorrow night?"

Ed scowled at Bridge.

Jacob's confused look quickly turned to a smile. "You know it. Wouldn't miss it for the world."

"Good. I can't wait." She turned toward the doctor. "You don't know what I see in him? He's not *you.* He's a *real* man."

Doctor Young stomped over to his desk. Grabbing the phone, he aggressively punched numbers. "Nate? I need to speak to you about one of your paramedics," he said, glaring at Jacob.

I've done it now.

TWENTY

SHIFTING IN THE chair, Jacob waited for Nate to finish his phone call. Looking around the office, he tried to keep his mind from focusing on the certain trouble that loomed over him. No matter how many times he'd been called into Nate's office, he couldn't get used to the constant persecution.

Nate sat back in his seat, rubbing his temples as he spoke on the phone. "Yes. I understand. I don't completely agree. What about…I know, but…okay. I understand."

He leaned forward, hung up the phone and sighed. "You've done it this time, Jacob. Doctor Young has gone straight to the top. He's filed a grievance against you for administering pain medications to an undiagnosed abdominal pain and for not placing the football player in c-spine. I have to suspend you for a shift."

"That's complete bull." Jacob sat on the edge of the chair. "This is all personal."

Nate gazed at him, confused. "What are you talking about?"

Jacob leaned back in his seat. "This is more of a personal attack rather than a professional one. It's a long story."

"I'm all ears."

Jacob spent the next thirty minutes explaining everything to him. Nate remained speechless.

"Let me get this right, you think Doctor Young is trying to kill you and he's using his position as an ER doctor to torment you?"

Jacob nodded.

"Hmm." Nate sat back in his chair. "I've heard some outlandish

147

stories in my time, but this one takes the cake." He leaned forward resting his elbows on his desk. "Why can't you just accept responsibility for your actions and your punishment?"

"I don't think I screwed up. If I'm wrong, I will accept my punishment. Did he end up with any type of spinal injuries?"

"That's not the point."

"That *is* the point," Jacob growled.

"I've known Doctor Young for a long time. He's never been the type of person to hold personal grudges. As far as him trying to kill you, that's ridiculous."

Jacob felt the veins in his forehead pulsing. No matter what he said, or what proof he could provide, Nate would never believe him. "That's *your* opinion."

"Being that I'm your boss, my opinion is the only one that matters." Nate sifted through a stack of papers and pulled out a sheet of paper. He slid it across his desk.

Jacob leaned forward, picked it up, and began to read it. "What's this?"

"It's your official written disciplinary action. And it will go in your permanent employee file. You'll need to sign it."

After spending several minutes scanning over the document, Jacob slid it back across the desk. "I don't agree with it. I'm not going to sign it."

Nate exhaled. "You don't have a choice. This isn't a democracy. If you don't sign it, you'll be suspended until you do. The EMS Board has decided this is the correct line of action." He rocked back and forth in his chair. "It's a written warning Jacob, not a termination letter. Sign the damn thing and enjoy your day off."

Jacob reached across the desk, took out his pen and scribbled his signature across the bottom of the page. "Are we done here?"

"Yes."

Jacob stood and stomped toward the door.

"Jacob."

"Yeah?"

"I'd keep your story about Doctor Young to yourself. He's a pillar in the community. I'd hate to see it cost you employment here."

Jacob walked out of the door and slammed it shut behind him. *You're wrong. This is all wrong. Small town politics at its best*

James met up with Jacob at the car rental store. The repairs on his truck were finished and James agreed to give him a ride to the repair shop.

Jacob sat on a bench in front of the business as James pulled up.

"You going my way, big boy?" James asked, laughing.

A small smile cracked his stern face. "Only if you're driving."

"Get in. You look like you just lost your best friend. What's up?"

"I've been suspended for a shift," Jacob solemnly said as he got into the truck.

Shock washed across James' face. "Are you serious?"

"As a heart attack."

"For what?"

"Apparently, Doctor Young called Nate and filed a grievance against me for not putting the football player into c-spine. That, coupled with giving narcotics to an undiagnosed abdominal pain, they've decided to suspend me."

James squeezed the steering wheel and his knuckles turned white. "That's a bunch of crap. I don't agree with that at all."

"Neither do I."

"What did you say?"

Flashes of their conversation rolled through his mind. "There wasn't anything I could say that would change his mind. I signed the written warning."

James shook his head. "I wouldn't have."

"I didn't have a choice," Jacob growled. "I would remain suspended until I signed it."

"I'm going to have a talk with Nate. I don't agree with this at all."

Jacob turned toward James. "Don't do that. It will only make things worse. It's only one shift. An extra day off is the way I'm going to look at it."

They arrived at the repair shop and Jacob got out of the truck. "Thanks for the lift."

"What are you doing tonight? Want to come over for a BBQ?" asked James.

Jacob rested his elbows on the open window of the truck. "Sorry, but I have plans."

"Dare I ask?"

"I'm going out with Bridge tonight."

"You haven't learned your lesson yet, I take it?"

"Nope, and I'm not going to."

Jacob smoothed his clothes one last time. Deciding to go casual, he donned a green t-shirt and blue jeans. Taking in a deep breath, he slowly exhaled and pushed the doorbell. A few moments later, Bridge opened the door. As usual, her beauty astounded him. He stood in front of her, speechless.

"What?"

"You're...so beautiful."

Her skin turned the color of the red blouse she wore. "Oh stop it. I'm not that beautiful."

"Yes...yes you are." Jacob couldn't take his eyes off her and butterflies filled his stomach.

"Why thank you, sir. Are you ready?"

A smile stretched across Jacob's lips.

"Are you okay?"

"I'm better now that I get to see you."

Bridge blushed again. "You sure know how to make a girl feel good."

"I call it as I see it."

She grabbed her purse from a table, walked outside, and locked her front door. She walked past Jacob toward his truck. He dashed beyond her and opened the door for her.

"You're such a gentleman. I like that." She stepped into his truck and he shut the door.

Jacob walked around the back of his truck. He noticed down the block, parked on the side of the road, a white car that resembled the one Doctor Young owned. He waved. The car squealed around the corner and disappeared. The windows were tinted and Jacob couldn't make out who drove the car.

He got into the truck.

"Who were you waving at?" Bridge asked.

"Thought I saw someone I knew."

Silence stagnated the air. Bridge looked out the window as they drove down the road. Occasionally, she would slip a half-hearted smile in Jacob's direction. He reached up and tuned the radio to a country music station. Bridge glanced over at him and smiled.

"I know you don't like this type of music. You can turn it to a different station if you want to. I don't mind. It's a nice gesture though." She reached over and clasped Jacob's hand. Her touch sent electricity flowing through his body.

Jacob pulled into the parking lot of the restaurant.

"No burgers again?"

"I told you a long time ago that if you went out with me again I'd upgrade you." Feeling quite pleased with himself, he got out of the truck, sauntered over, and opened Bridge's door.

"Thank you, sir."

"It's my pleasure."

She climbed out of his truck and gave him an approving smile. Jacob raced ahead of her so he could open the door for her. As they walked into the restaurant, there were several people seated at tables anxiously awaiting their meals. Servers sped across the floor working hard for their tips.

Once seated, Jacob picked up a menu and glanced it over. Across the table from him, Bridge sat looking at him.

Why isn't she looking at the menu?

Suddenly, a light bulb appeared above Jacob's head and he knew what she wanted.

A few moments later, a server approached their table. "Evening, folks. My name is Amanda. I'll be taking care of ya tonight. What can I get ya?"

"We would each like a glass of Chardonnay and an order of crab cakes for an appetizer. The young lady will have the lobster and I will have the king crab."

"I'll get your order going. Your drinks and appetizers will be out shortly," she said and took the menus from the table.

Bridge continued to smile at Jacob. "I'm quite impressed. I like a man who can take charge."

"What can I say? I'm a take charge kind of guy."

A few minutes later, the server returned with their wine and crab cakes.

Jacob picked up his glass. "A toast?"

Bridge picked up hers. "Sure. What shall we toast to?"

"To friends and hopefully more."

They clinked their glasses together, each taking a drink. Jacob set his glass down, picked up a crab cake, and shoved the entire thing into his mouth.

"Are you hungry?"

Jacob stopped chewing and tried to gulp down the contents. *I can only imagine what she's thinking right now.*

Jacob took another swig of his wine to wash down the crab cake.

"You don't have to worry about trying to impress me. You've done a fine job, sir."

Jacob relaxed.

The server returned to their table with the main course. Once she set each plate down, she paused for a moment. "I hope I'm not being rude, but how long have you two been together?"

"We're not together," Jacob quickly answered.

"We're just friends," Bridge chimed in.

The server shook her head. "If you say so. You two look cute together."

Bridge's cheeks turned red.

"I have to pee," Jacob blurted out.

Bridge laughed hysterically. "You're too cute."

"No, I actually have to pee," he said as he stood.

"Don't stiff me with the bill."

"You don't have to worry about that. I'll be back in a jiffy."

As Jacob stood at the urinal, he couldn't stop smiling. For the first time he felt as if he was gaining momentum with Bridge. He washed his hands and exited the restroom.

As he walked around the corner, Jacob noticed Doctor Young sitting at the table berating Bridge. She sat silently and hung her head. Jacob walked toward their table, burning with anger.

"What do you see in him?"

"You need to leave, now," Jacob commanded, standing over Ed.

"Mind your own business. I'm having a conversation with my woman."

"She's not your woman any longer. She dumped you, remember?"

"Leave us alone, ambulance driver."

Fury and anger washed over Jacob. His fists clenched. "You can either walk out of here, or be carried out. Your choice."

Silence came over the restaurant. Patrons curiously looked on. Jacob hoped he chose the latter. Nothing more in the world would make him happy than to beat Ed Young senseless.

Young shook his head and stood. "This is far from over."

He looked down at Bridge. "Enjoy your slumming with this gurney jockey." He turned and walked out of the restaurant.

Jacob sat back down. "The nerve of that guy."

Bridge looked up, tears rolled down her cheeks. "I've lost my appetite. Can we call it a night?"

Jacob sighed. "Sure."

Their server approached the table. "Is everything okay?"

"Yeah. Can we get a few to-go boxes and the check please?"

"You bet."

Jacob looked across the table at Bridge. It broke his heart to see her so upset. She didn't deserve this. A few moments later, the server returned with their check and a few boxes. Jacob pulled out his credit card and handed it to her.

"It's none of my business, but you don't deserve to be treated that way. That man is a jerk. You have a good guy here so hold onto him," the server told Bridge.

As they left the restaurant, Jacob opened the truck door for Bridge. She walked over, still hanging her head. Jacob reached down, put his hand under her chin, and lifted her face up toward him. Her eyes filled with sadness.

"Don't let him get to you. You're a strong and independent woman."

She smiled weakly and got into the truck.

As they drove down the road, she looked out of the window, not speaking.

Jacob pulled into her driveway and Bridge sat looking out the window. He got out, walked over, and opened her door. He followed closely behind her, holding their dinner boxes. Stopping at her front door she turned, a few tears still on her cheek. Jacob reached up and wiped them off.

"You're beautiful. You know that?"

"I don't feel beautiful."

"Well, you are."

Bridge unlocked her door and walked inside. Jacob stood in the doorway unsure of what to do. After setting her keys down, she turned toward him.

"Thank you for tonight. I had a great time. I'm sorry for…."

Jacob reached up and pressed a finger against her soft lips. "It's okay. You don't need to apologize. I had a great time, too."

He dropped the leftovers, pulled her into his arms, and pushed her up against the wall. Breathing heavily, he searched her eyes for answers.

Leaning down, he softly planted his lips onto hers. At first, she pulled back with hesitation. As he tenderly kissed her, she returned the gesture. Each of them ran head first into the thralls of passion. Jacob scooped her up into his arms, still passionately kissing her. Bridge pulled him in close to her.

Walking into her bedroom, Jacob laid her down on her bed. Fear and excitement glittered in her eyes. "Do you think this is a good idea?"

"Yes. I want you and I'm going to have you," Jacob said, as he pulled the shirt over his head.

Bridge smiled.

TWENTY-ONE

THE SUN PEEKED through the blinds, waking Jacob. Reaching up, he wiped the sleep out of his eyes. He rolled over and Bridge wasn't there.

Jacob slipped on some clothes and then walked out to the living room. Bridge sat at her kitchen table sipping on a cup of coffee. She glanced at Jacob and then looked down at the table.

"Good morning, gorgeous," Jacob said, as he leaned down to kiss her on the forehead, but she pulled away.

He sat down in a chair next to her. He stared at her, confused. They had a wonderful night together and then made love. Why is she acting like this?

"Morning," Bridge answered as she continued sipping on her coffee.

"Something wrong?" He feared her answer.

She wouldn't make eye contact with him. "Last night was a mistake. It shouldn't have happened."

Jacob leaned back in the chair. "What do you mean it was a mistake? You didn't act like it was last night."

"I was vulnerable. I'm sorry."

Jacob sighed. "What kind of games are you playing with me?"

Bridge sipped her coffee. "I'm not. It's a mistake that can never happen again."

He clasped his hands behind his head. "You're unbelievable."

"I said I'm sorry. What else do you want me to say?"

Jacob leaned on the table, reached for Bridge's hand, but she pulled it away.

"So this is how it's going to be?"

"I think you should leave. I don't know if we can be friends any longer. This changes everything."

Jacob sprung from the chair. "You're damn right it changes everything." He walked back into her bedroom to retrieve the remainder of his clothes that littered the floor.

Bridge continued to sip on her coffee.

Jacob stomped out of her bedroom and opened the front door. "This is bull crap, Bridge," he shouted. "I don't know why you're fighting your feelings. Last night was wonderful and you know it. You can sit there and say it's a mistake all you want to, but I don't believe you."

He walked through the door and slammed it shut behind him. As he stomped to his truck, he noticed the same white car as Young drove, sitting on the shoulder down the road with a license plate missing.

You picked the wrong day to mess with me.

Jacob put his shoes on and jumped into his truck, racing toward the white car. The windows were darkly tinted and Jacob couldn't see the driver, though he already knew. The white car pulled out onto the residential street and sped away.

Run as fast as you can. You won't get away from me.

Jacob pushed down on the accelerator and his speedometer read sixty miles per hour. The white car drifted around the corner without letting off the gas. Jacob followed closely behind.

The end of the street intersected with Broadway, a busy four-lane road. The white car blew through the stop sign, turned left, and narrowly avoided a collision with an eighteen-wheeler. Jacob slammed on his brakes and waited for the intersection to clear. The white car raced down the street weaving in and out of traffic.

"Come on," Jacob shouted as he waited for an opening to cross.

Once the traffic cleared, Jacob pushed down on the gas pedal and attempted to catch up to the escaping white car. He quickly made up the half-mile distance between them. His knuckles were white from the death grip he had on the steering wheel. Droplets of sweat beaded on his forehead.

Rushing past car after car, Jacob finally caught up to the fleeing vehicle. They were approaching a major intersection that had a history of hellacious traffic accidents, but neither vehicle let off the gas pedal.

The light was red.

I'm not backing down. One of us is going to die and it won't be me.

The driver of the white car accelerated and shot through the intersection, narrowly avoiding a collision with two trucks. Jacob approached and noticed several more vehicles entering the intersection. He slammed on the brakes, juddering to a stop just short of the cross walk.

"Damn it, damn it, damn it," Jacob yelled as he punched the dash of his truck.

The next morning, Jacob strolled across the parking lot toward the station. He had served his one shift suspension and couldn't wait to get back the ambulance. A smiling James greeted him in the ambulance bay. Most people dreaded going to work, but not Jacob. This was the one place that nothing in the world could touch him, his world, and his sanctuary.

"Nice to have you back, brother," James said, bear hugging him.

"Put me down," Jacob grunted.

"Sorry. Just glad to see you, man." James released the death grip around his partner.

"I guess you missed me?"

"Like a poke in the eye with a hot stick."

Jacob walked past him into the station and set his belongings on the bed in his room. He joined James in the ambulance and grabbed the narcotics box to do the daily count.

"Something wrong?" James asked.

Jacob flipped through the drugs. "Nope."

"I can tell when something is wrong with you. What's going on, man?"

Jacob tossed the last drug back into the box, closed it, and placed it back in the fridge. "I don't feel like talking right now."

James shook his head. "I know you better than that. Tell me what's on your mind."

"I went out with Bridge last night."

"That's a good thing."

"Yeah, but it gets worse."

"Oh?"

Jacob leaned back against the seat and his shoulders slumped. "I stayed the night with her. One thing led to another and...we had sex."

"And you're upset about that?"

"When I woke up she wasn't in bed. I got dressed and found her drinking coffee. She told me it was all a mistake and we couldn't be friends anymore."

James' face went blank. "Oh my. That's not what you want to hear."

"Yeah. I don't know what to do." He looked up at James. "I think I'm falling in love with her."

Usually James offered relationship advice, but now he was

speechless. Station tones blared across the speakers.

"Medic-57, we have an abdominal pain call at 510 Park View Terrace."

Jacob climbed out the back of the ambulance, got into the passenger seat, and picked up the radio microphone.

"Medic-57 is en-route."

James climbed into the driver side. "Copy that Medic-57. You have a male patient complaining of profuse abdominal pain. He believes he has kidney stones."

Traffic offered no resistance and they raced toward the address with ease. The address was on the Upper East Side. It was considered the ritzy side of town. The streets lined with six-figure homes, neatly groomed lawns, and cars in the driveways that cost more than Jacob and James' annual salary combined.

They pulled up to the address. The white car with tinted windows in the driveway caught Jacob's attention.

"You've got to be kidding me," shouted Jacob.

"What?" James asked, confused.

Before the ambulance stopped rolling, Jacob jumped out the truck and ran toward the house. "Medic-57 is on scene." James announced and then ran after Jacob.

A firefighter walked out of the house shaking his head. "That man is in some serious pain."

"Who is it?" Jacob asked.

"I don't know his name. He's in the bedroom."

Jacob entered the house. Several paintings covered the walls. The ceilings were high and vaulted. White leather furniture stood in the living room. As Jacob made his way through the house, he could hear a man moaning. By the sounds of it, he was in excruciating pain.

"Hello? Paramedics," Jacob shouted.

"We're back here," a voice answered from the back of the house.

Jacob followed the direction of the voice. Walking down a narrow hallway, he could see an open door at the end. As he entered the room, he saw a man lying on his side with his back to him.

"What's going on?" Jacob asked. Two firefighters were tending to the man.

"Oh….I'm in so much pain," the man bellowed.

His voice sounds familiar.

Jacob walked around to the other side of the bed. Doctor Young was on his side writhing in pain.

Are you kidding me?

"He's complaining of flank pain that is radiating to his groin area," said one of the firefighters.

"Hello, sir, I'm a paramedic. What's going on?"

"Oh, it's you. Just my luck," Young said, shaking his head as he recognized Jacob.

"Do you know each other?" a firefighter asked.

"You can say that," said Jacob.

"I'm in so much...." Young started to say, and then he rolled over to the edge of his bed and vomited.

James walked into the room. "Jacob, what the hell? Why did you...." He noticed the man on the bed. "Oh, I see."

Ed Young rolled back and forth on the bed. "Are you just going to sit there? Give me something for pain and get me to the hospital."

"Can you two help me with the cot?" James asked the firefighters. They nodded and followed him out to the ambulance.

"Ohhh...I'm hurting. Do something," Young commanded.

"Mr. Young, once we get the cot in here, we'll get you moved to it and on your way to the hospital," Jacob said, smiling.

"Ohhh." He leaned over the side of his bed and vomited again, and then rolled over onto his back. "I'm *Doctor Young!*"

"I'm sorry you're in so much pain, Mr. Young."

"It's *Doctor Young*. I've earned the title."

Jacob leaned down next to him. "You're not a doctor out here, Mr. Young."

Ed rolled his eyes. James returned with the cot. They positioned it next to his bed, avoiding the pile of gastric contents that littered the floor. Young, profusely sweating, skin pale, rolled out of his bed and knelt, rocking back and forth. "Kill me now, please."

I would love nothing more, but I like my career.

Jacob stood over him. "Mr. Young, we need to move you to the cot. The longer you wait, the more your pain is going to increase. Let me give you a hand," Jacob said, reaching for his arm.

Doctor Young pushed it away. "I don't need your help. I can do this myself."

Slowly, he stood, bent over and vomited once more, but this time on his bed. After a few heaves, he plopped down on the cot, pulled his legs up, and rolled onto his side.

James raised the rail and fastened the seat belts across him. Two firefighters raised the cot and then navigated it through his house out to the ambulance. Once lifted inside, James started to climb into the back.

Jacob grabbed his arm. "I'll take this one."

"I don't know, man. It's not a good idea," James said.

"I've got this."

"Okay. If you say so." He climbed out and Jacob entered the back of the ambulance from the side door.

"I'm ready. Let's get going," said Jacob.

James closed the doors to the ambulance.

"Where are you hurting at, Mr. Young?" Jacob asked.

Doctor Young rolled back and forth holding his back. "I have kidney stones, you idiot. Give me something for pain," he ordered.

James pulled out of the driveway and headed toward the hospital.

"What idiot is driving? Tell him to take it easy!"

Jacob couldn't help himself. Seeing Ed Young in agony amused him. If it had been another patient, he would've been more compassionate. "I'm sorry, but we're built for speed, not comfort."

"Oh, please help me."

Jacob retrieved the IV supplies and spiked a bag of saline. "I need your arm so I can start an IV."

Ed surrendered his right arm.

With the IV started, Jacob opened up the saline and watched it drip in rapid succession. Fluid resuscitation was a common practice with people who suffered from kidney stones.

"Oh...please give me something for pain," Young pleaded.

Sitting on the bench seat next to him, Jacob leaned down close to him. "I'm sorry, but I can't give you anything for pain. My protocol specifically states that I am not able to administer pain medication for undiagnosed abdominal pain."

Doctor Young begged him for relief with his eyes. "I have kidney stones, you idiot. I'm a doctor. Give me pain medication, now."

Jacob couldn't help himself. He enjoyed the doctor's pain. "Like I said, I can't give you...."

"I'm your medical control doctor. Give me meds now. It's an order."

Jacob looked him squarely in his eyes. "You had me suspended for giving a man pain meds even though I knew the cause of his pain. You're not a doctor out here; you're a patient. I will not go against protocol just because it suits you. You want pain meds? You can wait until an emergency room physician evaluates you. Are you still feeling nauseated?"

Doctor Young nodded.

Jacob grabbed his medication box and pulled out a vial of Phenergan. He drew it up and plunged the needle into the IV line. "Before I administer this, do you have any drug allergies?"

"No."

Jacob slowly dispersed the medication into the IV tubing.

"How much are you giving me?"

"Twenty-five milligrams."

A few moments later, Young rested his head on the cot, not rocking as much. After several minutes, they arrived at Magic County Hospital and Jacob climbed out the back of the ambulance. He only wished the ride would've been longer so he could've enjoyed Ed's misery a bit more. Talk about poetic justice.

James looked at Doctor Young and he was sleeping. "What did you give him?"

"Phenergan."

"How much?"

"Twenty-five milligrams."

"That's a little much, don't you think?"

Jacob looked at him and smiled. "No. You saw him puking several times. I simply wanted my patient to stop throwing up."

James smiled. They pulled him out of the ambulance and pushed the cot toward the ambulance entrance.

Young looked up. "Where are we?"

"The hospital, sir," Jacob answered.

The doctor rested his head back on the cot. "Quit calling me sir. I don't like you and you don't like me."

You got that right.

As they entered the emergency room, several nurses watched curiously. "Whatcha got...oh. Is that you, Doctor Young?" the nurse asked.

"Yeah," he grumbled.

"Take him to trauma-one."

Jacob nodded.

On their way to the room, Jacob looked over at the main nurse's desk. Bridge stared at him and she was shocked. He was still angry with her, but seeing her lightened his mood.

Once inside of the room, they readied to move him over. "You're going to feel a few bumps as we move you over, sir," James said.

Bridge walked into the room holding a chart. First she looked at Jacob and then over to Ed, speechless. They lifted him up and gently sat him down on the awaiting bed.

"Is this going to be your patient?" Jacob asked Bridge, smirking.

"Yeah."

"Flank pain with vomiting. I administered twenty-five milligrams of Phenergan to him via IV. He hasn't vomited since receiving the medication."

The doctor lifted his head and regarded Bridge. "Great. This is par for the course." Resting his head on the bed, he began to groan in pain. "Can I get some pain medication, please?"

Bridge walked over next to the bed. "Once the doctor evaluates you, he can order you some."

He groaned. "I'm a doctor, damn it. Give me pain meds."

"You can wait your turn. There are many sick people in here. You're not special," Bridge said.

Jacob smiled and then followed James out of the room. With their cot reassembled, they walked out of the ambulance entrance toward their unit. For the first time in several weeks, gratification filled him. Part of him felt guilty for feeling that way; the other part jumped up and down for joy.

Bridge dashed out of the ER. "Jacob."

He ignored her and continued to walk through the parking lot.

Bridge continued. "Jacob, don't ignore me. I know you can hear me."

He kept walking. James looked back toward her and then back at Jacob.

"Jacob Myers. Stop walking away from me when I'm talking to you."

He stopped and turned around. "What?"

Bridge stomped toward him.

"I've got the cot if you need a minute," James said.

Jacob nodded and turned toward Bridge. "What do you want?"

Standing in front of him, Bridge took a moment to catch her breath. "I told you I'm sorry. I don't know what else to say."

"You said plenty." Jacob turned away from her and walked toward the ambulance.

Bridge grabbed his arm and flung him around. "Why are you so damn stubborn?"

Jacob shook his head.

"What? Spit it out!"

Jacob shifted nervously. "I can't be your friend. If I can't have you, then I don't want anything at all. You don't understand."

"Make me understand."

"Bridge...I...."

She looked curiously into his eyes.

"You hurt me," he said. "That night was special to me. It wasn't just about sex. It was deeper than that."

Bridge's shoulders slumped. "I can't get into a relationship right now. I just got out of one."

Jacob laughed. "What are you afraid of?"

She looked at the ground.

Shaking his head he started to walk away. "I don't have time for this. I'm outta here."

"Jacob, wait."

"What?"

"You don't understand. I...."

Jacob walked up to her, pulled her into his arms and placed his lips on hers, kissing her passionately. A warm feeling rushed through his body. The touch of her lips felt heavenly.

She tried to push away, but he pulled her closer to him. Her resistance melted in his embrace. Reaching up, Bridge pulled Jacob closer and reciprocated the kiss.

James watched in awe.

After several minutes of kissing, Jacob pulled back and looked into her eyes. Her body limp with euphoria of the moment, she draped speechless in his arms.

"How did that feel?" Jacob asked with a smile.

Bridge pulled Jacob back into her arms and kissed him again.

TWENTY-TWO

ON HIS WAY home, Jacob's cell phone rang. He pulled it out of his pocket and flipped it open.

"Hello?"

"Hey, bub. How are you doing?" Kenzie asked. Her voice trembled.

"Good. Everything okay?"

She began to cry. "No. Dad isn't doing well. You need to come home."

Jacob shuddered at the thought of losing his father. Since his move to Idaho, they hadn't spoken much. His life had become so busy, but that wasn't an excuse since he was only a phone call away.

"Sis, I can't. I have a life here, a career."

"I don't think you understand. Dad is struggling with the chemo treatments. There's no guarantee he'll be alive tomorrow," Kenzie hissed.

"I can't just pick up and move away. I wish I could be there. You have no idea."

"You've been gone for over ten years. What did Dad do when you got hurt? He dropped everything and rushed to be by your side."

Everything Kenzie said was true. While Jacob was hospitalized, his father stayed with him as long as he could until he had to go back to work. If it wasn't for his father pushing him, the outcome may have been different.

"I'll see what I can do, sis."

"Good. I'm scared, Jacob. I'm afraid we're going to lose him. We can't. We just can't." His sister sobbed heavily.

"I'll call you back later."

"Okay," Kenzie said and then hung up the phone.

Jacob sat in his recliner and his sick father weighed heavily on his mind. He had to go home, even if only for a short time. Jacob dialed Nate. After a few rings, he answered.

"Hello?"

"Hey, Nate. It's Jacob. I need some time off. My dad is sick and I need to go home for a visit."

"Is he okay?"

"He has leukemia. I need to go home and see him. Will that be okay?"

"Sure. I'll cover your shifts for the next couple of days. I wish I could give you more time, but we're shorthanded right now. Go see your dad."

"Thank you, Nate."

Jacob zipped his suitcase closed. Waiting for Bridge to arrive, he checked to make sure he had the plane ticket he ordered online. His father moved to Muldrow, Oklahoma shortly after his return to Missouri. Blake met Savannah, a wonderfully devout Christian woman, and they wed a short time later.

Blake could be a difficult man to live with, but Savannah changed all of that with her loving ways. At times, she had trouble tolerating him, but she loved him and accepted his flaws. Once she dug through his stubbornness and bullheadedness, she found a loving man that completed her in ways no other man had been able to do. Together, they were a perfect match.

Kenzie wasn't Jacob's sister by blood, but by marriage. In their family, they didn't acknowledge the term "step." They were a loving and accepting family.

Standing five foot ten, with shoulder length, dirty blonde hair and full lips, several men pursued her. She was beautiful and confident. Kenzie spoke her mind and not many people appreciated her abruptness.

A short time later, Jacob's doorbell rang.

"Hi," Bridge said softly.

"Hey. Come in."

Jacob closed the door, turned around, and Bridge pulled him into her arms. The smell of her hair enticed him. Holding her felt so natural and welcome. He didn't know what to call their relationship, but he had high hopes that it would grow into an exclusive one.

Bridge's hands slid down his arms and she leaned back. "I'm

worried about you."

"Don't be. Worry about my dad." Jacob glanced at his watch. "Crap! We need to get going or I'm going to miss my flight." Jacob rushed to his bedroom, retrieved his suitcase, and returned to the living room.

"You have everything?"

He patted his pockets and glanced through his suitcase. "I think so. Let's go."

Jacob gazed out the window as they drove toward the airport. Occasionally, he would glance over at Bridge and smile. His mind fixated on his father, and nothing else mattered at that moment. More questions than answers flooded his head. The mere thought of losing his father to cancer forced his eyes to well up with tears. He needed to be strong for his father.

They arrived at the airport and Bridge pulled up to the unloading zone. Jacob sighed and glanced over at Bridge.

"Here we are," Bridge quietly said.

"Yeah. Guess I need to get going. Thank you for giving me a ride."

"Anything for a friend."

What exactly are we? I'm so confused.

"Kissing friends, right?"

"Something like that."

Jacob reached across and gave her a hug. As he pulled back, Bridge leaned forward and lightly kissed him on the lips. The softness of her lips threw him into a whirlwind. For a brief moment, he forgot about his ill father. She had that effect on him.

"See you in a few days." He got out of her car and shut the door.

"Jacob," Bridge yelled.

He leaned down in the open window. "Yeah?"

"Miss me."

"You know I will." Walking into the terminal, he looked back. Bridge sat in her car smiling at him. He waved.

Jacob attempted to take a nap during the flight, but he couldn't fall asleep. His mind flooded with thoughts and worries about his dad. For his sister to call him, it must've been grave. They were no longer close, as he had spent the last ten years away. He often missed them and wished he could've gone home for more visits, especially now. It never failed. Every time he had the money to take the trip, something would come up that prohibited him from doing so. Still, he felt guilty and couldn't lose his dad.

Jacob stepped off the plane and looked around the terminal. Several people were in heart-felt embraces around him, making it difficult locate to his sister. The crowd thinned and he saw his sister leaning against a wall. She ran and jumped into his arms.

"Bubba! I'm so glad you're here."

"Gee, sis. Did you miss me or what?"

"Maybe a little. Don't get a big head."

Jacob grabbed her shoulders. "Sis, what happened?"

A serious look washed over her face. "What?"

"You grew up and you're hot," Jacob said playfully.

Kenzie hit Jacob on the arm. "Ok, stop it."

Jacob grabbed his suitcase and followed Kenzie through the terminal. He flew into Fort Smith, Arkansas, which had a much smaller airport than Boise and it didn't take them long to make their way to the main parking lot.

"My car is over here." Kenzie pointed to a black Cadillac.

"Nice car, sis."

"I work hard for my money. I deserve a few nice things," Kenzie said proudly.

She opened the trunk and Jacob placed his suitcase into it. He walked over and climbed into the passenger seat of the car. He didn't feel comfortable driving an expensive car.

As they drove down the road, Jacob noticed that Fort Smith resembled Boise, only not as green. His dad lived in a small town twenty-minutes south of Fort Smith. There were two hospitals in town: Regency Medical Center and River Mercy Hospital. His father's physician admitted him to Regency.

Looking out the window, Jacob's excitement to see his sister subsided and replaced with fear. His father had always been a strong man. Seeing him sick would not settle well with him.

Ten minutes later, they arrived at Regency. The hospital was on Rogers Avenue and Seventy Second Street and it spanned over three city blocks. The five-story hospital consisted of red brick and the landscape lined with cherry blossoms. Kenzie pulled into the parking lot.

Jacob leaned his head against the headrest and took in a deep breath. "How bad is he?"

Kenzie hung her head and played with her car keys. "I'm not going to lie. He's pretty sick. Dad is on his third round of chemo."

"Why didn't anyone call me?"

Kenzie shook her head. "We shouldn't have to. It's not that difficult to keep in touch."

"I've been busy and dealing with some stuff."

"It doesn't take much to pick up a phone."

Jacob knew arguing with his sister would prove to be futile. It was silent in the car. Looking out the window, Jacob noticed several people hurriedly walking through the parking lot. An ambulance screamed down the road, turned into the parking lot, and raced toward the ambulance entrance. That grabbed his attention.

"You ready?" Kenzie asked.

"Yeah." He climbed out of the car and followed Kenzie across the black asphalt.

It resembled any other hospital he had seen, just different faces. Unaccustomed to the humidity, sweat beaded on his forehead. When they entered the hospital, a knot formed in his throat. As a child, Jacob always thought of his father as Superman, never being ill his entire life. He wasn't sure how he was going to take seeing his father laid up in a hospital bed.

Kenzie walked at a feverish pace, occasionally looking back to see if Jacob kept up. Her stride had a purpose. Once on the elevator, one of the hospitals clergy members joined them. Briefly making eye contact, Jacob smiled.

"How are you today, son?" he asked.

"Fine," Jacob lied. With each passing of the floors, Jacob's stomach formed knots. Part of him was excited to see his father, but he feared what he was going to see.

They arrived on the fifth floor. Kenzie rushed out of the elevator and Jacob followed closely behind. The stench of death lingered in the air. Each room had a cart parked next to the door that contained boxes of gowns, gloves and masks. Halfway down the hall, Kenzie stopped. She reached into the various boxes on top of the cart, pulling out its contents.

"Before you go in, you have to put on a gown, mask, and a pair of gloves."

"Why?"

"Because the chemo has destroyed his immune system. He's highly susceptible to infections. You're the medical professional. Figured you knew this already," she said as she donned the gown.

Jacob wasn't in the mood to argue with her, so he ignored her comments. Once he had everything on, Kenzie opened the door and Jacob followed.

Savannah, Blake's wife, sat in a chair next to the bed. Holding his hand, she looked up as they entered the room. Jacob could see a smile on her face under the mask.

"I'm so glad you could come, Jacob. It will mean so much to him when he wakes up seeing you here," Savannah said.

Jacob nodded. As he approached the bed, the man lying in it didn't resemble his father in the least, but a mere shell of the man he had admired all of his life. Tears flooded his eyes. He reached up and wiped them away. He approached the bed. Blake's hair had completely fallen out. His eyes were sunken into his skull. His lips were dry and cracked, starving for moisture. Blake had always been a bigger man. Now he was skin and bones. At the young age of fifty-six, his body resembled that of a man in his late eighties.

Jacob couldn't take it any longer. He rushed out of the room.

He leaned against the wall and crumpled to the floor, bursting into tears. Kenzie walked outside, knelt down in front of him, and then pulled him into her arms. For several minutes, Jacob cried. Each time he felt the urge going away, his eyes would well up with more tears and he wept more. Flooded with such emotions was foreign to him. Jacob wasn't an expressive person. He prided himself with how keeping his emotions under control was an easy task over the past few years. It was different this time. His father was dying. Jacob choked down the sobs and wiped away the tears.

"Are you okay, bubba?"

"Yeah. I'll be fine. I'm sorry. I'm such a wuss."

"No. You're human. It's good to see that you still have a heart. I worry all of the paramedic stuff would make you cold."

Jacob leaned his head back against the wall and let out a deep breath. "I can't see him like this."

"Get used to it, bubba. He's going to be this way for a while. His doctor is hopeful he'll recover, but he's having a hard time with the treatments."

"Just what he didn't want, to be sick and lose all of his hair."

The door to his room opened and Savannah walked outside. "Jacob, he's awake and wants to see you."

Jacob wiped his eyes. "I can't let him see me crying. He raised me to be tough."

Kenzie laughed. "It's okay. Women like men who can cry."

Jacob walked toward the door. Before opening it, he took a deep breath in and let it slowly escape through his lips. He walked through the door and approached the bed.

Blake looked up at him and smiled. "I'm so glad to see you son," he weakly said as he reached for Jacob's hand.

Jacob wanted to reach for his father, but he didn't know if it was safe.

"It's okay. You can touch me. I won't break."

Jacob laughed and took his father's hand into his. Blake weakly gripped his hand. He used to be strong and firm. Jacob fought back the tears. "How are you feeling?"

"Living the dream."

Jacob laughed. "I could think of a lot better dreams to have."

"I'm glad you could make it. I feel better already."

"I don't know why you're just lying in bed, Dad. I've had worse scratches on my eyeball."

Blake laughed and then coughed. He released Jacob's hand and covered his mouth. His pale skin turned red as he gasped for air.

"Are you okay?"

Blake breathed in heavily. "Yeah. I'm fine."

Jacob walked around to the other side of the bed and plopped down in a chair. Studying his father, his heart sank.

"How long are you staying?"

"The director said I could only have a few shifts off. I wish I could stay longer."

Blake reached up to grab Jacob's hand, and gave him a reassuring smile. Even at his weakest point of his life, Blake was more concerned with his son's feelings rather than his own health. Tears began to trickle down Jacob's cheek. He turned his head trying to hide them from his father.

Blake drifted off to sleep. Jacob sat back in the chair watching his father breathe. Never in his life had he been more scared than right at that moment. Jacob's entire world revolved around his father. They were the best of friends.

God, I don't even know why I am praying to you because I don't believe in you, but my dad does. Spare him of this suffering and please heal him. We can't lose him.

TWENTY-THREE

FOR THE NEXT two days, Jacob never left his father's side. Blake slept most of the time. It didn't matter to him as long as he sat next to his father, and any time he woke up, Jacob relished the brief moments of consciousness.

Kenzie grew increasingly irritated with Jacob. She felt that he needed to pack up and move home. Anytime she brought up the subject, Jacob would try to find something else to talk about. She was a strong willed woman who wouldn't budge on her beliefs.

Deep down inside Jacob wanted to move home, or at least closer. Since his spinal cord injury, he missed his family. It was much easier said than done.

Jacob had his bags packed up and ready to go. Sitting next to his sleeping father, his cell phone rang. Retrieving it from his pocket, it was Bridge. He jumped up from the chair and dashed out of the room.

"Hello?"

"Hey, you. How's it going?"

Jacob sighed. "Okay, I guess. My dad has been sleeping a lot since I've been here."

"Is he doing better?"

"The same. I spoke with his oncologist and he believes Dad could make a full recovery. Right now, he's been sick and is having trouble with all of the chemo. He's in complete isolation. Can't even touch him with my bare hand," Jacob answered.

"I know it's hard. Wish I could cheer you up."

"You could."

"How?"

"Letting me kiss those sweet lips of yours," Jacob said devilishly.

"We're friends, remember?"

"Kissing friends."

"Jacob, you crack me up."

"Just saying. Don't forget to pick me up from the airport tonight."

"How could I forget?"

Kenzie walked up to Jacob, slid her hands into her pockets, and glared at him.

"Hey, I have to go. See you tonight."

"See you then."

Jacob hung up his phone and slid it into his front pocket. "What?"

"Nothing." Kenzie slid by him and started to put on the isolation outfit.

Jacob walked up behind her. "Sis, what's wrong?"

Once the gown was on, Kenzie slipped her hands into the gloves, grabbed a mask, and pulled it over her face. "I'm glad to see you're ready to run out of here. Dad is in there fighting for his life and all you're doing is pretending like everything is okay." She brushed by Jacob and walked into their father's room.

Jacob changed his gloves, pulled the mask back over his face, and joined her. Kenzie stood at the foot of the bed lightly rubbing their father's legs. Jacob noticed her shoulders bobbing up and down—she was crying. He walked up behind his sister and put his hands on her shoulders, but she pulled away.

"Sis, I'm not happy about leaving. I don't have a choice. I have to go back to work."

Kenzie faced him. "You *do* have a choice. Of course, just as always, you're more worried about your own life instead of ours."

Jacob's eyes narrowed. "You're wrong. I love my family, but I have responsibilities to take care of."

He walked over and sat down on a chair next to the bed. Blake's eyes flickered to life. He looked up over at Jacob and smiled. "Hi, son."

Jacob leaned forward in his seat and grasped his hand. "I'm right here, Dad. Are you doing okay?"

Blake smiled weakly. "Yeah. I'm fine." He looked up at Kenzie. "Why are you two fighting?"

"It's nothing for you to worry about."

"Young lady, you will not talk to me in that tone. I am your father. I may be sick, but I still have enough strength to get out of this bed and paddle your butt."

Jacob laughed.

Blake shifted his attention to Jacob. "What's so funny? It goes for you, too. Both of you need to quit fighting."

Jacob hung his head. Even as an adult, his father had a way of making him feel like he was three years old all over again. Silence overtook the room.

"Kenzie, give me a few minutes alone with your brother."

"But...."

"Don't argue with me, young lady. Step outside so I can talk to Jacob."

She glared at her brother for a moment, turned, and walked out of the room. Jacob looked curiously at his father.

Blake turned back toward Jacob. "Son, I love you. I understand you have to go back to work. There is no reason for you to sit here and watch me wither away. My life is in God's hands now. I know you don't have a belief in God, but I've been praying for you every night."

How can you expect me to believe in God when all I see is death on a daily basis? Now you're sick. Why would he do that to you? Jacob thought, sitting quietly in the chair listening to his father.

"Don't you worry about me and don't let your sister get you down. She's just worried about me, is all."

Jacob's eyes filled with tears. Holding his breath, he tried to choke down the eruption of crying that brewed deep inside of him. He laid his head on his father's shoulder. He wanted to take away his father's sickness. Blake ran his fingers through Jacob's hair. The two sat quietly in the room loving on each other. Thoughts of quitting his job in Idaho and moving home invaded his mind. After several minutes, Jacob leaned up and wiped his eyes.

Blake smiled. "I'm going to be okay. Don't you worry. I'm too stubborn to go anywhere."

Jacob laughed. "You got that right, old man."

"Go tell your sister to come in here."

"Sure thing, Dad."

Jacob stepped out and found Kenzie a few feet down the hall. Still brewing with anger, she walked past Jacob and into the room. Jacob leaned his back against the wall and fished his phone out of his front pocket. Certain that Kenzie was going to be in with their dad for a while, he decided to text Bridge.

Hey, gorgeous. I can't wait to see you—Jacob.

Me either. Something I want to talk to you about.-Bridge.

Care to fill me in?—Jacob.

No. You can wait to find out.—Bridge.

That isn't right. You can't leave me hanging like that—Jacob.

I'm a woman. I can do whatever I want to—Bridge.

Jacob closed his phone as Kenzie walked out of their father's room, tears streaming down her cheeks. "Let's go or you're going to miss your flight. We couldn't allow that to happen."

She stomped down the hallway toward the elevators. Jacob wanted to say one last goodbye. He opened the door to see his father sitting on the edge of the bed sweating and vomiting into a pail. Jacob closed the door and walked down the hall to catch up with his sister.

Silence loomed in the elevator. Kenzie wouldn't look at Jacob. Other people in the elevator could sense the tension as well. They looked at the floor or pretended to check the time on their watches. The elevator doors opened and Kenzie rushed through them. She stormed through the lobby, out the front doors, and through the parking lot to her car. Jacob nearly had to sprint to keep up with her. Once inside of the car, Jacob had enough.

"What the hell is wrong with you?"

Kenzie looked over at him, and then erupted into tears. She leaned forward and rested her head on Jacob's shoulder. His anger quickly became sadness for his sister. She wasn't mad at him; she was scared to death of losing their father, the same as he was.

For several minutes, she cried.

Looking at his watch, he realized they were going to be cutting it close if they didn't leave soon and Jacob didn't want to miss his flight.

"Sis. We need to get going. I can't be late. Do you want me to drive?"

Kenzie pulled back and wiped both of her eyes. "No, I'll be fine." After a few minutes of drying her eyes, she slipped on her seatbelt, and then headed toward the airport.

"He's going to be fine, you know. Dad is a fighter."

Kenzie continued to look forward, concentrating on the traffic in front of her. "I hope you're right. I'm sorry I've been so mean to you for the past few days. I just wish you were here to be with us."

"I know. Me too."

A short time later, they arrived at the airport. Kenzie pulled into the off-loading area. Jacob walked around to the trunk and retrieved his suitcase. Kenzie stood in front of him half-smiling.

Jacob pulled her into his arms and squeezed tight. "I love you, sis."

"I love you too," she whispered into his ear.

Jacob pulled back, picked up his suitcase, and disappeared into the terminal. Once he made it through security, he raced toward the gate. This was one time he was thankful for a small airport. In Boise, he would've missed his plane. He made it just in time and found his seat on the plane. After putting his suitcase in the overhead bin, he pulled out his phone to text Bridge one last time.

On the plane. Be home soon. Can't wait to see you—Jacob.

Me too. See you in a bit—Bridge.

Jacob powered down his phone and placed it back in his pants pocket. The flight only took two hours and he couldn't wait to see Bridge again. He couldn't get whatever Bridge said she wanted to talk to him about out of his mind. Regardless, he would be home soon. He was going to kiss her soft lips, friends or not.

TWENTY-FOUR

JACOB GREW MORE and more eager for the plane to land. The closer they got to Boise, the more his stomach filled with butterflies; he couldn't wait to see Bridge's beautiful face. Regardless if she only considered them friends, he was going to pull her into his arms and kiss her. With each passing moment, his feelings for her grew stronger.

As the plane taxied toward the gate, Jacob couldn't wait to rip off his seatbelt and get out. With his hand on his seatbelt, he watched the sign signaling they could unfasten and retrieve their luggage. It felt like an eternity until the plane came to a rest. A voice came over the speaker thanking them for flying and they were free to move around the cabin.

Jacob unfastened his seat belt, stood, grabbed his suitcase from the overhead compartment, and started toward the front of the plane. Seated near the rear of the plane, several people had the same plans and cluttered the aisle. Jacob's frustration escalated. He wanted Bridge in his arms, but was going to have to wait a few more minutes.

The closer he drew to the exit, the more excited he became. He wanted more than anything to bull over people to get off the plane, but he chose to try and be more patient. Passing each seat, people looked up at him awaiting a chance to step into the aisle, but he pretended not to see them. He prided himself on being a courteous man, but there wasn't any time for that now. He wanted off the plane.

Finally, approaching the plane doors, Jacob nodded and smiled at the attendants as they thanked him for flying with their service. Rushing down the jet way bridge, Jacob rushed past people in anticipation of seeing Bridge.

Once he entered the terminal, he scanned the crowd looking for her beautiful face. He couldn't find her. Several people were in happy embraces. Jacob continued to look the terminal for Bridge. After several minutes of searching, he pulled his cell phone out and dialed her number. It went straight to voicemail. Excitement swapped places with disappointment. He continued to walk around the terminal. He tried several more times to call Bridge, but it continued to go straight to voicemail. He sat down on a seat, confused. She said she would be there to pick him up. Dialing her number again, it went to voicemail once more.

Maybe she's trying to call me.

The terminal thinned out and there were only a few people walking around, but still no Bridge. He tried texting her : no answer. After thirty minutes, Jacob decided to call James.

"Hello?"

"Hey James, it's Jacob. Can you come to the airport and pick me up? Bridge was supposed to be here, but I haven't been able to find her," Jacob said disappointed.

"You try calling her?"

"Yeah. It just goes straight to voicemail. She's not answering text messages either."

"I can do that. Give me a few minutes and I'll be on the way."

"Thank you, brother. I appreciate it. Sorry I have to bother you."

"It's no bother. Be there in a jiffy."

Jacob tried calling Bridge several more times and it continued to go to voicemail. He looked at his messages and it showed she hadn't read them yet. He began to worry.

Thirty minutes later, James strolled into the terminal. Jacob picked up his suitcase and then walked toward him. Disappointment lined his face.

"Don't be so happy to see me," James said, smiling.

"Sorry. Just wish I knew what was going on with Bridge."

Jacob walked up and gave his friend a hug. They turned and walked toward the main terminal.

"How's your dad doing?"

"He's okay. Having a hard time with chemo, but he's tough."

"I'll keep him in my prayers."

Jacob nodded.

As they drove down the road toward Jacob's house, he stared out the window. His mind was racing and he was worried. It wasn't like her to ignore him. A hundred scenarios raced through his mind.

Am I overreacting? Maybe her phone is dead.

After James dropped him off at his house, Jacob walked inside, dropped his suitcase by the door, and plopped down in his recliner. He pulled the cell phone out of his pocket; still no messages from Bridge.

It was out of character for her to blow him off. An uneasiness settled over him. Throughout the night, Jacob continued to try calling and texting her, but she didn't answer. His eyes became heavy and he drifted off to sleep.

The next morning, Jacob woke up to the alarm on his cell phone. After wiping the sleep from his eyes, he grabbed his phone and didn't have any missed calls or messages. He dialed Bridge's number and it went straight to voicemail. Something wasn't right. He jumped out of bed, showered, got dressed, grabbed his gear and headed out to his truck. Looking at his watch, he still had forty-five minutes before his shift started, so he decided to go by her house to check on her.

Jacob weaved in and out of traffic. He wanted to get to her house and didn't want to risk being late to work. Part of him hoped she was there and then the other part hoped she wasn't. Afraid of appearing to be stalking her, he had to satisfy his curiosity and make sure nothing was seriously wrong. As he turned the corner on her street, a knot formed in his throat. Her car was in the driveway. Slowly approaching her house, Jacob tried to think of a witty reason why he showed up on her doorstep. He parked in front of her house, took in a deep breath, and then exited his truck. As he walked up her driveway, he glanced around her neighborhood. Nothing seemed out of place, and more importantly, no white car in its usual parking spot down the street.

He stopped next to her car and placed a hand on the hood, it was cold. With a perplexed look on his face, he headed toward her front door. A million scenarios raced through his mind. He rang the doorbell. A minute passed by, no answer. He rang it again...still no answer. Looking through the window in the door, he couldn't see any movement in the house.

He knocked. Another minute passed. Still no answer.

Jacob decided to walk around her house to see if he could see through any of the windows. After looking through each window, he still couldn't see if she was home. Glancing down at his watch, he noticed he was running out of time before he risked being late for work.

Nothing inside of him wanted to leave. Pulling his phone out of his pocket, he dialed her number and it went to voicemail. Filled with frustration, Jacob decided to get to work.

Once inside of his truck, he sat and stared at her house.

Nothing was making any sense. She didn't show up to pick him up and now, she wasn't answering the door.

Against his better judgment, he decided to head into work.

Once Jacob arrived at the station, his mood was bleak. He was so excited to see Bridge, but for the life of him, he couldn't figure out what was going on. He grabbed his gear and headed into the station. Walking inside, he went straight to his room. He didn't acknowledge James, who was in the kitchen cooking breakfast. The smell of sausage and eggs wafted through the station. Once his gear was stowed inside of his room, he walked out to the kitchen table and plopped down in a chair. He couldn't fight off the uneasiness that filled his stomach.

James curiously looked at him. "What's going on?"

Jacob sighed. "I went by Bridge's house."

"And?"

"Her car was there, but she wasn't."

"I wouldn't think too much into it. She may be sick or something."

Jacob shook his head. "No. Something isn't right. I can feel it."

James continued to cook breakfast. "You hungry?" He scrambled eggs and flipped the sausage over.

"No. My stomach is in knots. Thank you, though."

Jacob was never one to turn down food, especially home cooked food. James dished up the food onto two plates, carried them over to the table, and sat one down in front of him.

"You need to eat. I can't eat all of this food by myself," James demanded.

Jacob picked up a fork and poked at the sausage on his plate. James shrugged his shoulders and ate, but Jacob sat quietly playing with his food.

James sat back in his seat. "You're probably worrying for nothing. She's most likely at work already."

"I hope you're right. If she is there, she has a lot of explaining to do."

James' eyebrows raised. "You're starting to sound like a boyfriend."

Jacob laughed. "We're just friends."

"That doesn't sound too convincing. You falling for this woman?" James asked as he rested his elbows on the table.

"I...."

The station tones blared over the speakers. "Medic-57, you have a call at 9010 Ashwood Place. You have a ninety year old female that had a syncopal episode."

James started shoveling food into his mouth. Jacob pushed his plate away from him and headed toward the ambulance bay. He wasn't in the mood to run calls. Being worried about Bridge consumed his every thought.

Jacob climbed into the driver's seat. "Medic-57 is en-route."

"Dispatch copies," the female voice answered.

A moment later, James opened the passenger door and climbed into the ambulance. He reached down, held his stomach, and let out a thunderous belch.

"You feel better?" Jacob asked.

"Yes, I do. Compliments to the chef," he said with a satisfied look on his face.

Morning commuter traffic was rather heavy by Boise standards. Cars pulled to the right with ease. Jacob drove to the call in a half daze, unable to shake the feeling that something was terribly wrong. He pulled up in front of the house. There wasn't a fire truck on scene. Jacob looked over at James, confused. He shrugged his shoulders.

"Medic-57 to dispatch."

"Go ahead."

"We're on scene. Be advised fire isn't here."

"They're at low census due to a large field fire," the dispatcher answered.

Jacob and James climbed out of the ambulance, grabbed their gear, and walked toward the house. It was a single story brick home with a neatly manicured lawn.

Jacob knocked on the door. "Paramedics," he shouted.

"Come in," a woman answered.

Jacob and James walked inside. An elderly woman sat on the couch, holding an ice pack on her forehead.

Jacob knelt down in front of her. "What's going on, ma'am?"

"I lost my balance and fell. Silly me."

"Are you hurting anywhere?"

"Yes. My head." She pulled the ice pack back and revealed a large purplish mass protruding above her left eye.

James sat on the couch next to her. "I'm going to check your vital signs. Is that okay?"

"Yes, young man. That would be fine," she said as she patted him on the knee.

James placed the blood pressure cuff on her arm and listened to it with a stethoscope. She sat calmly on the couch enjoying the attention of the two men.

"What did you strike your head on?" Jacob asked.

She giggled. "I feel so foolish."

Jacob reached up and took her hand. "Don't be, ma'am. Accidents happen."

"You're making me feel like an old woman when you call me ma'am. My name is Doris."

"Okay, Doris. What happened?"

"I leaned down to pick something up from the carpet. When I stood, I got dizzy, fell down and struck my head on the dresser," she said while rubbing her forehead.

James deflated the blood pressure cuff. "Her pressure is 146/78 with a heart rate of 72." He replaced the equipment into their bag.

Jacob reached back behind her and started pushing on the back of her neck. "Are you hurting here, Doris?"

"No."

Jacob slid his hand down along her spine. "Any pain here?"

"No. I think I'll be fine."

Jacob knelt down in front of her. Looking at her, something didn't feel right. Other than the hematoma on her forehead, he didn't find any other significant signs of trauma, but something didn't sit well in his gut. His old partner told him that a paramedic's first line of defense was his gut feeling. If it told you something wasn't right, you'd better be listening.

"You know, Doris, I think we should run you in and get you checked out," Jacob said.

She smiled. "I appreciate your concern, but I think I'll be just fine, young man."

He looked over at James for guidance, but he only shrugged his shoulders.

Jacob grabbed one of her hands. "Doris, I would feel better if you'd just let us take you in and get checked out. What's the worst thing that can happen? You find out you're okay? Think of it this way, you're getting to hang out with a couple of handsome men."

Doris laughed and patted Jacob's hands. "Okay, young man. I'll go with you."

"We'll be right back. You just sit there and look beautiful," Jacob said.

Doris blushed. "I'll do my best. But at my age, that will be difficult."

James grabbed their bag and the two men walked outside to their ambulance. They grabbed the cot and pushed it just outside of her front door. Once back inside, Doris was standing in front of a mirror in her living room.

"My goodness, my hair is a mess," she said.

Jacob smiled. "You look fine, ma'am…I mean, Doris."

She gave him an approving smile and sat on the cot. They pushed her out to the ambulance and loaded her into the back. Jacob climbed into the back with her. He sat down on the bench seat next to her; she smiled and patted him on the leg once more.

"Code one to Magic County," Jacob said.

James nodded, closed the doors, and then climbed into the driver's seat. "Medic-57, to dispatch, we'll be en-route to the hospital."

"Dispatch copies."

While on the way to the hospital, Jacob took her vital signs a few more times, and nothing changed. He couldn't decide if his gut feeling was about his patient, or Bridge. He felt sick to his stomach. They arrived at the hospital and James opened the back doors.

"Hope that ride wasn't too rough, Doris," James said.

She smiled. "Not at all, young man."

Pushing her through the parking lot, Jacob hoped he would see Bridge smiling at him once they entered the emergency room. Relief would be his first reaction and then anger would take over. Stopping at the main nurse's desk, Jacob glanced around the emergency room hoping to catch a glimpse of Bridge, but he didn't see her.

"What you boys got?" a nurse asked from behind the desk.

Jacob strolled over to her, breathless with anticipation. "Is Bridge here?"

"No. She didn't call or show up today."

Jacob's heart sank. His mind spun out of control, something was definitely wrong. Sitting at the doctor's desk was Doctor Young, glaring at him.

Jacob stared at him. *Just what I needed today.*

"Hey, snap out of it. What do you have?" the nurse impatiently asked.

"Ninety year old woman who struck her head on a dresser. No loss of consciousness, neck, or back pain," Jacob answered.

Doris sat on the cot, still smiling.

"Sounds easy enough. Take her to room seven. I'll be there in a minute to check her in."

Pushing the cot toward the room they were assigned, Jacob glanced over his shoulder. Doctor Young still glared at him. Once inside of the room, Jacob prepared to move Doris. He untucked all of the sheets and waited on James to do the same.

"What do you want me to do?" Doris asked.

"Sit there and look beautiful," Jacob said.

"Oh you're too kind," Doris said as she playfully slapped Jacob's arm.

Young stormed into the room as they moved her over to the bed. He bumped into Jacob as he walked past him. "Hello, ma'am. I'm Doctor Young. What brings you into the emergency room today?"

"I feel so foolish. I bumped my head on the dresser. These wonderful boys convinced me to come to the hospital," Doris answered.

"I see." Doctor Young pulled out a pen light and shined it into her eyes; she squinted. He reached around to the back of her neck. "Does this hurt?" he asked.

"No."

Doctor Young turned and faced Jacob. "Why didn't you c-spine her?"

"No need to. She didn't have any neck or back pain," Jacob answered.

Doctor Young shook his head. "Haven't you ever heard that the elderly have degenerative nerves and don't feel pain like a younger person?"

Jacob sighed. "Like I said, she didn't have any pain."

The nurse walked into the room. "Sorry, had a phone call."

Was it Bridge? Please say it was!

Doctor Young snatched the chart from the nurse and began to scribble on it. "I want a head CT, no contrast and a CT of her neck stat," he snapped.

He turned toward Jacob. "Don't leave. I want to see the results before you run out of here." He shook his head and left.

"Did I miss something?" the nurse asked.

Jacob shrugged.

James pushed the cot out of the room, grabbed a new set of linens, and walked outside. Jacob grabbed his paperwork and walked over to the nurse's station.

A few minutes later, the nurse walked out of Doris' room. She walked over, got on the phone and placed a verbal order for the head and neck CT that Doctor Young wanted. A tech came out of Doris' room and pushed her toward the x-ray department. She was still smiling.

Jacob walked around the desk and sat down next to the nurse. "So, Bridge didn't call or show up?"

"No. It isn't like her either. I've tried calling her several times, but it goes straight to voicemail. If she doesn't call soon she could lose her job. Our department head isn't tolerant of no-call no-show," the nurse said.

Jacob began to do his paperwork. He was instructed not to leave and he wasn't about to. Doris was brought back to her room, still smiling.

She was the type of patient Jacob enjoyed the most.

Several minutes later, Doctor Young shot up from behind his desk and stomped over to where Jacob was sitting.

"You idiot," he yelled.

Jacob turned toward him. "What?"

"She has an unstable C-1 fracture. You should've put her into full c-spine!"

The emergency room grew quiet. Patients and nurses curiously watched. Jacob could feel his blood pressure rising. Every time he turned around, Doctor Young was berating him. It all stemmed from his hatred for Jacob.

Jacob stood. "I will not be talked to that way. We made a command decision and I stand by it."

"Nurse, get a c-collar onto this patient now, please," ordered Young. "As for you, Jacob, I'll be calling Nate. He needs to do a little house cleaning with his incompetent paramedics."

Redness washed over Jacob's face. "I will not tolerate you berating me in front of everyone."

It was quiet enough a pin dropping could be heard in the emergency room.

Ed Young smiled and backed up a few feet. "I hear you can't find Bridge. Maybe she got smart and left your sorry butt."

Jacob started to lunge at him, but James grabbed him from behind, stopping him dead in his tracks.

Doctor Young turned, walked back toward his desk, and started to whistle. Yet again, the doctor got the best of him.

Bridge, where in the hell are you?

TWENTY-FIVE

THE NEXT MORNING when Jacob went off shift, he tossed his gear in his truck, and raced toward Bridge's house. The staff at the hospital didn't seem too worried she didn't call or show up for work, but Jacob was worried sick.

He pulled onto her street and rushed to her house. Her car was still in the driveway. It was eerily quiet in her neighborhood. Jacob pulled his truck into the driveway. He jumped out and walked over to her car. Touching the hood, it was still cold. He tried to open the doors, but they were locked. He pulled his cell phone out and tried to call her, but it went straight to voicemail. Frustration brewed in him. He peered through the window on the front door, but still couldn't see any movement. After ringing the doorbell several times, he knocked on the door with such force it shook the windows in the house and still no answer.

Jacob walked around to the back of the house; looking in every window, he approached hoping to catch a glimpse of something. He grabbed the cool brass door handle on the back door and it was locked. He looked around on the ground and found a rock that was a little bit bigger than his hand. Picking it up, he looked around. Jacob approached the door, swung back, and crashed the rock through the window. Glass toppled all over the back patio and inside of the kitchen. He reached in, unlocked the door, and went inside. Glass crunched under his feet.

She's going to be pissed at me for this. Oh well.

Jacob made his way through each room, looking for something that would be a clue as to where she was. Each room remained tidy, as if she hadn't been there in several days. Bridge was a neat freak and she believed everything had its place and it belonged there. He walked into her bedroom and found the bed neatly made. It appeared she hadn't slept in it for some time. That added to his anxiety. As he walked around the rest of her house, he couldn't shake the feeling that something was terribly wrong.

Jacob sat down on her couch, not sure what to do next. It didn't make sense that she would go this long without talking to him. Especially not showing up for work, and then his cell phone rang.

He pulled it from his pocket and it was Bridge.

"Hey. Where are you? I've been so damn worried...."

"Jacob, listen to me.I need your help. Get a pen and paper."

He ran into the kitchen and opened several drawers before he finally found a pen and paper. He rested the phone on his shoulder.

"Come to 11209 State Highway 79. There's an old farm house there. Get on the highway heading south out of town. About five miles outside of the city limits, you'll pass over a river. It's the first farm house on the right. It sits off the road. Come now, I need you," Bridge said with a quivering voice.

"Are you okay? What's going on? Where have you...."

The phone went dead.

"Hello? Bridge?" Jacob looked at his phone.

CALL ENDED.

He redialed Bridge's number and it went straight to voice mail. Frustrated, Jacob ran out the back door, around the house, and jumped into his truck. Squealing out of the driveway, he slammed his truck into drive and raced down the road, narrowly missing a blue Crown Vic traveling toward him.

Jacob's mind raced as he headed toward the address Bridge gave him. He tried calling her a few more times, but it continued to go straight to voicemail. After a few minutes of driving, Jacob decided to check on a suspicion he had. He dialed the hospital.

"Emergency room," a woman answered.

"Hey. This is Jacob from Magic County EMS. Is Doctor Young working today?" he asked, holding his breath for the answer.

"No. He didn't come in today. He called in sick."

Jacob gulped. "Thank you."

As he sped down the curvy road, he watched for the river that Bridge told him about. A million things ran through his mind. Was Doctor Young capable of hurting her? At this point, Jacob was convinced it was a definite possibility.

A few minutes later, he approached the river and crossed the bridge. He studied the right side of the road looking for a mailbox. Checking the address on the piece of paper, he glanced up just in time to see the numbers he was trying to locate scrolled across the side of a mailbox. He slammed on the brakes and skidded across the asphalt. The smell of burnt rubber invaded the cab of his truck. He backed up and stopped at the mailbox. It was the address he was looking for. The driveway consisted of gravel and weeds. It appeared no one had brush hogged the property for a long time. His heart thumped in his chest.

What kind of trouble are you in, Bridge?

Jacob stared down the driveway for several minutes trying to decide if he should call the police. The house wasn't visible from the highway. His male ego took over; he turned and began to drive down the gravel road. Trees hung low over the drive making it difficult to see anything in the distance. Slowly he crept down the driveway, still not able to see the house. An uneasiness began to roll through his stomach. A few minutes later, a large two-story house came into view, paint peeling from the sides, shutters broken, and windows shattered. As Jacob approached the house, a white car with tinted windows came into view without any license plates.

Jacob punched the gas and sped toward the front of the house. Slamming on the brakes, he skidded to a stop next to the car. A large cloud of dust floated over his truck. Jacob jumped out of the truck and ran up the stairs. He turned the rusty doorknob, but it wouldn't open. He scurried over to a window and looked inside. He saw Bridge tied to a chair with her hands bound behind her. His heart leapt into his throat. Jacob ran back to the front door, lifted up his foot, and kicked the door as hard as he could, knocking it open. A man stood behind Bridge with a knife in his hand. Terror filled her eyes and tears streamed down her cheeks.

Jacob stared at the man, and he couldn't command his muscles to move. He looked familiar, but couldn't place how he knew him.

The man stared at Jacob with hate in his eyes. "You look surprised. Can't remember who I am?"

Jacob shook his head. "No. Who are you? What are you doing to Bridge?"

The man's eyes narrowed. "You don't remember the family of the people you've killed?"

Jacob searched his memory, but he couldn't place the man. "Do I know you?"

The man laughed. "You should. You killed my wife," he growled.

Suddenly, Jacob realized who he was. His wife was the patient that died from the abdominal aneurysm. Remembering the call, the man had threatened him in the emergency room, saying he was going to pay. It all made sense to Jacob now. The brake lines cut, being run off the road into the river, but he couldn't figure out why the man kidnapped Bridge. It never was Doctor Young trying to kill him; the disgruntled husband was the culprit.

Bridge shook her head from side to side and had a piece of tape over her mouth. Jacob could hear her muffled sobbing.

Jacob held his hands in front of him and slowly walked toward the man.

"Stop," he ordered, pointing the knife toward Jacob. "You come one step closer, and I'm going to cut her damn throat. Do you love her?"

Jacob stopped. His throat constricted and he couldn't breathe. "Sir, what are you talking about?"

"Do you love her?"

Jacob looked confused. "Who?"

The man pressed the knife firmly into Bridge's throat. "Her," he said looking down at Bridge. *"Do you love her?"* the man asked in an icy voice.

Jacob looked into her eyes. "She's a friend."

The man smiled. "Then I guess you won't mind if I kill her then, would you?" He pressed the blade against her neck once again. A trickle of blood ran down the side of her neck.

Jacob could no longer fight his feelings. "Yes...I love her."

Tears flowed down her cheeks.

The man's eyes narrowed and he smiled. "Good. Then you'll soon find out what it's like to lose someone you love." He pulled Bridge's head back, exposing her throat. A sliver of light reflected off the blade and traced across Jacob's face.

Jacob's body tensed. "Wait," he shouted.

The man looked up at him quizzically. The desperate situation demanded a desperate action.

"Your wife didn't love you."

The man stopped and glared at him. *"What* did you say?"

"The last thing she said was she wanted to die. She was tired of you and wanted out."

The man's lips began to quiver and a tear slid down his cheek. "Don't you say that about her. Don't you dare!" he shouted, pointing the knife at Jacob.

"Does the truth hurt? Frankly, I don't blame her. How did she ever put up with you for as long as she did?"

The man stomped toward Jacob. "How dare you. I'm going to kill you first and then her."

He grabbed Jacob and slammed him into the wall. Plaster caved in behind his back. He struggled not to lose his balance, but fell to the ground with the man lying on top of him.

Jacob looked up in time to see the blade plunging toward his face. He moved his head and the steel blade plunged into the floor. Panting heavily, Jacob reached up and shoved a finger into the man's eye socket. A skin-crawling shriek ripped out of the man's open mouth. Jacob squirmed out from under him and tried to crawl away. The man grabbed his ankle; Jacob reared back his free foot and kicked him in the face. The man toppled over onto his back.

Bridge struggled to wiggle her hands out of the ropes, but wasn't able to.

Jacob ran over to her and tried to free her hands. He looked up and noticed her eyes wide and she was screaming from under the tape. He spun around to find the man standing directly behind him, one eye closed with blood flowing from it.

"This isn't over yet," the man said.

The crazed look in his eyes sent a shiver down Jacob's spine. His hands were trembling and his heart thumped in his chest.

The man lunged forward. Jacob tried to back up, tripped, and fell down. The man jumped on top of him. With the butt of the knife, he struck Jacob on the forehead and his vision became blurry. Raising the knife over his head in both hands, he brought the steel blade down toward Jacob's chest.

Two thunderous cracks echoed through the house, and the man dropped the knife.

He grabbed his chest where blood flowed from two holes.

Jacob looked toward the front door and saw Detective Morrison standing in the doorway with a smoking gun in his hands. The man fell off Jacob and onto the floor.

Jacob scrambled up and rushed over to Bridge. He pulled the tape off her mouth.

"Are you okay?"

"Yeah."

Jacob untied her hands and feet. She reached up, covered her mouth with her hands, and burst into tears. Jacob pulled her into his arms holding her close as she wept. For several minutes, she cried.

Detective Morrison walked over to the man's body pointing his gun at him, kicked the knife away, and then leaned down pressing on the side of his neck checking for a pulse.

"Are you two okay?"

Jacob nodded.

Detective Morrison walked outside and made a phone call on his cell. Jacob couldn't hear what he was saying. A few minutes later, he returned into the house. "The coroner is on his way. I've got an ambulance en-route to check on you, ma'am."

She wiped the tears off her face. "I don't need one. I'm fine." She looked toward Jacob. "I have my own paramedic right here."

A short time later, several more police officers and the coroner arrived at the house. The investigators took pictures of the man's body, while two other detectives asked Bridge several questions. Jacob sat on the porch holding a bandage to his forehead.

Detective Morrison sat down next to him. "I owe you an apology," he said, looking out into the distance.

"No, you don't. Thank you for saving my life, I mean our lives. How did you know where we were?"

"I happened to be in the area when we received a report of someone breaking into a house. As it turns out, it was Bridge's house. I saw you leave in a big hurry, so I decided to follow you. I lost you, but when I saw the tire marks on the pavement, I took a wild guess and went down the driveway. Guess I got lucky," he said, laughing.

Jacob reached up and patted him on the back. "No. We got lucky. Thank you."

"I was wrong. Someone was trying to kill you and I'm sorry."

"Water under the bridge," Jacob replied.

Bridge walked up to the two men.

Detective Morrison smiled. "I'll need you to come to the station and file an official report," he said to Bridge. "I'll leave you two alone." He got up and walked over to a group of police officers talking.

Bridge stood in front of Jacob. "My knight in shining armor."

Jacob laughed. "You mean your friend in shining armor?"

Bridge sat next to Jacob. "I have to ask you something. Was it true everything you said about that guy's wife hating him?"

"No. It was a horrible thing to say, but I had to get him away from you. What happened?"

Bridge looked at the ground. "That guy knocked on my door. When I answered it, he held a rag over my face. The next thing I knew, I woke up here tied to the chair. He kept talking about his wife and how he was going to enjoy killing you. He said over and over you killed his wife."

"I'm sorry you were dragged into this."

Bridge smiled. "Don't apologize. It wasn't your fault. He had issues. I didn't want to call you, but he left me no choice. He said if I didn't, he was going to cut my throat and still kill you." Bridge grabbed Jacob's hands. "Did you mean the other thing you said?"

Jacob pulled her close to him and looked into her eyes. "Yes. I love you."

Bridge smiled. "I'm falling in love with you, too."

Jacob's heart jumped for joy. "Then why have you been pushing me away?"

"A proper woman doesn't give in that easily. Have to make you work for it," she said with a satisfied look on her face.

"Shut up and kiss me," Jacob ordered.

"Yes, *sir.*"

TWENTY-SIX

FOR THE NEXT month, Jacob and Bridge's relationship flourished. They spent every waking moment together. Once Bridge quit fighting her feelings for him, their friendship blossomed into a wonderful relationship. A night didn't go by that they weren't spending the night at one another's house if Jacob wasn't on duty.

Doctor Young still went after Jacob every given opportunity. Jacob ignored his hatred and chalked it up to jealousy. He found a wonderful woman and wasn't going to let anything stand in the way of his happiness.

The shrill sound of his alarm clock shot Jacob out of bed like a cannon. Bridge, unfazed, continued to sleep next to him. Leaning down on one elbow, he reached down and moved a few strands of hair out of her face. She looked angelic and peaceful. He could stare at her for a lifetime and planned to do so. He slipped quietly out of bed, slid on a pair of shorts, and walked out of his bedroom. Wanting to surprise her, Jacob went into the kitchen to make her breakfast.

His step had a little pep in it. The thought of Bridge gave his life a new meaning. One day he wanted to marry her. He wondered if it was too soon to feel that way. Shrugging off the doubt, he began to prepare her breakfast. A short time later, she came out of his room wearing one of his t-shirts. He stopped preparing the breakfast and stared at her.

"What?" she asked, half asleep.

"Nothing. You're just so beautiful. That's all."

She rolled her eyes. "No one looks good first thing in the morning." She ran her fingers through the bird's nest that was her hair.

"You do. My shirt looks better on you."

Bridge blushed. "It's too early for flattery." She walked into the kitchen and took Jacob into her arms. "What are you doing?"

"Making my beautiful woman some breakfast."

"I'm going to go brush my teeth. Smells like a cat crapped in my mouth." She turned and walked toward the bedroom.

"Please do. I don't like kissing a nasty mouth," Jacob said smiling.

Bridge rolled her eyes at him and then disappeared into the bedroom. He often thought about being in a relationship with Bridge, but he never dreamed he could knock down her walls.

After breakfast, Jacob got dressed, grabbed his bags, and walked to the front door. She followed behind him. She grabbed his butt and he jumped.

"I'm going to miss you."

"I can see why you would. I'm pretty awesome."

She reached up, pulled Jacob down to her, and kissed him passionately on his lips.

Electricity rolled through him. Grabbing his bags, Jacob turned and headed toward his truck.

Standing at the door she watched him leave.

As Jacob strolled through the station parking lot, James sat outside on a chair. "You sure look happy."

Jacob stopped and looked around him. "Are you talking to me?"

"Smart alec," James growled.

Jacob walked inside, put his bags in his room, and joined his partner outside.

James looked up at him. "Things still going well with Bridge?"

"Yup. Couldn't be happier. When is it too soon to be thinking of marriage?"

James' jaw dropped. "You thinking about popping the question?"

"Yeah."

"That's a pretty big step. You sure you're ready for that?"

"I think so. I don't know if she feels as strongly as I do though."

James stood. "Think long and hard about it before you pop the question. It could drive a wedge between you two."

Jacob had never thought about that. It was the last thing he wanted to happen, but he was ready for the next step.

Station tones squelched through the speakers. "Medic-57, we have a fifty-six year old female patient at 785 Tinker Circle with a possible stroke."

James walked over to the ambulance and grabbed the microphone. "Medic-57, we'll be en-route."

Jacob joined him and climbed into the passenger seat. As they raced toward the address, Jacob sat looking out the window. Would she break it off with him if he asked her to marry him? Was that even a possibility?

His mind should've been focused on the call, but he couldn't stop thinking about Bridge. Was it too soon to ask her for her hand in marriage? Part of him thought so, but the other part of him couldn't wait to pop the question.

As they arrived on scene, a man ran out the front door waving his arms in the air. A fire truck was parked in front of the house. "Like we couldn't see the big truck in front," James said shaking his head. "Medic-57. We're on scene."

Jacob climbed out of the passenger seat and walked toward the back of the ambulance. The man ran up to him, short of breath, and grabbed his arm.

"You have to hurry. My wife isn't breathing right. Her face is drooping on one side and she's drooling."

Jacob pulled his arm from the man's fierce grip. "When did that start?"

"She was fine twenty minutes ago. I took a shower, and when I came out, I found her like this. Please hurry," the man pleaded.

Jacob stared at the man for a moment. The fear in his eyes tugged at his heart. For a brief moment, Jacob could relate. If this had happened to Bridge, he would be lost.

James nonchalantly walked around to the back of the ambulance. He looked over at the panicking man and shook his head. "What's going on?"

"Sounds like a stroke. Symptoms started about twenty minutes ago," Jacob answered.

Jacob threw the gear on the cot, pulled it out of the ambulance, and then they pushed it toward the house. The man ran ahead of them, opened the door, and impatiently waited on them. Once inside, Jacob looked over at the couch. An elderly looking woman lay on it, head turned to the side, drool dripping out of her mouth. One of the firefighters placed a non-rebreather onto her face.

James walked around Jacob and looked at the woman. He walked over and shook the woman's shoulder.

"Ma'am, can you talk to me. What's going on?" James asked. She didn't answer. Her eyes stared blankly off to the right.

"She hasn't answered us either since we got here," a firefighter said.

The frantic husband stood behind them. "Is she okay? What's going on with her?"

James asked, "Does she have any history of anything?"

"Um...high blood pressure, I think."

"Can you gather her medications for us, please? We're going to get her loaded onto the cot and then take her out to our ambulance," James said.

The man nodded and then ran down the hallway.

"She's stroking. Let's get her out to the truck," James said, with seriousness in his voice.

With the help of the firefighters, they picked up the woman, placed her on the cot, and then pushed her out of the house toward the ambulance. Once she was loaded into their truck, they each began to grab equipment.

They worked methodically together. In their short time as partners, they had grown to know what the other was thinking without speaking. Jacob pricked the woman's finger and touched the drop of blood to the glucometer.

"Blood sugar is 128," he told James.

James attached the cardiac monitor to the woman and obtained a set of vital signs. Her condition hadn't improved. Laying in front of them was a woman teetering on the brink of death.

"Blood pressure is 220/120. Heart rate is 130." James said.

They sat for a moment looking at one another. The unspoken language between them said it all. James grabbed an OPA and tried to place it in her mouth, but she gagged.

"We need to knock her down and RSI her," Jacob said.

James agreed.

"What do you want me to do?" the firefighter asked.

Jacob handed a saline bag and tubing to the firefighter. He assembled it and handed it back to Jacob.

James pulled out the intubation kit and prepared to tube her.

Jacob was able to establish an IV with ease. He connected the IV tubing to the saline lock and ran fluid wide open. Saline dripped at a rapid rate into the chamber of the tubing.

James had the intubation equipment prepared and was ready.

Jacob assembled the Lidocaine and administered one-hundred milligrams of the drug. Then he grabbed the Versed and pushed five milligrams of the drug into the tubing. James watched him intently.

"You ready?" Jacob asked.

James nodded.

Jacob pushed the needle into the IV tubing and flushed in 150mg of Succinylcholine. Her face began to twitch. After thirty seconds, her face stopped twitching, and her breathing stopped.

James slid the laryngoscope into her mouth. After a few seconds, he slid the tube into her throat. He pulled out the stylette, attached a bag valve mask to the end of the tube, and began to ventilate. Each time he squeezed the bag, her chest would rise and fall, and misting appeared in the tube - all signs that the tube was properly placed.

"I think we're good," James said.

Jacob grabbed the tube holder, slipped it around her neck and attached it securely, holding the tube in place. The husband opened up the back doors of the ambulance.

He stared at them and his lips began to quiver. "What's going on? What have you done?"

"She wasn't breathing well so we gave her some medications that allowed us to intubate her. We're breathing for her now. Give us a few more minutes and we'll get her going to the hospital," Jacob said.

"Was it necessary?"

"Yes. I know it's scary looking, but this was something we needed to do to make sure she was breathing sufficiently. Why don't you go ahead and leave for the hospital. We'll be behind you shortly," Jacob said.

The man nodded and slammed the doors shut. A few moments later, he squealed out of the driveway and raced down his street.

"I think we should give her Vecuronium so she doesn't buck the tube. The Succs isn't going to last long," Jacob said.

"Sounds good to me. Let's give her 10mg of it," James ordered.

Jacob retrieved the medication. Vecuronium was a long lasting paralytic that would keep her muscles paralyzed for an hour.

Once he had drawn up the saline, he grabbed the vial of powder and began to push it into the vial. There was a lot of resistance and he was only able to get half of the saline into it. Jacob turned the vial upside down and looked closely at it to see if the needle was all of the way in. Unsure of what was causing the resistance, he pulled the syringe out of the vial and the drug sprayed him in the face.

The vial crashing to the floor caught James' attention. "What's wrong?"

Jacob looked at him blankly. "The Vecuronium just sprayed in my face."

He leaned back against the wall of the ambulance. "I'm going to stop breathing," he said, panting. The firefighter stood across from Jacob with his eyes the size of softballs.

"Come bag this woman," James ordered.

The firefighter stared at Jacob in shock.

"Hey!" James screamed. *"Come bag this woman!"*

The firefighter walked around the cot, took the bag valve mask from James, and began to ventilate the woman.

James rushed over to Jacob. "It's going to be okay, buddy." He pulled Jacob over and laid him flat on his back on the bench seat.

James opened the side door. "Hey, captain."

"Yeah?" the captain answered.

"I need one of your firefighters to drive us to the hospital, now!"

He had a puzzled look on his face. "Okay. What's going on?"

"No time to explain. Just get him in the front and drive. We need to leave," James yelled.

The captain nodded. A few moments later, another firefighter climbed into the driver's seat of the ambulance.

"Don't kill us, but get us to the hospital as quickly as you can," James ordered.

"You got it," the firefighter said. He switched the ambulance into drive, accelerated and sped down the road toward the hospital.

James knelt down next to Jacob. "How ya feeling, buddy?"

He continued panting. "I'm…going…down," Jacob answered.

James placed a pulse oximeter onto Jacob's finger and it read one-hundred percent. He reached down and grasped his wrist for fifteen seconds; his heart rate was one-hundred forty beats.

"Keep concentrating on breathing. You're going to be okay," James said reassuringly.

Jacob felt that he was going to stop breathing at any moment and he was terrified. Knowing that the medication didn't do anything for sedation, he would feel his muscles seize up and stop breathing.

"She's starting to bite the tube," the firefighter said.

"Crap," James yelled. He grabbed the drug kit, pulled out another Vecuronium and a saline flush. He plunged the needle into the vial and dispersed the saline into it. Withdrawing the needle, he shook the vial vigorously to mix the drug. Once the powder was in water form, he reinserted the needle and withdrew the medication.

Jacob continued to pant.

Sliding the needle into the woman's IV tubing, he dispersed the medication.

She stopped biting the tube. James sighed with relief. "She won't be doing that anymore. Keep ventilating her. You're doing a great job."

The firefighter nodded.

James turned back toward Jacob. "How ya doing, buddy?"

"I'm…okay…I…guess."

James leaned down close to him. "Look, if the drug was going to hit you, it would've by now. I think you're going to be okay. Try slowing down your breathing."

James took a moment to call in a report to the hospital. A few nurses met them at the ambulance bay with a cot. Once they unloaded the woman, the firefighter and a nurse pushed her into the hospital. Another nurse stayed and helped move Jacob to the awaiting cot. He was still panting, but breathing none the less.

"Take him to trauma-one," a nurse ordered as they passed by the main desk in the emergency room. Once in the room, a nurse began to hook him up to the cardiac monitor. She didn't say much to him. Jacob was embarrassed.

"I'll be back in later to check on you. The doctor will be in shortly," the nurse said.

"Who's the doctor?" Jacob asked, afraid of what the answer was going to be.

"I am," Doctor Young said, standing at the door. He looked down at Jacob with a smirk on his face.

Just my luck. The punches keep coming.

Jacob rested his head against the pillow.

"Had a little accident, did ya?" Young asked snidely.

Jacob had calmed his breathing down. "You can say that."

"What happened?"

You know exactly what happened. I'm sure you're enjoying this.

"Accidentaly sprayed Vecuronium in my face."

Doctor Young approached the bed, placed a stethoscope into his ears, leaned down, and placed the bell on Jacob's chest. "Take a deep breath."

Jacob inhaled and then exhaled deeply.

"Again," Young said after he moved the bell to the other side of his chest.

Jacob followed his instructions.

Doctor Young pulled the stethoscope out of his ears and smiled at Jacob. "You're going to be fine. The chance of you getting enough of that drug into your eyes to stop your breathing is nearly impossible." He grabbed a chart and began to scribble on it. "Basically, you had an anxiety attack. I'll discharge you shortly."

Jacob couldn't look him in the eyes. He knew Young enjoyed it. The doctor shook his head. "And Bridge chose you over me? What a joke," he said, laughing as he walked out of the room.

Jacob felt humiliated. When the drug sprayed him in the face, he was sure it would've been absorbed enough to stop his breathing. Worse yet, he had to face Doctor Young. He didn't want Bridge to know. The embarrassment would be too much to handle. The last thing he wanted was for her to look at him differently.

James walked into his room. "How ya doing?"

"Fine. How's our patient doing?"

James walked over and pulled up a chair next to the bed. "She's in CT now. The firefighter that rode in with us was a great help."

Jacob nodded. "I'm sorry. Guess I freaked out."

"It's okay. It happens. Just glad I didn't have to intubate you as well."

"Where is he?" a woman yelled from down the hall.

Jacob looked at James. "You didn't!"

"I did."

"Why?" Jacob asked.

"She's your girlfriend. She has a right to know. I had the charge nurse call her."

"I don't care what you think," shouted Bridge. "Where is he?"

A moment later, she stormed into the room. Standing at the foot of the bed, she looked at him with tears trickling down her cheeks. She rushed around to the side of the bed and pulled him into her arms.

"I was so scared," she said, sobbing.

"I'm fine. There's no reason to be upset. It was an accident."

She leaned back, looking at him. He brushed her tears away.

"I couldn't handle it if something happened to you."

"I'm fine. You don't have to be so worried. I'm Superman, baby."

Bridge's face tensed. "Why weren't you wearing goggles?"

Her question took him by surprise. "I never do."

She slugged him in the arm. "You have to be careful. You may not be so lucky next time."

Jacob felt foolish again. "Okay. It won't happen again."

Ed Young walked into the room. "I'm discharging you. No reason for you to take up space from patients who need to be seen in the ER."

Bridge turned and faced him. "What is your problem? He deserves to be here just as much as anyone else."

Young smirked. "I guess the clinic for idiots was completely full today."

"I don't *care* if you're angry," she said. "I don't care how you feel about me, or Jacob. He's a human being that deserves to be treated just like anyone else. Do you talk to all of your patients this way?"

Doctor Young glared at Jacob and then looked back at Bridge. "You're not worth my time. Have fun being with an incompetent man."

Bridge walked up to Ed. "Don't you ever talk about my man that way again. You had your chance and you blew it. You're not even half the man he is. Get over yourself."

The doctor walked out of the room.

Bridge turned around and sat down on the bed with Jacob.

"You're sexy when you're angry. You're turning me on."

"Shut up. Don't get me started on you next."

TWENTY-SEVEN

JACOB REJOINED HIS partner on the ambulance after he was discharged from the hospital. Nate couldn't stop laughing at him. It was a relief because Jacob was certain Nate was going to discipline him....again. He walked out to his truck and loaded his gear in the back.

His cell phone rang. He pulled it out his pocket. It was Bridge.

"Hey, sexy."

Bridge laughed. "I will never get tired of hearing that. You off work yet?"

"Just loaded my stuff into my truck. What's up?"

"Can you come by the emergency room? I have something I need to talk to you about."

"Sure. I'll be there in ten minutes."

"Great. See you in a bit."

Jacob smiled, put the phone back in his pocket, and then headed toward the hospital. On his way to see Bridge, the anticipation was killing him. He couldn't wait to see her and find out what she had to say. His life had made a drastic change. Since he and Bridge had been together, he'd never been happier in his life. Each day he thought of ways he could make her smile and make her happy. He couldn't imagine his life without her in it.

He arrived at the hospital and walked through the ambulance entrance. The emergency room was buzzing. Nurses hustled in and out of rooms. He walked up to the main nurse's desk where Bridge sat working on a computer. Jacob looked behind her to see Doctor Young glaring at him.

Bridge looked up. "Hey, handsome."

Jacob's heart skipped a beat and he looked at her curiously. "What did you need to talk to me about?"

Bridge walked around the desk and took Jacob's hand. "Let's go outside so we can talk privately." She led him out of the ambulance entrance into the parking lot. She walked over and leaned against a wall. "Don't be mad at what I'm going to tell you. Promise?"

The anticipation was killing him. "How could I ever be mad at you?"

"I didn't say anything because I didn't want to jinx it. I interviewed with LifeStar Air Medical as a flight nurse."

"And?"

An enormous smile lit up her face. "I got the job. I start my training with them the end of this week."

Jacob was happy for her. The twinkle in her eye when she told him was worth a thousand words. He pulled her into his arms. "You're going to make a great flight nurse." He looked her up and down. "Not to mention, you're going to be so hot in the flight suit."

Bridge playfully slapped him on the arm. "Oh, Jacob, stop."

"What? I'm just sayin."

"Thank you. That means a lot to me."

He pulled her close to him and looked her in the eyes. "I love you."

"I love you, too."

For the past two weeks Bridge had been in Salt Lake City, Utah going through her flight training. He missed her dearly. When he wasn't at work, he was at home bored out of his mind. Part of him was jealous of her. Only the best medical professionals were hired to be flight nurses and paramedics. Knowing he wouldn't be seeing her smiling face working in the emergency room bothered him. Still, he was proud of her because she was a great nurse.

Jacob's cell phone rang. It was Kenzie.

"Hey, sis. How's it going?"

"Not good. Dad isn't doing too well. Jacob, you need to come home. I don't know if he's going to survive this," her voice trembled.

"Sis, you know I can't do that. I have a life here, a career. I wish I could be there, but I can't."

Kenzie sighed. Her voice was stern. "I'm so tired of hearing about how you can't do this, you can't do that. Your dad needs you. Your *family* needs you."

Jacob grew tired of Kenzie's constant badgering. He loved his father more than life, but it wasn't possible for him to rush home. "I wish you could understand."

"I do understand. You're selfish. I don't even know why I tried." Kenzie hung up the phone.

Jacob closed his phone and sat down in his recliner. His heart hurt. He wanted more than anything to be there for his dad.

James and Jacob sat in the day room at the station. They finished the check-off and their daily chores were complete. The system was busy and they were the only available unit to take calls. Their station was centrally located so posting wasn't necessary.

Jacob flipped through his cardiology book while James was fast asleep in the recliner. He felt the need to brush up on the basics when they had down time. Being proficient at his job required constant training and education. He didn't want to traipse through his career and not be the best paramedic possible.

Jacob laughed as James shot out of his recliner when the station tones blared.

"Medic-57, we have an unknown medical at 752 Grapevine Terrace. Male stated he needed an ambulance and hung up the phone."

Jacob lay his textbook on the table and strolled to the ambulance. A few moments later, James joined him.

"I hate those station tones sometimes. Going to give me a heart attack, I swear," James complained.

"Want some cheese with that whine?"

James glared at him. "Sometimes I hate you."

"No you don't."

"You're right, I don't and it pisses me off."

"Medic-57 is en-route."

"Dispatch copies."

On the way to the call, James's head bobbed up and down. Jacob found it funny that he couldn't stay awake. There was no way he could sleep through the sirens blaring and the constant jostling of the ambulance as it bounced down the road.

A short time later, they arrived on scene. The house was in an upper middle class neighborhood. The houses were simple, but well kept. Jacob found the address they were dispatched to. It was a brick home with a nicely maintained landscape and a chain link fence surrounding the property.

Right away, Jacob noticed the fire department wasn't on scene. He reached over and nudged James. "Hey, sleeping beauty. Time to wake up."

James wiped the sleep from his eyes and yawned. "We're here already?"

"Yes, sir. We are." He retrieved the radio microphone. "Medic-57 to dispatch. We're on scene. Be advised, fire isn't here."

"Dispatch copies."

The two men exited their ambulance and met at the back doors. Jacob had become accustomed to the fire department always being there to lend a helping hand. They were useful more often than not.

They pushed their cot, loaded with their equipment, up the sidewalk and through the gate. Stopping at the bottom of the steps leading to the porch, Jacob walked up and tried to open the door, but it was locked. He peered through the window and was unable to see anything. James stood behind him still half-asleep. He knocked and rang the doorbell several times. Still, no answer.

Jacob grabbed his radio. "Medic-57 to dispatch. No one is answering the door. Please send law enforcement to our location. We may need a forcible entry."

"Dispatch copies."

Jacob turned toward James. "I'm going to walk around back and see if there's another door that may be open."

"Sounds good to me. I'm going to stay here and wait for the police to arrive." He sat down on the steps and rested his head against a concrete pillar.

Jacob jumped down off the porch and walked around the side of the house. The neighborhood was eerily quiet. The only sounds were that of the birds chirping as they playfully flew around. He peered into each window he passed, but he couldn't see anything due to thick white blinds blocking his view.

Jacob walked around the back of the house and stopped in his tracks. Lying on the ground motionless was a man's body with its head in a huge flowerpot. He ran over and knelt down next to the body. He grabbed the wrist and checked for a pulse—there wasn't one.

"James! In the backyard. I found a body!"

A few moments later, his partner joined him. "What the...."

Jacob glanced over and found a gun in the man's hand underneath the flowerpot. Blood poured out onto the hot concrete. He knelt down closer and looked up into the flowerpot. He noticed a single gunshot entering under the man's chin. He grabbed his radio. "Medic-57 to dispatch, advise law enforcement we have a suicide and a weapon is involved."

"Dispatch copies. Fire and police should arrive on scene shortly."

Jacob looked over his shoulder at James. "We need to get that gun out of the way so we can work on him."

James shook his head. "I don't know, man. I don't think it's a good idea. Does he have a pulse?"

"No."

"We should leave everything where we found it. This is a crime scene now."

Jacob didn't agree. "I'm moving the gun."

He reached down, pulled the man's hand out of the flowerpot, removed the gun from his lifeless grip, and placed it on the ground next to his body. James stood behind him watching, but not offering any help. Jacob pulled the flowerpot off his head. Blood and brain matter filled the bottom. He noticed the bottom of the pot had been filled with concrete, which struck him as odd. Pressing his fingers against the man's neck—there wasn't a pulse.

"Don't just stand there. Get our equipment," Jacob ordered.

James ran back to the front of the house. Jacob knew what the monitor was going to say; the man was dead. Lying on the ground in front of him was a frail man that appeared to be in his fifties he guessed. There was a single gunshot wound just under his chin with an exit at the top of his head. He moved around to the shoulders of the man and studied the exit wound. The gunshot blew virtually the entire top of his head off.

James returned with their bag and monitor. After placing the leads on him, just as he suspected, it showed asystole. There was no need to attempt any resuscitation due to the man showing brain matter. Jacob ran a copy of the strip and turned off the monitor. James continued to stand behind him in shock.

On a table behind the house, Jacob noticed some things that had been strategically placed on it. He walked over and found a note with several names and phone numbers on it. He picked it up and studied it. Listed on the paper, next to the names, was the man's relatives. He also listed the funeral home and contact information.

Jacob sat the paper back down. Sitting on the table was an old wind up clock with the time stopped. A piece of paper next to it read, *Please note time of death.* The time listed was when they were dispatched to the house.

James walked over and stood next to Jacob looking at the items on the table. Both men stood quietly next to one another.

"This guy meant business. He wanted to die and for us to find him sooner rather than later," James said.

Jacob was in shock. They had been sent on suicide calls all of the time. More often than not, they were cries for help or attention. This was a first for him. Two police cars screeched to a halt in front of the house. They ran around and joined Jacob and James in the back yard.

"What do..." the officer stared at the man on the ground. "Did you guys move anything?"

"I moved the gun. It's sitting next to his body. It was in his hand and inside of the flowerpot," Jacob answered.

"Haven't you ever heard not to touch or move anything?"

"I didn't have a choice. We couldn't very well work on him with the gun in the way."

The officer angrily shook his head. He turned toward his partner. "Take the other medic and sit him in the back of your car. I'll take this one to mine," he said, pointing at Jacob.

James followed the officer to the front of the house and sat down in his car. Jacob followed the other officer and did the same.

The fire department arrived on scene, but the officers sent them away. Jacob felt it was odd that he and James were kept away from one another. He knew the officer was angry with him, but didn't see the point of being sequestered in separate cars. Twenty minutes passed by and several more officers arrived on scene. The yard had been draped with yellow tape that said, CRIME SCENE DO NOT CROSS. Several more minutes passed by until a man in a suit opened the door and motioned Jacob to step out.

"My name is Detective Lancaster with the police department. Mind telling me what happened?"

"We were dispatched to this house for an unknown medical call. You can verify that with our dispatch center."

"Go on."

Jacob gulped. "The door was locked. After several knocks on the door, I decided to walk around back to see if we could make entry. I found that man lying on the ground with a flowerpot over his head and a gun in his hand."

"At what point did you find it necessary to move the gun?"

"I needed to assess him to see if resuscitation was necessary. I very well couldn't do that with a gun in the way, so I moved it."

The detective sucked in a deep breath and exhaled. "Crime scene 101, you don't touch or move anything. Sometimes you damn paramedics don't think."

Jacob knew that. It was an odd situation, but he did what he felt was right. And he didn't feel safe having a gun so close to him that it could accidentally discharge and mortally wound him as well.

"Have a seat. I'll be with you in a few minutes," Detective

Lancaster said, pointing to the back seat of the patrol car.

Jacob sat back down and the detective slammed the door shut. He noticed several officers talking to one another and looking at him. He couldn't understand why they were treating James and him like criminals.

A few minutes later, Detective Lancaster returned. He opened the door and Jacob stepped out of the car.

"Your stories match up. This appears to be a simple suicide." The detective's voice grew harsh and deep. "Next time, I suggest you leave my damn crime scene alone and don't touch anything. Do you understand?"

Jacob nodded.

"You and your partner can go. If we need anything else, we'll be in touch."

Jacob walked back to the ambulance and James was sitting inside. He climbed in and looked over at his partner, who gave him a disapproving look.

"What?"

"I *told* you not to move the gun. You should listen to me more often," James growled.

Jacob cleared them from the scene with dispatch and headed back to their station. James looked out the window, but wasn't talking.

"I'm sorry," Jacob said.

"It's okay. I understand why you moved the gun, but we have to work with these guys. It isn't wise pissing them off."

"I know. There's something that bothers me though."

"What's that?" James asked.

"What is so bad that drove the man to want to die? I mean, he laid everything out for us to find and called 911 right before he killed himself."

"Makes you wonder."

"He even filled the flowerpot with concrete. I'm guessing so the bullet didn't travel anywhere and hurt someone else. That takes some planning."

Jacob was baffled. He couldn't understand why a man would want to die that bad. Each time he was on shift, he was exposed to different things. Just when he thought he'd seen it all, he was reminded that he hadn't seen the tip of the iceberg yet.

TWENTY-EIGHT

THE TIME HAD finally come. Bridge's plane was scheduled to land back in Boise at ten o'clock that night. Jacob waited eagerly at the airport for her flight to arrive. Standing in the terminal, he had a dozen red roses in his hand. Excited to see her, he couldn't sit still. Pacing back and forth, he looked at his watch and he still had twenty more minutes until her flight would land. He decided to walk around the terminal.

He enjoyed people watching. By looking at them, he could tell some of the medical problems they had. Barrel chested man with yellow tinged fingers probably has COPD. Obese woman devouring an ice cream sundae possibly has diabetes. Man sitting and picking the sores off his face probably a meth addict. It was distracting him from thinking about Bridge. Looking down at his watch, Jacob realized it was time for her plane to arrive. He quickly walked through the terminal toward the gate. His heart began to race. He couldn't wait to wrap his arms around her.

As he arrived at the gate, people had already begun to exit the plane. Looking around, he didn't see her yet. Disappointment rushed through him. People happily greeted and embraced their loved ones around him. A few moments later, Bridge walked out of the jet way looking for Jacob. He stood back for a moment admiring her beauty. As she turned around, he ran up behind her trying to not to give away that he was there. He took her into his arms.

She happily wrapped her arms around him and began to kiss him. A soothing warmness washed over him. They sat down after several minutes of the heated exchange.

"Hello, stranger."

A smile encompassed her entire face. "Hello to *you*. I've missed you so much."

"I've missed you. How was your training?"

Bridge rolled her eyes. "Oh gosh. I used to think I was a good nurse until I went through all of those classes. I don't know *anything.*"

Jacob shook his head. "I highly doubt that. You know your stuff."

"Doesn't feel like it. I did learn quite a bit though. I didn't miss one intubation," she said proudly.

Jacob began to laugh. "Look at you go. I'm so proud of you."

"Thank you." Jacob pulled her back into his arms and looked into her eyes. "You know what?"

"What?"

"I love you."

"I love you, too."

Jacob pulled the flowers, out showing them to her.

"Aww, thank you. They're beautiful." She held them close to her face and inhaled deeply.

"Not nearly as beautiful as you." Jacob pulled her close and began to kiss her again. He couldn't get enough of her kisses and her touch.

Jacob grabbed her bag and they headed out of the airport. He walked with his arm around her shoulder. He didn't want to let her go in fear of losing her. As they drove down the road, Bridge told Jacob about everything that she had learned. The excitement that sparkled in her eyes when she spoke about it intrigued him. She had such a passion for her new job. It reminded Jacob of how eager he was when he first started in the field and was hungry for knowledge. They came to a stop at a red light. Bridge continued to boast about all of her newfound knowledge.

Their conversation was interrupted by the sound of screeching tires. Jacob looked up in time to see a full size truck run a red light and T-bone a small compact car on the passenger side. The car rolled over several times until it came to rest on its top.

"Call 911," Jacob yelled to Bridge as he exited his truck and ran toward the car.

He noticed gas leaking onto the pavement, and there were small flames shooting up from the undercarriage of the car. Jacob knelt down to look inside.

A young woman, who looked to be in her early twenties, hung upside down in the car being held by her seatbelt. She was unconscious. Jacob crawled on his stomach into the car and reached up, trying to unfasten her seatbelt.

It was stuck.

The flames were growing. The smell of gas had gotten substantially stronger. He began to panic. Crawling back out of the car, Jacob looked back over at his truck and Bridge was still on the phone.

"Bring me my trauma shears from the glove compartment," Jacob shouted to Bridge. She nodded. A few seconds later, she handed them to him.

"Fire department and paramedics are on their way. What do you want me to do?"

"Get back to my truck," Jacob ordered.

"Let me...."

"Don't argue with me. Do it *now.* "

Bridge looked displeased. She stomped off like a scolded two year old. Jacob slid onto his back and scooted back inside of the car. Several cars stopped and curiously looked on, but no one offered Jacob any help.

He shook the woman's shoulder. "Ma'am, can you hear me?"

Still no answer.

The smell of gasoline flooded the car. Jacob's shirt was soaked with sweat from the heat building up. The orange glow from the flames illuminated the asphalt. Jacob shook the woman's shoulder roughly, but still no answer.

He took the trauma shears and began to cut the seat belt. The sound of sirens in the distance raced toward the accident. There was no time to wait. Jacob continued to cut. The orange glow grew brighter; the heat was unbearable.

"Jacob, get out of there," Bridge screamed.

By the tone of her voice, he knew he was running out of time. At any moment, the car could burst into flames. Jacob feverishly cut through the seatbelt, but he wasn't making any progress.

I have to get sharper shears. This is ridiculous.

Finally, he cut through the seatbelt and the woman fell down on top of him. Placing his arms around her back, he began to wiggle his way out of the window. The petite woman slid easily past the steering wheel.

"You have to get out now! " Bridge screamed in terror.

Jacob continued to scoot himself and the woman out of the window. Looking up, the flames were shooting well above the car. Finally out, Jacob reached down, picked up the woman, threw her over his shoulder, and began to run clear of the blazing inferno. As Jacob ran toward Bridge, the car exploded, knocking him to the ground.

Bridge ran up to Jacob. "Are you okay?"

He shook his head, got up to his knees, and began to pat himself all over his body checking for injuries.

An ambulance and a fire truck arrived on scene. The firefighters pulled a hose from their engine and began to spray water on the blazing car. Two paramedics approached Jacob and the woman he pulled from the car. He didn't recognize them.

"I'm fine. Don't worry about me. Just take care of her."

Bridge pulled Jacob into her arms. She held onto him tightly. After a few moments, she looked up at him.

"Are you okay?"

"Yeah."

"Are you sure?" she asked, with a tear streaming down her cheek.

Jacob grabbed both of her arms. "Yes. I'm sure."

She smiled and held onto him so tightly he could barely breathe.

Once Jacob gave his statement to the police, he was free to go. They got into his truck and continued driving toward Bridge's house. She reached over and tightly held his hand.

When they arrived at her house, Jacob grabbed her suitcase and followed her to the front door. Walking inside, he set her bag down on the floor, and turned around to see Bridge grinning at him.

"What?"

"You're a hero. You saved that woman's life."

Jacob shook his head. "I'm no hero. I did what anyone else would've done."

"No you didn't. If you didn't notice, no one offered to lift a finger helping you," she said in a matter-of-fact voice.

"I guess my instincts took over."

"Well, you're my hero. Watching you turned me on."

"You sounded more scared than anything."

Bridge reached up and caressed his face. "How about you be my hero tonight?"

A boyish grin slid across his face. He picked her up. "I'd love to. You need saving?"

"Yes I do, Mr. Paramedic. I'm in need of some medical attention."

Jacob walked over, kicked open her bedroom door, and then flung Bridge onto the bed. "I think I'm just the man for the job."

TWENTY-NINE

THE ALARM ON Jacob's phone woke him from a deep sleep. He rolled over, reaching out for Bridge, but she wasn't there. He sat up in the bed looking around the room. She walked out of the bathroom primping her hair. Wearing her blue flight suit, Jacob couldn't take his eyes off her.

"What?" she asked.

"You're so beautiful."

She blushed. "Oh stop it. I told you back in Phoenix, I'm not that hot. Moderately cute at best."

"I beg to differ."

Her cheeks glowed red. She walked over and sat on the bed next to Jacob. He reached up and pulled her down next to him. Grabbing the zipper on the front of her flight suit, Jacob began to pull it down.

"What's under here?"

Bridge grabbed his hand. "Stop it. You're going to mess up my hair. I have to look good for my first day on the helicopter." She zipped up her flight suit, sat up, and straightened her hair.

"Who are you trying to impress?"

Bridge reached down and caressed Jacob's cheek. "Only you, baby." She looked at her watch and leaped out of the bed. "I have to go or I'm going to be late."

Jacob frowned. "I wanted to see what you're wearing under your flight suit."

"Nothing."

"Tease."

She walked toward the bedroom door.

"Hey. Aren't you going to give me a kiss goodbye?"

"I'm running late."

"You never know when it could be the last time you see me. You might want to rethink that."

She turned around, walked back to the bed, leaned down, and gave him a kiss. "Don't talk like that. I just found you, and I'm not planning on going anywhere."

"You'd better not, or I will come find you. After all, I moved all the way up here just for you."

Bridge endearingly smiled at him. "That makes me one lucky girl. I love you."

Leaning up on one elbow in the bed he stated, "I love you, too. Don't forget it."

"I won't."

A few moments later Jacob heard the front door open and then close. He laid back down in bed. This was the happiest he'd ever been in his life; it was a dream come true. He'd been through so much over the past few years. Now, he was finally in a happy place in his life.

As time wore on, he knew he wanted to marry her. Was she ready? Did she feel as strongly as he did? Only one way to find out.

Jacob arrived at the station in a virtual skip through the parking lot. James stood in front of the bay, shaking his head and laughing.

"You look like you're about to burst."

Jacob strolled up to him. "I can't help it. I'm a happy man. I decided something this morning."

James took a few steps back. "You're not about to profess your undying love for me, are you?"

Jacob laughed. "Brother, I don't bat for that team."

"Phew! Had me scared there for a minute."

"If I did though, you wouldn't be my type."

James stepped forward. "Oh yeah? Why not?"

"You're not good looking enough for me."

James stuck out his chest. "I happen to think I'm pretty hot."

"Whatever helps you sleep at night."

They each shared a hearty laugh. Jacob was thankful James was his partner. Not only was he a seasoned paramedic, but he also proved to be a good friend. A day didn't go by that Jacob didn't stop thinking about Stitch. If he were alive, the three of them would have had some great times together.

"Tell me about this epiphany you had."

"I'm going to ask Bridge to marry me."

James looked shocked. "Are you sure? Have you thought this all the way through?"

"I'm sure. It all came to me this morning. She's the woman I want to spend the rest of my life with."

"I think it's too soon, but it's your decision, brother."

Jacob knew in his heart it was the right choice. He'd felt strongly for Bridge from the moment he had met her. She understood him. She understood his job. Their relationship had taken off like a rocket heading for the moon. When he saw her tied up in the chair, from that moment on he knew he couldn't live without her.

Jacob's shift was an uneventful one. They only had one call in twenty-four hours. That wasn't normal for their station, but he wasn't complaining. As he headed home, he couldn't wait to see Bridge. She had several flights for her first shift and they weren't able to speak much. Even though he didn't talk to her, she was always on his mind.

Pulling into his driveway, Bridge's car was there. His heart skipped a beat. She stepped out of her car still looking as beautiful as she was when he saw her last. Jacob got out of his truck and walked around to her. He pulled her into his arms and kissed her.

"Are you happy to see me or something?" she asked.

"If you only knew. How was your first shift?"

Bridge sighed. "It was busy. I don't know how you do these twenty-four hour shifts. We only got a few hours of sleep."

"Welcome to my world. You hungry?"

"Feed me, please. Then, can we take a nap?" she asked, looking up at him.

"Sure thing."

After breakfast, they each got undressed and crawled into bed. Jacob pulled Bridge into his arms, her face resting on his chest.

"Ever thought about getting married?" Jacob asked.

Bridge shot up and looked at him. "Are you...."

"No," Jacob answered. "Do you see me with a ring?"

Disappointment came over Bridge's face. She laid her head back down on Jacob's chest. "I've thought about it. Why do you ask?"

"No reason. I was just wondering."

"Only way you'll ever know is if you ask."

Jacob held her close to him. He wanted more than anything to pop the question, but he wouldn't dare think of doing that without a ring. They drifted off to sleep.

He woke up to Bridge getting dressed. "What time is it?"

"Three o'clock. I need to go home and do some laundry. What are your plans for the rest of the day?" Bridge asked as she slid her flight suit back on.

"I need to go and pay some bills. Want to take care of that for me?"

Bridge laughed. "I'll pass on that. You work tomorrow?"

"Yeah. You?"

"Yes." She sat down on the end of the bed. "It's crazy. I look forward to work now. Does it ever wear off?" she asked as she zipped up her boots.

"I don't know about wearing off. You get used to it after a while and it feels more like a job."

Bridge leaned down and kissed Jacob. Her lips sent shivers down his spine. "I love you, my hero."

"How many times do I have to say I'm not a hero?"

"You're *my* hero."

The next morning, Jacob woke up to the annoying sound of the alarm on his cell phone. It was time to get ready for work. He rolled over in bed, opened up his nightstand, and pulled out the ring box. He had purchased a beautiful one, a half-carat diamond ring, the day before. Looking at it, he could see it on Bridge's finger in his mind's eye and she was going to be surprised.

It was another beautiful morning. The sun shone brightly through the clear blue sky. Jacob was excited to ask Bridge to marry him. He wasn't sure when he was going to propose. He got ready for work and headed for the station. It was difficult for him to control his excitement; asking her to marry him was all that was on his mind.

Jacob had a little extra pep in his step while walking through the station parking lot. He wanted to go to Bridge right then and pop the question. Being on duty made that possibility difficult, not to mention she was on the helicopter that day as well.

James sat on a chair just outside of the ambulance bay reading a newspaper. He looked up as Jacob approached him with a grin on his face.

"What's in your pocket?" James asked.

"Nothing."

James put down his paper, walked toward Jacob, and reached into the front pocket of his pants. "What is it? Let me see!" he demanded.

Jacob tried desperately to fight him off, but it didn't work. James pulled the ring box out of his pocket and opened it. A smile splashed across his face.

"You didn't."

Jacob reached over and swiped the box out of his hands. "Yes, I did."

"You sly dog," James said as he punched Jacob in the arm.

"I told you I wanted to ask her to marry me." Jacob rubbed his arm.

"When are you going to do it?"

"I don't know," Jacob answered, shaking his head. "I would go to her right now and ask her if it was possible. Probably not the most romantic way to do it."

"It's not always about romance, brother. I'm sure she wouldn't care."

The station tones blared over the speakers. "Medic-57, we have a structure fire with multiple possible entrapments at 1057 Van Neys Road. Fire department and law enforcement are en-route."

James bolted toward the ambulance and Jacob followed closely behind.

"That's a few blocks from here," James said. "Medic-57, to dispatch, we're en-route."

"Dispatch copies. We have three more ambulances en-route as well."

James pulled out of the bay. They both looked to the east and saw thick black smoke billowing into the sky.

"That's not good," Jacob said. He pulled the ring box out of his pocket and put it in the glove compartment.

James pulled the ambulance out onto the main road and raced toward the address. Traffic was light. They pulled onto Van Neys Road; halfway down the block there were already four police cars on scene. James pulled their ambulance ahead of the residence and threw it into park.

"Medic-57, we're on scene."

"Dispatch copies."

Both men exited the ambulance. A single-story wood structure stood before them fully engulfed in flames. There were several officers standing at the back door trying to go inside, but the treacherous heat prohibited them from entering.

James ran up to the back of the house. "Anyone inside?"

"Yeah. A dad and two small kids. Where's the damn fire department?" the officer screamed.

"Medic-57 to dispatch, what's the ETA on the fire department?" James asked. "We have three people trapped in the house and it's fully engulfed."

"ETA is less than five minutes."

"We don't *have* five minutes. Tell them to expedite!"

Jacob stood behind James in complete disbelief. He wanted to storm into the house, but that would prove fatal without the proper equipment on. Glass shattered, wood popped, and thick black smoke swirled around in the air. The heat had grown so intense the men had to back away from the house.

A few minutes later, three fire trucks arrived on scene. The firefighters exited their trucks, pulled out fire hoses, and went to work. Two firemen went into the burning inferno, while two others stood crouched at the back door.

After several minutes, they ran out the back of the house holding two small children. They placed them on the ground and ran back into the house once again.

Jacob and James approached the children. Their skin was charred black from their heads to their toes. James reached down and felt for a pulse on each kid, but there wasn't one. He grimly looked up at Jacob.

"They're gone," he said choking back the tears.

"We're not even going to try?" Jacob asked.

He placed a hand on Jacob's shoulder. "They were in there too long. There's nothing we can do."

The house raged in flames despite the efforts of the firefighters dousing it with water. The two firemen ran out the back of the house, this time empty handed.

James walked over to them. "No one else in the house?"

One of the firefighters pulled off his helmet, a hood, and then his mask. His face was red and saturated with sweat. "Can't see anything. The roof is about to give. It wasn't safe. We had to get out of there," he said, panting.

Jacob stared at the inferno. He had never felt more helpless in all of his life. Lying on the ground were two innocent children, dead.

James cancelled the other incoming ambulances; there was no need for them to respond. It took the fire department just over an hour to extinguish the flames. The house was barely standing, had no roof, and was heavily charred. The coroner arrived, took a statement from James, and then took the deceased children away from the scene. There wasn't a dry eye in sight.

During rehab, the firefighters found a man on the floor just past the room where they had found the children, his body barely recognizable. It was calls like this that made Jacob question why he chose this job. There was so much death, sadness, and despair. The media flocked to the scene and were trying to grab any person they could to ascertain information on the fire. The fire department's public information officer hadn't arrived on scene yet.

James grabbed Jacob's arm. "Let's get out of here."

Jacob nodded. "Sounds good to me."

They climbed into the ambulance, cleared the scene on the radio with dispatch, and headed toward their station. Neither man spoke.

Once back at the station, they each sat in the ambulance staring out the bay. Death was a hard pill to swallow and even worse when kids were involved.

"I need to go see Bridge."

James turned toward him. "Now? Isn't she working?"

"Yeah. Take me to the hanger."

"That's not in our area."

"I don't care." Jacob turned toward James, his face blank. "Take me there now."

James shrugged his shoulders. "Okay. If we get into trouble, this is all on you, brother."

Driving down the road, Jacob couldn't stop thinking about how fragile life was and there were no guarantees for tomorrow. A short time later, they arrived at the hanger. The helicopter engines roared to life. James pulled the ambulance around to the back.

"I'll be back in a minute."

James nodded.

Bridge and the flight paramedic were coming out of the hanger, donning their flight helmets. Bridge stopped and looked at Jacob, surprised. "What are you doing here?"

"I had to see you. We just had a bad call," Jacob said loudly, competing with the deafening engines of the helicopter.

She frowned. "We heard. You okay?"

"Yeah, I guess." He reached into his pocket, but the ring box wasn't there.

"Can you give me a minute?" Bridge asked her partner.

"Make it quick. We have a call," the flight paramedic answered as he continued to walk toward the helicopter.

Crap! How could I forget the ring in the ambulance?

Bridge looked at him confused. "Something wrong?"

"I need to grab something from the ambulance. Can you wait a second?"

"Bridgette. We need to go. Come on!" the flight paramedic yelled.

"I'm sorry. I've gotta go. Call me later?" Bridge asked. She started to walk toward the helicopter. She stopped, and ran back to Jacob. "There's something I need to tell you. I wanted to wait until we had more time, but I can't. Jacob, we're having a baby," she said smiling. "I'm pregnant!"

"You're *what?*" His head swirled. He couldn't believe his ears.

"Bridgette, let's go." the paramedic yelled from the helicopter.

"Give me a minute," Bridge snapped back at him.

"Yes, Jacob. You're going to be a daddy. I left yesterday to go and have a pregnancy test done. I was late on my period. I didn't want to say anything until I was certain."

Jacob was speechless. He was about to surprise Bridge with a marriage proposal. Instead, she got the upper hand and surprised him with much more monumental news. Jacob reached down and placed his hand on her stomach.

"Are you happy?" Bridge asked. "Please, say something,"

Jacob looked up into her eyes. "Yes. I'm happy. Wow!"

"Now, Bridgette!"

"Baby, I've gotta go. Call me later." She turned and ran toward the helicopter.

"Wait. I love...." Jacob tried to say, but Bridge had already climbed into the helicopter and shut the door.

The engines roared with power, lifted off the ground, and disappeared into the sky. Jacob stood in shock on the tarmac. He walked back to the ambulance and climbed in. Jacob stared out the window.

"Everything okay?" James asked.

Jacob turned toward him. "Bridge is pregnant."

James' mouth dropped open. "Seriously?"

"Yeah."

James slapped him on the shoulder. "Congratulations, buddy!"

"Thank you."

While on their way back to the station, Jacob's shock was replaced with happiness. The realization of becoming a father excited him. Asking Bridge to marry him had more meaning than ever. He was about to become a father and hopefully a husband. His life took a huge turn for the better. At first, he questioned himself for moving to Idaho. Now, he realized it was the best decision he ever could've made.

"Medic-57, we have a patient transfer from Magic County Hospital to Springhill nursing home. You have an eighty-eight year old female seen in the emergency room for pneumonia. She'll be in trauma four."

"Medic-57, show us en-route," James answered.

Jacob had a permanent smile plastered on his face. He reached into the glove compartment and retrieved the ring. He couldn't wait to propose to Bridge, the mother of his child.

James pulled the ambulance into the parking lot. "Medic-57, we're on scene."

"Dispatch copies."

The two men climbed out of the ambulance, pulled out the cot, and headed toward the ambulance entrance. Jacob was walking on air; he couldn't contain his excitement.

Wouldn't this news just cook Doctor Young's goose? I hope he's on duty.

As they walked into the emergency room, Jacob noticed several nurses huddled at the main desk holding each other and crying. James and Jacob looked at one another confused.

The charge nurse walked around the desk, approached Jacob and hugged him. "I'm so sorry. Oh, God, I'm so sorry," she said weeping.

Jacob glanced at James. He shrugged his shoulders and pulled free from the nurse. "What are you sorry for?" Jacob looked over and noticed Doctor Young staring at him with a smirk on his face.

She reached up and dabbed her eyes with a tissue. "She was such a wonderful nurse. Are you okay?"

Jacob looked at her still confused. "I have no idea who, or what you're talking about."

Her face grew blank. "Haven't you heard?"

"Heard what?" Jacob asked. His irritation grew.

"Oh, God. You don't know."

"Don't know what?"

Her lips began to quiver. "The helicopter Bridge was flying in just crashed in Pulsar County on their way to a call."

Jacob's knees went weak. He grabbed onto the nurse to help steady himself. "Is she okay?"

Tears welled up in her eyes. "They all died. I'm so sorry. I thought you knew."

Jacob looked over at James. His world came crashing down. Not more than thirty minutes ago, he was talking to her. Found out he was going to be a father. Now, the woman he loved and was about to ask to marry him was dead.

Doctor Young walked over from his desk and stood in front of Jacob. "Sucks to be you," he said with a smile on his face.

Jacob's pain and anguish transformed into complete rage. He grabbed Doctor Young, slammed him into a wall, and began punching him repeatedly in the face. Blood sprayed from his nose. He went limp, and fell to the ground. Jacob stood over him and continued to punch him—all he could see was red. Bones crunched under the force of the blows.

Two security guards rushed over, grabbed Jacob, and dragged him

227

through the emergency room.

"How dare you! I'm going to kill you!" Jacob screamed as the security guards pulled him out of the ER.

The two men dragged him to the security office and shut the door. Jacob heard it lock from the outside. Pacing back and forth, he couldn't contain his rage. Jacob pushed everything off the desk onto the floor. Papers floated through the air.

He leaned against the wall and collapsed to the floor. Holding his face with his hands, he burst into tears. He just lost the woman of his dreams who was carrying his child. He couldn't imagine life without her.

Why do you keep doing this to me, God? Why? What have I done to you to deserve this? Why?

Jacob cried until there were no more tears in his body. He sat on the floor, back against the wall and stared blankly into the air.

The door unlocked and Detective Morrison walked into the room. Looking around the room at the mess Jacob had made, he shook his head. He walked over, pulled out a chair, and sat down in front of him. "First of all, I'm sorry for your loss."

Jacob looked up at him. "Like *you* care."

Morrison shook his head. "I do care. I understand your anger. We've got quite a mess here right now, but I think I fixed it."

"What do you mean?" Jacob softly asked.

"You did quite the number on Doctor Young. You've broken his nose and he has multiple facial fractures. He wanted you locked up."

"So?" Jacob had no reason to care anymore. He lost everything that meant anything to him. If it weren't for the security guards, he would've beaten Young until his body fell onto the floor lifeless.

"I've spoken to him. I urged him to reconsider and he's agreed to drop the charges with one condition."

"What's that?"

"You have to leave Boise and never come back."

Jacob shook his head and laughed. Was that all he had to do? He had thoughts of running past the detective and finishing off the job, but what good would that do? He stared at the floor for a long moment. "Okay then. Looks like I have nothing else here. I'm going back where I belong, back to Oklahoma."

ABOUT THE AUTHOR

Jerrid Edgington is a Paramedic for Le Flore County EMS in Poteau, Oklahoma. He's been in EMS for a total of eighteen years with sixteen of those years as a Paramedic. Jerrid spent several years playing semi-pro football, officiated high school football/ basketball for thirteen years, and enjoys woodworking building furniture for his home.

Jerrid aspired to write a book for several years and had several unsuccessful attempts until one day the story of Jacob Myers took on a life of its own and Jerrid couldn't stop writing. Resuscitation is the second book in the Racing the Reaper Series.

Connect with the author on his blog:
http://www.authorjerridedgington.com

Catch *Racing the Reaper* Book One:

http://www.amazon.com/dp/B00GQD9S94

After a life altering accident, Jacob Myers he feels he is meant for something greater than the boring grind of an office job. Through his recovery process he comes to a decision to become an EMT.

In the fast paced world of emergency services, Jacob nearly buckles from the pressure and begins making one mistake after another. He wonders if the stress of holding other lives in his hands is too much for him.

Just as he thinks he is conquering the new challenges, things turn dark when a former patient stalks him and accuses him of sexual assault

Will Jacob clear his name and rid his life of this mentally unbalanced woman or will he be trapped and imprisoned for something he didn't do?

◇◇◇

Read an excerpt from the exciting third book in the Reaper Series, *Reaper's Requiem.*

◇◇◇

JACOB SAT AT his desk in triage at Regency Medical Center. He popped four Ibuprofen into his mouth to ease the pain that pulsed in his temples. Another night of marathon drinking, another hangover. A woman ran across the lobby and smacked into his desk.

"I need to see a doctor, now," the woman screamed. She leaned against the desk, panting.

"What seems to be the problem, ma'am?" Jacob asked.

"I have a cockroach in my ear. It's going to eat into my brain. Get a doctor out here." She tugged on her right ear. Other patients in the waiting room stared in her direction.

Jacob fought hard not to laugh. He grinned and shook his head. Grabbing a packet, he slid it across the desk toward her. "I'll need for you to fill out this information and bring it back to me when you're done."

The woman stared at him in disbelief. "Are you serious? I need a doctor. Do you know what a medical emergency is?"

There were several things he yearned to say to her, but it would cost him his job. "Yes, I do, and you don't have one. Now, if you don't mind, please fill out this packet and return it to me when you're finished."

The woman snatched the packet from the desk. "You're unbelievable. If anything happens to me, you will be hearing from my attorney."

Jacob grinned. "Looking forward to it. Have a seat and wait like everyone else in this waiting room."

As the woman walked away from the desk, Jacob pushed down the urge to laugh. Several other people in the waiting room shook their heads. He leaned back in his seat and thumbed through a magazine that Tom had left at the desk.

When Jacob began working at the hospital, Tom tried to befriend him, but it didn't take long for Jacob to see his true colors. A police officer who had trouble functioning on the street, Tom began his second career as a paramedic working the night shift at the triage desk. And to date, he had several harassment complaints against him from several females in the nursing staff. Jacob's blood pressure would rise every time he saw Tom get too close to a nurse and he couldn't understand why the hospital administration allow Tom to keep his job. He must have something on them—Jacob thought. He glanced at his watch; he had eleven and a half hours left until he continued his nightly ritual of drinking himself into oblivion.

A few minutes later, the woman returned to the desk. She flung the packet at Jacob; it landed in his lap. He glared at her.

"Never mind. I got the bug out myself, no thanks to you," the woman yelled.

"Good. Then you saved the working man from having to flip your bill, since you probably don't have insurance and wouldn't pay for it anyway."

The woman's eyes narrowed. "I thought people in the medical

profession were supposed to be caring and compassionate?"

"I'm fresh out of caring today. Just your luck."

The woman threw her hands into the air and stormed out of the waiting room.

Jacob went back to reading the magazine. When he worked on the ambulance, he never would've spoken to a patient that way. After losing Bridge, nothing else in his life mattered. He could've easily gotten another job as a paramedic, but the fire that drove him to help others had since been extinguished. He was okay with the thought of never stepping foot into another ambulance for as long as he lived.